UN

Now the city was plunged into the horrors of war—the streets running with blood, women and children with frenzied eyes wandering aimlessly, animals and men racing in frantic gallop toward unknown destinations. The disciplined troops of the Firozian army moved in groups from one position to another, strange islands of unity, these blocks of men marching in order amid a land that was suddenly torn asunder with as much force as an earthquake, except the devastation came from above instead of below . . .

Choking black smoke soon hung over Gnomon as it had over Firoze. The twin cities were now both shattered by the crushing blows of seaborne artillery. The Vargan ships continued to circle and fire . . .

Don't miss the first *Shadow World* adventure . . .

The Burning Goddess

SHADOW WORLD Novels
by Ian Hammell from Ace Books

THE BURNING GODDESS
CLOCK STRIKES SWORD

SHADOW WORLD

CLOCK STRIKES SWORD

IAN HAMMELL

ACE BOOKS, NEW YORK

*My thanks to Stephen Billias, without whom this book
would never have been written.*

This book is an Ace original edition,
and has never been previously published.

CLOCK STRIKES SWORD

An Ace Book / published by arrangement with
Bill Fawcett & Associates

PRINTING HISTORY
Ace edition / January 1995

ISBN: 0-441-00136-X

ACE®
Ace Books are published by The Berkley Publishing Group,
200 Madison Avenue, New York, NY 10016.
ACE and the "A" design are trademarks belonging to
Charter Communications, Inc.

PRINTED IN THE UNITED STATES OF AMERICA

10 9 8 7 6 5 4 3 2 1

for Bela

1

IT STARTED AS A DEEP RUMBLE THAT only the nervous, stamping animals heard, emanating from deep underground, a low groan that was precursor to the angry roaring sound that crescendoed and bellowed (inanimate creature of rock and stone under pressure) until men held their ears and moaned in a dim echo of the rolling chaos beneath them. The world split open, and out came fire and red, flowing lava, and a mountain fell into the sea and all was in upheaval and tumbling down. And (great mysterious paradox) the splitting of the world made the world one again, for the mountain barrier between Firoze and Gnomon was removed, and when the up-flung dust had settled and the world had ceased its quaking and shaking, behold, there was a great breach in the Impasse.

The next day two explorers from Firoze ventured into the gap, an immense boulder field strewn with pebbles the size of houses, still smoldering of the hot earth from which they were torn. An occasional quiver in the earth made footing uncertain and the way treacherous, as the newborn, unsteady rocks shifted and crashed all around them. The Firozians, bold and long of stride, gave each other the appearance that they were unconcerned by the danger. One was a near-giant named Beroth, with a black beard, thick legs and arms, and fleshy features that made his eyes too small for his face. He looked rough and crude, yet the smaller, younger man showed him the deference one would accord a superior. The second man was also a muscular fellow called Coker, who only looked smallish because he accompanied the behemoth beside him. Both wore two swords, a long sword in a leather scabbard and a short sword unsheathed at the belt. Both carried unslung bows and quivers of arrows on their backs, but for now they were not hunting. They walked boldly along the mountain trail.

"You must have struck your anvil too loudly, Beroth," the second man said to the first. "You've shattered the ground of your own estate with those blows."

"Not even I can bring down a mountain, Coker," the first man, Beroth, responded. "I defer to Nature, which can make fearful wood creatures of us all."

In the faces of both men was something slightly unpleasant, a certainty—or was it cruelty, arrogance, or merely that trait of royal breeding—that makes men feel innately superior, sometimes rightly, sometimes not?

"When even the ground beneath your feet is no longer dependable, what can you trust?" the smaller man wondered aloud.

"Not a Gno-man," answered his companion, Beroth, and both men laughed heartily at the crude joke.

"The Impasse has fallen. The spine of the island is broken. What next? Will the very stars drop out of the sky and leave us darkness?" Coker mused.

"The Impasse range still stands, thank the gods. This is only a tiny gap," Beroth replied.

"Through which may pour the tiny men of Gnomon, to annoy us like the gnats of summer."

"Have you ever met one?"

"Gnat or Gnomon? Once. At a trading fair. Dainty little fellow, he was, with sharpy eyes. I disliked him immediately."

Suddenly Beroth interrupted his companion. "Look there!" An old ram with fine curved horns had wandered through the cleft, picking its way carefully over the still unsettled rock.

"The Gnomons may be small and skinny but their sheep are nice and fat," Beroth grunted.

"That one would yield four fine spitted legs of mutton," Coker agreed.

"First shot takes the hindquarters," said Beroth, declaring a competition and reaching behind him for his unstrung bow. Both men raced to bend and brace their bows. At almost the same time they slid arrows from their quivers and launched them recklessly at the peaceful animal, which looked as if it were enjoying the view of territory it had never before seen. Beroth's arrow caught it above the shoulder—it was the killing shot. Coker's arrow plunged into the ram's woolly belly, but the creature was already dropping to its knees in its death throes.

"Hey, Coker! I'll throw you a kidney or two, for that's where you struck him, you worthless marksman you!" Beroth shouted gleefully as he ran ahead. They hadn't expected such easy pickings on this day. Beroth grasped the dying animal by its horns and pried back its head to slit its throat. Hot blood splattered over the still-warm rocks. Within minutes the two hunters had

skinned and butchered the ram, taking the bloody
fleece, the hindquarters, and forequarters, and leaving a
pile of bones and gore that attracted the attention of carrion birds drifting high overhead, who soon began to
describe slow wheeling circles in the sky, the ancient
signal of death.

Across the Impasse, a boy whistled for his lost flock.
Runny Platho was a frail-looking little fellow with a
pinched face and a slightly sunken chest, but his spin-
dly legs were strong from scrambling over the mountains near his father's home. Usually the sheep followed
him patiently wherever he led them, but today they
were skittish and truculent.

"It must be the earth-moving that has made them so,"
Runny said earnestly to his dog Maycome. "And
where's old Whitehead? He wouldn't abandon the little
ones, even if he's restless as they are." The dog looked
up lovingly at his young master, barked once, and set
off ahead to round up the scattered lambs. Runny followed his dog up the incline toward the ridge top,
where the surefooted sheep liked to nibble at tufts of
sweet grass growing on exposed ledges and steep
slopes near the summit.

Never been this high up here before, Runny thought
to himself as he hugged the mountainside on all fours.
*The earthquake has changed everything. I bet if I go
just a little higher I'll be able to see the other side of
the island!* he thought with a thrill, for it was every
boy's dream to be an explorer. Sure enough, the trembling earth had shaken up the mountains and caused
them to settle just enough so that he could now inch his
way up to the crest. He peered over and saw a world
that no Gnomon, boy or man, had ever seen. A stark
land confronted him, less lush and green than his own
country, a wild place, rocky and desolate, but beautiful.
As he looked he thought he saw Whitehead the lead

ram disappear around into a dense thicket below the tree line.

"Oh no!" Runny cried to himself, and without thinking he ventured across the border to give chase. He was now in Firoze.

Sometime later, Maycome dashed into the yard where he lived, howling miserably. Endimin Platho rushed out of his house. "Where's the boy? Where's Runny?" he asked of the dog, who could not answer except to increase his mournful yowling. It was quite unusual for the dog to come back without his youthful master. Endimin was immediately worried.

Widowed some years before, Endimin had done his best to raise his two children, Aivlys, his daughter, and Runny, his son, but life was hard. Both children had gone to work from an early age, and Endimin regretted that he had not been able to send them to school properly, though he tutored them himself at home. Aivlys became a surrogate mother to Runny. She did all the domestic chores while the boy tended the meager flock, which supplemented the income from Endimin's business. Like so many other Gnomonese, Endimin Platho was a watchmaker, but competition was fierce and business was sporadic, even though Endimin's work was of high quality. He worked slowly, that was his problem. He desired perfection, and wouldn't settle for shoddy workmanship in his shop. As a result, he often lost impatient customers to other watchmakers who were less particular. Even now, with his son missing, Endimin hesitated to take precious time from his work, but the baying dog would not leave him alone.

"All right, Maycome, take me to him," Endimin implored the anxious animal. Maycome shot out of the yard. Endimin had difficulty following him toward the high grazing fields on the mountain slope above.

Runny whistled and called for his lost ram, but Whitehead was nowhere to be found. The boy wan-

dered deeper into Firoze, occasionally casting anxious
glances up at the sky, which pressed down onto him
with a gray pall unlike any weather he'd seen in sunny
Gnomon. The land here was also more threatening than
the grazing slopes of the Gnomon side of the Impasse,
which were steep, to be sure, but smooth. Everywhere
the earth was cracked and fissured, so that he was constantly climbing in and out of tricky ravines and small
canyons. The two sides of the island could not have
been more different. The only reminder that he was still
on his own island was the ever-present tangy scent of
the surrounding sea. Runny had to undertake a series of
wearying descents and ascents just to traverse a few
hundred yards of the mountainside laterally. He almost
gave up except that every once in a while he'd find a
tuft of Whitehead's uncombed wool caught in a thicket,
or he'd catch scent of the ram's unmistakable odor.
Then, rounding a corner, he came upon a terrible
scene—the head of Whitehead stuck upon a stave! His
body was no more than a messy pile of bloody scraps,
the intestines cast carelessly aside, the bloodstained
fleece abandoned in a pile. Slaughtered! The boy
wailed his grief once, loudly, and instantly was confronted by two huge men, who had apparently been
crouching just behind the flat boulder they'd used as
their butcher block.

"Well, if it isn't a Gnomonese cub, crying for its
mother's teat," Beroth laughed.

"The little imp is barely as big as my three-year-old,
he must be a dozen years at least," Coker added.

"You've killed my lead ram, you thieves!" Runny
shouted excitedly. Beroth's face darkened suddenly.

"Watch your tongue, brat. This animal was trespassing on my land, and I took it by rights."

"It was lost. I came after it, but I'm too late. Oh,
what will Father say?" Runny wailed.

"Go do your caterwauling in your own backyard,"

Coker teased him, but Runny was not yet ready to leave the dismembered corpse of his beloved pet. He threw his tiny arms around the severed head and buried his face in its discolored fur. "Oh, Whitehead, ye shouldn't have crossed the Impasse."

"Indeed!" Beroth muttered, for in truth he was discomfited by the thought of what he would have done had the situation been reversed, that is, if one of his animals had wandered away and been slain across the border in Gnomon. He felt sorry for the boy, but what was done was done.

"Let it be a lesson to you, youngster, that you must watch your flock carefully and guard it well." Beroth tried to speak gently, though with his gruff bass voice it was difficult to project tenderness. The boy was inconsolable.

"I was watching them," Runny cried, "but the new breach let him cross where I thought he never could, into this dark place, under these clouds, in these rocky gaps and gulches. Oh, it's all so strange and unfriendly!"

"This is Firoze!" Coker boomed. "Land of fierce men, sword makers, and sword wielders, not some sunny bower in soft Gnomon!"

"What care I for your boasting?" Runny sniffled. "I will have to explain to Father that men of Firoze stole our Whitehead!"

"I warned you not to use such language again!" Beroth roared. "What I find on my property is mine!" he shouted, and he started forward as if to throttle the youngster.

Startled, Runny rose quickly from where he'd sat clutching the dead ram's head. Unaware that behind him was another dropoff, he backpedaled away from the giant who approached him, until he stood unknowingly on the edge of a cliff face.

"Don't!—" Runny pleaded, but the enraged Firozian

lumbered forward. Too late, he saw the boy's predicament.

"Watch out!" Beroth shouted, but the terrified boy took another step backward, teetered on the brink, then slipped and plunged off the precipice with a weak cry. His tiny body bounced once against a projecting rock, then plummeted fifty feet to the bottom of the gully below. Beroth and Coker were momentarily stunned by the sudden disaster. When they had somewhat recovered their composure, they picked their way hurriedly down into the darkened ravine, a foul place where the trees were moist and laden with dripping moss. The child's lifeless body lay twisted and bloody, a silent recrimination of their thoughtless behavior.

"He should have been more careful," Coker said finally.

"Of course. I only intended to scare him a little. It was his own fault," Beroth agreed, but both men were chagrined by the sudden tragedy.

"What do we do with him?" Coker asked.

"Let's bury him right here. It will only mean more trouble for us if we take his body with us." Neither man thought of carrying the lifeless boy over the Impasse to look for his family—it was as if the barrier still existed, in their minds.

Runny Platho was laid to rest in a shallow grave deep in a nameless wild ravine, beneath the rough stones of Firoze, without family present; a lonely grave for one so young.

When Beroth and Coker had heaped up enough stones to keep the wild animals away, they scrambled out of the chasm, looked down once more on the final resting place of the Gnomonese boy, turned their backs, and walked away as if the episode were over and there were nothing more to be done. Neither of them carried home the butchered mutton, however; they felt at least that much remorse over the accident.

It was nearing twilight when Endimin Platho came searching for his son some hours later. Endimin felt extremely uncomfortable to be in Firoze—he had always regarded his rough neighbors on the other side of the Impasse with suspicion and a slight dismay. Maycome ran ahead, barking and yapping. There was the scent of blood in the air. Black carrion birds circled overhead in the distance. *What could they be after?* Endimin asked himself, troubled by the sight of the harbingers of death. Soon he came upon the remains of Whitehead, a startling and fearful scene, but puzzling, since the butchery seemed to no purpose, nothing had been taken. Maycome recognized the chopped-up body of his former charge, and did not lick the blood or tear at the entrails the way he might have. He was even more frenzied than before, and bayed loudly for Endimin to follow him, then plunged down into another of the endless crevices Endimin had wearily climbed in and out of while following the trail of Runny.

"Not down there, Maycome," Endimin called out, but the dog was insistent, rushing back and forth, up and down the steep banking, so Endimin skidded and tumbled his way down the embankment until he reached the shaded bottom of the declivity.

Nothing but ruination and misery here, Endimin thought to himself as he looked around the darkened dismal glen. "Come away, Maycome."

Maycome pawed miserably at a pile of stones.

"What is it, Maycome?" Endimin asked, and he felt a sudden chilling in his bones, as if the dampness of the place had crept into his very marrow.

The dog squealed and scratched so pathetically that Endimin was drawn to the spot, against his better wishes, for he felt uncomfortable at what he might discover. Then his heart broke, quietly, for there in that solemn depression, that lonely crag, he saw that Maycome's desperate scruffling had exposed Runny's tiny arm. As gently as he knew how, Endimin removed the stones that covered the body, while the dog waited silently a few yards away, as if he knew his sad task was finished. With infinite care, Endimin brushed away the dirt from his son's face and lifted him out of the carelessly constructed grave site.

Who would do this? What sort of men would bury a child so coldly, without even trying to find his family? Endimin asked himself. *And what will Aivlys do? She loved her little brother so.*

Endimin stumbled into his home several hours later, having climbed back through the gap in the Impasse and down the treacherous mountainside in darkness. Aivlys had prepared a hot meal for her father and brother and had waited up for them. She was prepared to scold Runny for staying out so late, but when she saw her father carrying the boy in his arms, she screamed and dropped a pan of bread she was carrying to the table.

"Not dead!" she screeched.

"Alas, yes," Endimin sighed, all the grief in his worn and sore body pouring out of his breaking voice.

"But how? Why? Why?"

"I don't know." Endimin told her briefly how he'd found the boy's body in a ravine on the Firoze side of the Impasse, and that he suspected Runny had been murdered, but he spared her the grievous details of the boy's unceremonious burial. "Help me here," Endimin pleaded. Aivlys removed the settings from the table so that Endimin could lay the body there. Somehow the neighbors had already found out about the boy's death. They began to arrive in twos and threes, some sympathetic, some just curious, all whispering or murmuring in low voices; they crowded into the small kitchen of Endimin's house, forming a ragged circle around the makeshift bier where Runny lay. Aivlys had retreated to the back room, where she threw herself on the bed to weep, but when she heard voices in the kitchen she came running out with a broom in her hands and threatened to beat the assembled crowd with it unless they left.

"Go away! Leave us alone with our grief. We don't want you here!" she screamed. Only a few of the closest friends of the family were spared her delirious anger. The rest fled before her flailing broom.

"Poor girl, she's gone mad," they said.

Endimin tried to quiet her, but Aivlys was lost in her own terrifying world of confusion and darkness. She was a pretty girl with brown hair, fair limbs, and lively eyes, but now her face was splotchy with stress and her eyes red from crying. Her younger brother had been a light to her, a cheerful presence who had laughed at her fearful, worrisome nature and had played with her and teased her innocently when she grew too serious or pensive. Who would lighten her feelings now? Ah, if only she was a man, she would take up a weapon and hunt for her brother's killers. What could she, a weak girl, do against the Firozian beasts? Still, she would find a way to take revenge. This she swore to herself as she lay on her bed, her fists clenching the bedding material in futile anger.

The next day Endimin Platho locked Maycome the dog in a penned-in lower pasture with the sheep, and set out again for Firoze. Once more he scaled the vertigo-inducing slopes where until yesterday his son Runny had led a peaceful flock to graze on the high hillsides. His shoulders were hunched, by both the long years of bending over his watchmaker's workbench and by the weight of sadness that pressed down on him like a physical burden. He trudged slowly up the incline, head down, without noticing the glorious beauty of the mountain dawn, as the sun splayed purple and orange streamers across the green landscape.

I should have brought the dog, Endimin thought, not

for protection but to diminish his loneliness. Many times when Runny was younger, Endimin had come up here, to teach him the ways of shepherding. The boy was quick to learn both the intricacies of disassembling and reconstructing timepieces and the more leisurely routines of the pastoral life. As father and son they had roamed the upper slopes of Gnomon, happily following the meandering flock as it munched the high meadow grass—it was a wonderful memory, and all that remained for Endimin.

Like Aivlys, he dreamed of revenge, but not by violence. Endimin was a respected elder in the civilized state of Gnomon. He abhorred brutality in any form, which made it all the more tragic that this savagery had been visited on his family. Crime, especially of a vicious nature, was almost unheard of in Gnomon. Disputes were settled peacefully, or in civil court, and general prosperity kept theft to a minimum. The city-state had a well-regulated commerce system that brought the greatest benefit to the most people, without favoring one faction over another, but also without discouraging the active participation of the astute businessmen whose enterprises fostered the well-being of all citizens.

But none of this was on Endimin's mind as he crossed the broken line of the Impasse and walked slowly into Firoze, picking his way among boulder fields. Before he reached the tree line, Endimin came to a ledge where the cliff dropped off dramatically, offering a view of the entire countryside and the sea beyond. From here Endimin could see the wall-ringed citadel of Firoze far below. Like Gnomon, Firoze was a city-state, with one major population and commerce center supporting a collection of smaller villages in the countryside. From above, it was easy to see the difference between the two cultures as reflected in their architecture. Unlike Gnomon, which was a gracefully designed capital of wide boulevards and tree-lined promenades, Firoze resembled an immense fortress, as though the original castle had simply expanded to encompass the outlying buildings and homes within its stone walls. There was something rough and crude, yet strong and unyielding, in the defensive, secure layout of Firoze, that contrasted sharply with the open, free feeling of the city of Gnomon. To Endimin's eyes there was something foreboding, dispiriting, and hostile in the sight of the grim battlements. His will faltered as he contemplated entering that dreaded place, which had become a fearful legend during the hundreds of years that the Impasse had separated the two city-states.

Not today, he thought. *I must know what happened first.* Reluctantly he turned to find his way back to the gap between the two worlds.

Sound travels clearly in the thin mountain air. Endimin had not proceeded more than a few hundred yards before he heard the grunts of someone at work moving heavy objects. Curious, Endimin approached cautiously until he could see the figure of an enormous man, heaving and straining as he moved boulder-sized rocks without the aid of levers or slings, hefting them by hand.

The same morning that Endimin had come to look for his son's slayers, Beroth had decided to make another tour of his high lands, and to try to place a wall of stones across the breach to prevent further encroachment by nosy Gnomons. He arrived after Endimin Platho had already passed through. Beroth heaved a pack of heavy tools onto a pile of stones, tucked up the sleeves of his jacket, and began to shove the boulders around as if they were playthings. It seemed an impossible task even for a giant of a man such as himself to attempt to repair what an earthshaker had rended, but Beroth was stubborn and methodical, a combination that served him well in the onerous task of rebuilding

a natural wall with his own hands. Now they confronted
each other, these two men whose lives were now inex-
tricably joined by the death of a little boy. They faced
each other from a few feet apart, Beroth looming and
leering over Endimin.

"A Gnomon! I'm building this wall to keep you out.
This is my land, the land of Beroth of Firoze. What are
you doing in Firozian territory?"

"Endimin Platho is my name. I came to look for the
men who murdered my boy."

Beroth dropped the pickax he had been using to split
granite slabs to make blocks for his wall.

"Your son was trespassing, as you are now. He fell.
It was an accident."

"Then why was his body hidden as if to cover up a
crime? Why didn't you bring him up out of that black
ravine, look for his kin? Isn't that the least you could
have done?" Endimin's calm insistency annoyed
Beroth, who would have preferred a good fight to this
methodical questioning.

"Suppose I did slay him? What could you do about
it, you weak creature? Go back to your women and
your country of watchmakers!"

"If you are guilty I'll pursue justice by every possible means. I'll walk into Firoze itself to file charges
against you."

"If you had any self-respect as a man you would attack me, even if it meant your own certain death, which
it would!"

"Yes, that would be your way. Our way is more civilized. We have a court for our grievances, and a system
of justice that must be honored, if we are not all to turn
into savages as we once were, as you still appear to
be."

"As you suggested, we too have a court, a bunch of
sniveling panderers whose sole function is to separate
people from their money. This supposed crime, which I

tell you was an accident, occurred here on my land, in Firoze. Let's see you secure justice in a Firozian court. You might as well try to milk a bull or glean eggs from a rooster. Take this bag of gold coins for recompense," Beroth said, reaching into his clothing to remove a leather purse he kept hung around his neck, but Endimin waved him off with a curt gesture.

"My son was worth more than any amount of coinage. I'll test your society's justice system. If I gain no satisfaction there, then I'll challenge you to a fight, even if it does mean my death!" Endimin took Beroth by surprise with these bold words, pushed past him, and clambered over the wall before the enraged giant could summon up a response.

2

THE NEXT DAY ENDIMIN CLIMBED THE mountains once again and entered Firoze, this time carefully skirting the place where Runny had crossed; Endimin searched and found another, lesser break in the Impasse farther down the mountainside. By sticking to a forest path, he saw no one and no one saw him until he was well down off the mountain and within sight of the rear gate, known as the Hill Gate, of Firoze. Most traffic entered through the front gate, called the Port Gate, which faced the harbor and the sea. As soon as he was spotted, Endimin was immediately surrounded by a crowd of Firozians who were buying and selling goods at the informal bazaar that sprang up at the city walls. As he walked toward the immense carved wooden (iron-reinforced) double doors of the Hill

Gate, Endimin observed that among the food for sale
was much more meat and many fewer vegetables than
at a comparable market in Gnomon. Goat meat, pig
meat, whole skinned rabbits, and an occasional fish
comprised the available viands. But the intrusive mob
gave him little time for much more than a cursory
glance, as they jostled for a look at the stranger who
had wandered in from the mountains.

"What sort of man are you?" a gangly lunk asked
him rudely.

"I am from Gnomon," Endimin responded with dignity. Immediately the wide-eyed children in the procession (for it had become a lengthy train with Endimin at
its head) burst into a derisive song:

> *Funny little Gno-mon,*
> *Poke him in the nose, man,*
> *He's so tiny*
> *You can knock him on his hiney!*

By the time he reached the Hill Gate, Endimin was
being trailed by several hundred Firozians, some hostile, some mocking, all curious and amazed at the boldness of the diminutive figure, whose neatly tailored,
close-fitting clothes made him look dapper and a little
effeminate compared to the Firozians, whose finest rai-
ments were barely more than animal skins sewn together or rough-hewn cloth.

At the entrance to the city Endimin found his way
barred by two imposing sentries in military outfits, each
holding one of Firoze's famous broadswords that were
nearly as long as Endimin was tall.

"What is your business here?" one of the guards
asked him coldly. Fearlessly, Endimin announced his
purpose:

"I have come to press charges against a Firozian citizen. For the murder of my son."

"What?!" Momentarily stunned by this response, the guard sputtered in his rage.

"The courts, where are the courts?" Endimin insisted.

Mastering his anger, the warrior began to laugh harshly. "Who knows? No one uses them. We settle our affairs with this," he said, brandishing the outsized blade. "The court is for cowards, craven mongers, and money changers."

"Nonetheless, you must have one. If you don't know where it is, who will?"

The crowd murmured at the bravery of the little man who did not flinch as the guard lifted his weapon threateningly—they had seen others chopped to pieces for lesser offenses. For a moment it looked as if Endimin was going to be split in two right there at the entrance to Firoze, but just then a more important personage, some Firozian nobleman with a retinue of armed horsemen, came charging toward the gate, and both Endimin and the guards were forced to jump out of the way to let them pass. The guards also snapped to attention, eyes forward, and while they were saluting the royal procession Endimin walked into the city unmolested. A squat youngster in breech pants tugged at his coat.

"I know where them courts is," he said.

"Show me," said Endimin.

"Got any o' them Gnome-apples?" the boy asked, looking for a reward. Endimin smiled faintly at the thought that even with the Impasse between them, the fame of the tasty fruits of the orchards of Gnomon had reached the ears of children in Firoze.

"Alas, I have not brought any fruit with me," he said, making a show of rummaging in his pockets. "I have a Gnomon copper ha'penny for you, but you won't be able to spend it here."

"That's okay—it's a prize."

"Indeed."

"Foller me." The boy took Endimin's hand in one the same size and led him down a narrow side street while Endimin mused that children, though they could be cruel, had no inborn prejudice against others, it must be taught them.

"Here it is. Ain't much to look at, is it?" his youthful guide giggled. In Gnomon, Endimin reflected, the Hall of Justice was the centerpiece of the Civic Plaza, an imposing but somehow inviting building that was the pride of the citizenry. The structure before him was a shabby one-story wooden frame in need of painting. It was located far from the center of Firoze, on a nameless side street that the boy had dragged him down against his will, because he didn't believe this could be the site of the judiciary system of a city-state the size of Firoze.

"Thanks, little fellow," Endimin said to the urchin who had led him here, for though the child looked and talked nothing like Runny, Endimin felt a warmth in his heart for all little boys.

"Thanks for the ha'penny!" the boy said, and dashed off, probably to show his playmates his newfound treasure, Endimin speculated.

Summoning up his courage again, Endimin took a deep breath and crossed the threshold into the court building. Narrow windows allowed only a sickly light into the front hall, where a bored-looking clerk sat behind a desk whittling linked rings out of a long stick. He opened his eyes wide when he saw the odd-looking stranger enter, a foreigner, but soon slouched back into calculated indifference. He waited for Endimin to speak, rather than asking him his business.

"I've come to file a complaint," Endimin said, breaking the awkward silence.

"You're joking," was the clerk's response.

"A serious complaint, the highest charge one man can make against another. My name is Endimin Platho, and I wish to charge Beroth of Firoze with the slaying of my son Runward Platho."

"Murder!"

"Yes."

"Just a moment." The clerk didn't exactly jump up, but Endimin noticed that there was an increased alacrity in his movements, as he disappeared down a dim hallway, to fetch a court officer, Endimin hoped. The clerk was gone for several minutes; Endimin looked around, but there was little to see in the barren hall without any sign of activity. After a few minutes the clerk returned with a glum look on his face, as if he were the bearer of bad news.

"I'm sorry, there's no one here to take your complaint."

"That's absurd. Who did you go to see just now?"

"I, uh, I looked for the duty judge but he's not here right now."

"This is preposterous. There must be someone. How can you call yourselves a civilized people when your justice system is so pathetically understaffed? I don't believe you."

"Hey now," the clerk whined, "I'm only telling you what—" and then he stopped, realizing that his next words would reveal him to be a liar.

"I am going to wait here until court comes into session," Endimin announced, and he sat down on the floor, since there was no chair in the reception hall other than the one occupied by the stunned clerk.

"You can't do that!" said the bewildered functionary, who had expected Endimin to accept his dismissal without protest, as any Firozian would do. Endimin did not move. Instead he folded his arms to emphasize his resoluteness.

"I'll call the sheriff," the clerical worker threatened. This warning alone would have frightened off the most persistent citizen of Firoze, for the sheriff was known to be a man of quick temper (what Firozian wasn't?) who carried with him a leather whip that he used unsparingly, but Endimin was unaware of the man's reputation.

"Please call him. Maybe he can explain why there's no justice in his jurisdiction." The clerk scurried off to summon the sheriff. He must have told everyone he met along the way of his strange visitor, because by the time he returned, Endimin once again found himself at the center of a jostling crowd of curiosity seekers. They mocked his cross-legged posture and uttered delighted predictions of what would happen to him once the sheriff arrived. To distract them, Endimin removed his gold pocket watch. A murmur rippled through the onlookers —many had heard of the famous watches of Gnomon, but none of the assembled had ever seen one. Satisfied that he had their attention, Endimin flipped a tiny switch in the upper casing, and the delicate instrument began to chime a soothing lullaby. The light, tinkling sound of tiny sprockets pinging against resonating metal reeds utterly fascinated the crowd, which remained spellbound until the moment was shattered by the heavy footsteps of the sheriff entering the hall.

"Where is this impudent foreigner? I'll lash him to the bone!" he bellowed. The mob drew back in fear. Endimin calmly replaced his pocket watch and waited for the sheriff to approach him. Without introducing himself, the sheriff picked up Endimin from where he sat in his nonviolent protest against the inequities of Firozian justice, and began to shout in his face, "What do you mean, dragging me away from my duties to come here?"

"These are your duties," Endimin tried to say, but he was choking because the sheriff had him by the throat.

"I'll flay your hide!" the sheriff shouted, and pressed him against the wall and was in the process of withdrawing his whip from the holster where he carried it when an amazing thing happened—the sheriff found himself clutching empty air and the crowd surged forward to look for the mischievous Gnomon, but he was gone, vanished, disappeared!

Endimin looked back from the hillside above Firoze. He could see search parties combing the streets for him, led by the sheriff, riding a miserable pony that was too small for his bulk, that suffered and stumbled at every step. They would never catch him today. By the time they climbed the mountain to look for him, Endimin would be approaching his home on the other side of the slope.

3

AIVLYS SIFTED A HANDFUL OF CORN-
meal together with wheat flour and
scooped a chunk of butter from the
churn to cut into the dough. Her
hands worked independently of her
mind, which was occupied with
thoughts of her lost brother. In the
days since his death, Aivlys felt as
though she were moving in a world of
ghosts, as if she too had been killed
and all around her were disembodied
spirits. She tried to be helpful and
consoling to her father, but he too was
silent and brooding. They coexisted in
the small farmhouse without much
talk or warmth between them, until
the morning that Endimin came out of
his bedroom to find Aivlys weeping
into the bread batter.

"Are ye substituting those tears for
salt, daughter?" he asked, trying to
cheer her with a joke.

"I'm sorry, Father. I'll throw this out and start over."

"No need, no need. Your tears are as pure as your soul, dear girl."

"I fear not, Father. I hunger for revenge."

"Seek justice, not retribution, Aivlys."

"But they drove you off when you tried to appeal to their court," Aivlys pointed out as she kneaded and patted the tear-moistened dough and began to shape it into a loaf.

"Yes, but I am not finished with them. I have a new plan for securing justice, in our courts, not theirs."

"How will you ever get those beasts to submit to Gnomonese litigation?"

"There are ways and there are ways," Endimin said mysteriously as he watched his daughter place a nicely formed oval mound of soon-to-be bread in the heated oven. "Aivlys, come here," he said with a sudden decisiveness in his voice that startled her out of a moody reverie. She approached him timidly. He took her by the shoulders and looked into her pensive, sorrow-worn face, *too serious for such a young one,* he thought.

"Aivlys, I have made a decision. No more baking and cleaning for you."

"What do you mean, Father? Who will take care of you? And what will I do?"

"We'll hire a housekeeper."

"And I? . . ."

"You are going to be a watchmaker," Endimin told her.

Aivlys clapped her hands together. Her face lost its usually melancholy expression and its gloomy cast was replaced with one of surprise and excitement. Her father's repair shop was a nearly magical place for her, with its neatly displayed tools, its many boxes and drawers of tiny parts, its smooth wooden tables, its magnifying glasses, and bright focused oil lamps.

"That's wonderful. I've always wanted to learn your trade. How did you know?"

"I didn't," Endimin answered honestly. "Girls aren't supposed to like those sorts of things."

"Oh, but I do. And anyway, I'm all you have now, Father."

"Yes. But you mustn't enter into this lightly, Aivlys. There is more to the watchmaker's trade than simple repair of clocks and watches."

"What do you mean?"

"There are spells and charms associated with our work," Endimin began, hesitantly, for in his heart he felt that it was his lost son who should have been receiving this knowledge.

"Go on, Father," Aivlys said, her eyes bright with anticipation. "I have heard old folk talk of these things, but I never knew that my own kin were privy—"

"You must promise never to use them in anger, or vengefully. This is a sacred trust I convey to you now." Aivlys nodded her head; she was aware that accepting this secret was an initiation into the heart of Gnomonese wisdom.

"A timepiece," Endimin said, "is much more than an object for keeping track of the hours. It represents the highest knowledge of our civilization, for from it spring all the other wonders of science. If you can count the hours you can organize, divide, and classify the multitude of things in this world. Many animals are endowed with a well-developed sense of time, to be sure, but theirs is limited to knowledge of what is good for them. Bats come out early in the evening when insects are aloft. Roosters crow at dawn—"

"Why, Father?"

"I don't know. They just do. Perhaps because it's their one moment to celebrate. Their spirit rises with the sun. But the men and women of Gnomon have learned that they can comprehend time without reference to the sun, and moreover, they can manipulate it, albeit ever so slightly, by means of our—"

"Watches?"

"No, dear, not our beautiful watches. These are only the creations that have enabled us to understand time. To bend and shape it to our wills, that took a mechanism much more sophisticated than our watches: our minds!"

"Is it magic?"

"Everything is magic. The unfurling of a curled-up bright green leaf, the smell of persimmons, the pull of the moon on the sea, ah, what pageantry! And all of it happening within the framework of Time."

"I, I don't understand." Aivlys looked crestfallen, as if she imagined that just by hearing these whispered secrets she would suddenly have understood all.

"Listen carefully. The people of Gnomon, after hundreds of years of study, have mastered several spells, among them, Stop Time, Slow Time, and No Time. Each has unique properties. Stop Time creates the appearance that everything has momentarily come to a halt around you, so that you can move quickly within the suspended moment. This is useful when you are threatened by imminent danger. For example, it allows you to reposition yourself out of the way of an attack. I used it yesterday to free myself from the clutches of the sheriff of Firoze. Slow Time has a slightly different effect: everything seems to slow down, so that a single moment plays itself out ever so slowly. This is useful if you are already engaged in combat with a faster, more agile opponent. It enables you to see his (or her) intention as it is born, and react, though you yourself are moving no faster than the events around you. No Time—No Time is the most powerful of these three. I am not ready to reveal its secrets to you yet. Study the first two for a while."

"All this talk suddenly about combat. I thought we

were a peaceful people." Aivlys had never thought of her mild-mannered, bench-bound craftsman father as a fighter.

"We are a peaceful folk," Endimin rejoined, "but we will fight when we have to. Fortunately that has not been necessary in your lifetime, or mine, but the ways of war have never completely left us, even if we work on watches, and not swords, like our militant brethren, the Firozians."

"Don't call them our brethren," Aivlys said hotly.

"Oh, but they are, my dear, more than you know. All men are brothers, especially on a small island like this. But brothers often quarrel. The Firozians are bigger, stronger, faster, more warlike. Our spells are our equalizer."

"Show me one," Aivlys whispered in fascination.

"All right, a simple demonstration of Stop Time. When I bow, you bow, too." Endimin bowed. Aivlys followed suit, and when she lifted up her head, he stood a hundred paces off, though Aivlys had not seen him move! He could not possibly have run so far so quickly. How had he gotten there?

This was how Endimin had escaped from the grip of the sheriff of Firoze. The whole great engine, the heart of the universe stopped in midpulse. In that gap, in that frozen moment between breathing in and breathing out, between systole and diastole, Endimin had been free when all else was restrained. It had to be an illusion, of course, but it was real, too. Aivlys was mystified. Endimin walked back toward her slowly while Aivlys waited, her heart aflutter and her mind feverish with questions.

"We have learned to take a slice of time and expand it, contract it, or, most difficult of all, make it disappear," Endimin explained. "As precise as our timepieces are, time itself is vague, elusive, a matter of

perception on the part of the one observing it. Time is
not in the watch, but in the watcher."

"I don't understand," Aivlys protested again.

"You must study and practice yourself the mysteries
of time. First of all, you must learn to use the watchmaker's tools. Runny, good lad that he was, was more
interested in running and playing outdoors than in the
tedious and painstaking work of constructing timepieces. You must take his place, be diligent and metic-
ulous, until you can see the insides of a watch as if you
were looking at the delicate tracery of your own veins.
Then will come understanding, and power."

"But I thought you said it wasn't in the watches—"

"True—"

"Then how—"

But Endimin would say no more. Aivlys knew that
she had been granted an honor not given to many
young girls, the opportunity to become one of the people for whom Gnomon was justly famous in this part of
the world; the watchmakers of Gnomon were known
throughout the western ocean of Emer. Traders came to
port on a regular basis to purchase their elaborate creations for wealthy collectors, among them the royalty of
other cultures who were unfamiliar with the workings
of the fancy, ornate devices. In some of these lands the
clocks were treated as toys, while in others they were
regarded with almost mystical reverence. To be a
Gnomonese clockmaker was a highly honored position,
not often filled by women, even though with their small
hands and aptitude for detail one would think they
would be perfect candidates for the job. Endimin had
lost his male heir, who even while alive had never
shown much interest in assuming his father's mantle, so
it was natural that he should turn to his only other
child, but still, Aivlys was moved by being chosen. She
vowed to herself that she would do everything she
could to make herself worthy of the position.

"Will you send me to the apprentice school?" she asked.

"No, I'm going to teach you myself."

Beginning that morning, Aivlys went to school in her father's workshop. With her nimble fingers and agile brain, she quickly learned the basics of watch repair— finding a broken spring here, a gear tooth snapped off there. Often, removing a speck of grease or grit in the wheels was the only adjustment necessary to put a malfunctioning watch back in service. Then Endimin had her learn all over again, blindfolded. Her hands learned what her eyes and mind thought they already knew. Soon she could identify the three hundred–odd parts of the most complicated mechanisms by feel alone. A mere touch would tell her what others could not detect with careful observation.

When she thought she was ready she asked her father again to teach about the spells, but he declined, saying only "Give it time," an appropriate but maddening response. Occasionally Aivlys still found herself overwhelmed with sadness at the loss of her brother. Endimin had forbidden her to climb the mountains behind their house, and had sold off most of the sheep to a neighboring farmer to give her less reason to even think of venturing up there. He kept her busy with clock repairs and housework so as to take her mind off her sorrow, but on occasion he would find her weeping at the workbench, and would slip out unseen so as not to disturb her in her grief.

Endimin was also at work on a plan to lure the Firozian murderer into Gnomon territory, where he would be incarcerated and brought to trial. He discussed his ideas with a small group of influential citizens of Gnomon who had heard about the case and expressed their willingness to help him. They met in a tea shop on a corner of the main city square, under the shadow of the civic administration building. The open

plaza was Gnomon's heart, a broad open area that
sometimes served as an open-air market, and other
times functioned as a meeting-place for the citizens.
The grand courthouse and offices of the city dominated
the square on one side; the remaining three sides were
occupied by smaller buildings, shops, private offices,
and the Clocktower Hotel for travelers. Because Gnomon was on an island and was a port of call, there were
a considerable number of businesses associated with
marine affairs: ship chandleries, freight carriers, seamen's employment agencies, fish markets, sail makers,
painters, lumber merchants, and, of course, numerous
watch and clock shops selling Gnomon's most famous
export.

Endimin ordered pastries and a pot of fresh-brewed
Stangian tea, the infused bark and leaves of a special
plant with soothing qualities that were said by some to
be medicinal. Half a dozen men gathered around a table
sipping from mugs and sampling from the plate of
baked goods. Other customers came in and left with
bags of tea or boxes of pastries.

"Well, my co-conspirators, I have given long thought
to how to rectify this outrage. It must be done with dignity, but also with cunning, for this Beroth is a formidable opponent: strong, agile, and not a fool."

"We need to put temptation in his way. What would
intrigue a man like him?"

"The prospect of bloodshed, for one thing," one man
commented. There was a murmur of general agreement
around the table. Although Endimin was the only one
to have recent contact with a citizen of Firoze, others
had encountered them in the past, with equally discouraging results. A few years back a Gnomonese fishing
boat had been swept around the coral reefs by unex-
pectedly strong currents and had foundered on Firozian
shores on the other side of the island. Firozian fishermen accused the Gnomonese of poaching and had exe-

cuted them on the spot, without benefit of legal
representation or procedure. This incident was typical
of relations between the two cultures—when they met,
it was usually the Gnomonese who suffered humiliation
and defeat, though their intentions were always peaceful.

"We could promise him a new weapon," one man
suggested. "New ways to kill have an allure for warlike
people."

"We could make him a sword," another craftsman offered.

"Yes, but he might use it on us," someone joked.
Several muttered their concurrence and drew out tobacco pouches and clay pipes. The teahouse was soon
filled with thick bluish smoke.

"No," said Endimin, "we need a subtler plan. Why
would Beroth risk coming to Gnomon for one of our
swords? He knows that blades made in Firoze are superior to any we could produce."

"And he probably doesn't know how to tell time, so
he doesn't need a clock," the jokester in the crowd
cracked, to general laughter. Encouraged, he continued:
"Do we need bait? Why don't we use what always
works on a man? A woman!" the prankster quipped, but
his remark was not greeted with laughter. It was well
known that Gnomon women were more delicate and refined than their coarser Firozian counterparts. The
slight stature of Gnomon men was perceived as weakness, but in Gnomon women the same daintiness gave
them a pale beauty that was unsurpassed among the
femininity of all the neighboring islands.

"We don't offer our womenfolk to the likes of him,"
was the gruff response from more than one of the con-
spirators gathered at the tea-shop table.

Undeterred, the pesky devil's advocate, Basco
Fournier, stood up to address his fellow tea drinkers.
He was a slight man, with sharp features and arched

eyebrows that fixed his face in a permanently quizzical expression, as if he were questioning everything in the world, all the time. "I speak joshingly, yet my purpose is serious," Basco taunted them. "We can't compete with the Firozians on the battlefield, nor do our crafts entice them. Only our wives and our daughters offer any attraction to them. As you all know, over the years we have discovered several of our ladies missing, with evidence pointing to abduction by men from Firoze. None of these crimes was ever solved, because we had no way to bring the evildoers to justice. Now, here is an opportunity to avenge ourselves for an even more heinous crime—the murder of an innocent. I say we use whatever wiles we have, even if that means putting our lives, and even the lives of our better halves, at risk."

"Fournier, you're mad," several protested, but Endimin rose slowly, faced the angry group, and said: "I agree with Fournier. Moreover, I am willing to offer my daughter Aivlys as the lure."

"What?"

"After you've already lost your son?"

"We can't let you do that!" With these and other remarks the men importuned Endimin against agreeing to Basco Fournier's wild and reckless plan.

"I have no intention of losing another child," Endimin said. "I plan to give her the proper preparation to defend herself. In short, even though she is a woman I propose to initiate her into the Watchmakers' Guild."

Instead of laughing at this ridiculous remark, the men instead nodded their heads and scratched at their beards, those that had them, and appeared satisfied with Endimin's answer.

"I will help you," Basco declared, suddenly serious.

Endimin circled the table to grip his hand. "I accept your offer. She has been practicing for several weeks now, and is ready for her first test. You can play the role of the enemy in our mock battle."

"It's a role I do not relish, yet I'll take it on for your benefit, and hers, and the lad Runny's, for I liked that boy. He used to come around to my shop on occasion, you know." Basco owned an odd little store down the lane from the teahouse, where boys could buy kites, marbles, spyglasses, whistles, and other items of interest to youngsters.

"Agreed."

That evening Endimin explained his actions to Aivlys as they sat at the dinner table. Lamps burning oil drawn from sea creatures should have glowed with warmth, but there was something hollow, cold, and empty in the wavering light. Both Endimin and his daughter still suffered from their loss, and no amount of soft illumination was strong enough to soothe their shattered spirits. Endimin knew that desire for retribution weighed as heavily on Aivlys's youthful soul as the hunger for justice gnawed on his heart.

"I offered your participation without asking you because I was sure you would be willing to do almost anything to see Runny's murderers brought to justice—"

"You are right, Father," said Aivlys, her eyes blazing.

"Now I must see if you are ready."

"But, Father," Aivlys protested, "you haven't taught me a thing about spells. I can take watches apart and put them together as well as anyone on Gnomon, I daresay, but I still know nothing of the powers you say we hold—and of which I've seen only one small demonstration by you."

"If you pass this test I will show you all, or almost all. The rest you will have to discover for yourself, within yourself."

"What kind of test can this be?"

"Basco Fournier will play the role of attacker, and you will defend yourself against him. When the right

moment comes, you will initiate a spell to protect yourself."

"Why couldn't you play that part?" Aivlys asked.

"I'm your father. You trust me too much. Fournier,
though he is known to you, is still by and large a stranger; you can't read him as easily as you could me."

"Read?" Aivlys asked.

"Divine my intentions. This is one of the keys of our
spells: timing!"

"You'll have to explain more to me."

"Even if you know the words for one of our enchantments, its power is null unless you use it at the proper
moment. That's what it's all about—finding the instant
that action is effective and applying the spell that fits."

"It's all so vague. . . . I like working on watches better, everything is so precise, so tiny and ordered and
regulated," said Aivlys, and her father agreed.

"Yes, and you must find that same precision in your
enchanting."

"Oooohhh, that's impossible," Aivlys moaned, and
she hung her head in worry.

"All things become easier with practice."

The next morning Basco Fournier sauntered up the
road to the Platho farm while Aivlys and Endimin were
sweeping the front porch after breakfast.

"I'm not ready, I'm not ready," Aivlys nearly
screamed, but her father insisted that she accompany
him to greet their visitor. Basco Fournier wore the same
puzzled expression that he displayed in the tea shop the
day before—it never left him, and neither did the twin-
kly, crinkly air of bemusement in his eyes. *He'll be
harder to fathom than my father,* Aivlys thought, but
she curtsied prettily and offered Basco a glass of goat's
milk and a morning biscuit, which he declined.

"Just some of that fine cold well water, darlin'."

Aivlys ran to the well and sent the bucket clanging
down into the hole. All she could think was *I'm not a*

sorceress. I'm just a young girl who knows how to fix watches. How can I try to use magic? I know nothing. But just before her father led her out to do battle with Basco Fournier, he whispered in her ear the words to the second spell, Slow Time.

"When you see him vulnerable, say to yourself: *'Time passes like molasses.'* "

"That's it?"

"That's it. Trust me, it will work. You are a Gnomon watchmaker. It's your heritage."

"But how will I know when to use it?"

"Use your feminine wiles, dear. Throw him off balance. Distract him. Make him think about something else besides fighting; then, when his mind wanders, strike!"

Still uncertain, Aivlys wandered out to the pasture where Basco Fournier stood. The quirky Fournier was flexing his stringy muscles and pretending to warm up for a fierce struggle, as though he and Aivlys were going to engage in hand-to-hand combat. When he saw her approaching he drew his sword, apparently determined to play his part to the hilt, so to speak. Aivlys, unarmed, wandered into his range and had to leap back to avoid a vicious midlevel swing from the surprisingly agile Fournier. The sword blade tore through the outer layer of Aivlys's sleeve, nearly slicing into her arm. She ran backward a few steps, more in shock than in fear, and screeched to her father, "He almost cut my arm off!"

Endimin Platho shrugged and watched silently, though he nodded his head imperceptibly to warn her that another attack was coming, which gave her just enough time to sidestep a downward thrust that would have split her in twain from head to hip.

"Mr. Fournier, have you gone mad? You could have killed me!" she gasped as she fought to catch her breath from the exertion of dodging the blow.

"That's the idea, m'dear." Again he advanced on her, sword poised in the stance of readiness for the cross-body attack. Aivlys finally realized that her father and Basco truly meant to test her. As Fournier prepared to utilize the cross-body blow, Aivlys licked her lips and blew him a kiss. He hesitated for a fraction of a second and his perpetually mocking eyes widened slightly, then he swung, but in the interim Aivlys saw her opening and recited to herself the words she had learned only minutes ago: *"Time passes like molasses."* The blade came at her as slowly as if Basco Fournier were moving underwater. Aivlys was able to turn away and at the same time grasp his outstretched hand that gripped the sword and twist it, hard. The sword fell from his hand and drifted to the ground like a feather. As soon as it touched earth the spell ended and time resumed its steady march, but Basco Fournier was unarmed and Aivlys stood with her foot triumphantly atop the fallen weapon.

"Well done, daughter!" Endimin cried out, and he came rushing up to embrace her, but she pushed him away angrily.

"If I wasn't quicker on my feet I might have died! Is this how you treat your only remaining child?"

Endimin's pained expression showed that he knew the demonstration might have gone too far, but curiously he refused to back down in the face of his daughter's rage. "What was done had to be done," he said quietly. "The Guild does not admit those who have not been tested under duress."

"The Guild?"

"You are not alone, daughter. As I tried to explain to you, there is a society of those who have obtained the hidden wisdom of the Gnomon. In order to enter it, you must prove yourself, as you have done. Tonight there will be a ceremony of initiation, and you will be inducted into the Watchmakers' Guild."

"I . . . ?"

"Yes. You passed the test."

"With colors flying," added Basco Fournier, who had been standing to the side rubbing his twisted wrist as father and daughter talked. "Even though I knew the nature of the test, I was caught unprepared, and you slipped the charm on me smoothly. An enemy would have succumbed even more easily."

"An enemy would likely be swinging a bigger sword and paying less attention to distractions," Endimin cautioned, but both Aivlys and Basco could see that he was pleased with her performance.

That evening Aivlys climbed the Clocktower above City Hall for the first time. Meetings of the Guild were held in a room near the top of the brick structure, windowless except for a single row of panes beneath the opening where the bells were arrayed. Inside the tower was a winding staircase that permitted no view until one reached this upper chamber. Access to the Clocktower was gained from the ground level through a door in the Mayor's Chambers, that led into the stairwell that proceeded in darkness uninterrupted up seventeen turns to a single door at the top of the stairs. It was the perfect meeting place for a secret society, even one as beneficent as the Gnomon Watchmakers' Guild. Firoze was ruled by their military; they had no civic government to speak of. Gnomon, on the other hand, was administered by a civilian group, not chosen by all the people, but instead inducted after nomination and selection from within the Guild. This was no more democratic than the Firozian method of rule by soldiery, but it had worked so well for so many years that no one complained about lack of representation, and everyone knew someone in the Guild.

The meeting room was sparsely decorated. Moonbeams struggled to penetrate the high windows that never received washing and supplement the dim candlelight from a dozen wicks laid out ceremonially on a round table in the center of the space. When Aivlys and her father arrived, the other members of the Guild were already seated in high-backed chairs around this table. Aivlys wanted to run to the windows to see the view from here above Gnomon, but the solemn demeanor of the men and the austere formality of the meeting place deterred her.

Among the attendees were several of the same men who had gathered at the tea shop the previous afternoon, only now instead of casual working dress or merchant's attire they wore black robes. As Aivlys waited she saw her father don one of these velvet garments, and suddenly it was as if she didn't know him, he was so serious and reserved. She felt herself the object of intense examination by these men, most of whom she had known since she was a little girl, who now stood in judgment of her. She shuffled her feet and kept her head up as her father had instructed her to do. The bells rang out the third quarter hour, and her heart raced at feeling the powerful reverberations so close by. Her entire life had been demarcated by the sound of those bells, which could be heard even up in the foothills where the Platho family lived, yet she had never heard them like this, shatteringly loud and ringingly pure, an almost physical sensation. There was another staircase that clung to one wall of the meeting room and snaked its way up to the bell tower; she would have loved to have scampered up there to see the huge swinging musical instruments in motion, but she held her ground and waited, for she knew that her patience was being tested.

Aivlys was still standing before them when the ringing of the hour began with the full cycle of the little melody that represented the four quarter hours, followed by the sonorous pealing of the hour bell, nine times in all. Nine o'clock. Not the witching hour, but

the hour of fulfillment and completion. The men around
the table rose with the first strike of the nine, and
formed a processional that encircled Aivlys. They had
draped their heads with the cowls of their robes and
hidden their faces with these hoods, but Aivlys could
still identify her father among the anonymous figures
by his familiar gait and the way he held his body. One
of the other men stepped forward to address her. The
others swayed and rocked gently on their heels while
murmuring a low chant. Aivlys couldn't quite make out
the words, but she heard her name more than once in
the monotonously hypnotic reverie that was created
by the quiet thrumming sound of their united voices. It
was a weird scene, here high above Gnomon, these
common townspeople playing out some mystic ritual
that was a throwback to an earlier time in history, when
the wisdom of the Gnomon was preserved by a few
monkish men. How would she feel tomorrow, Aivlys
wondered, when she saw Henri Blouchette, the court
cleric, on his way to a day of tedious, officious duties.
Would they nod at each other in secret remembrance of
this unlikely moment?

"What time is it?" the lead figure asked.

"Nine o'clock," Aivlys answered. *What a silly question, the bells had just rung. Anyone could count them.*

"What time is it?" she was asked again.

Aivlys was about to say something sassy when she
realized that there was a purpose to their inane query.
These men wanted to know how much she had absorbed of the mysteries her father had taught her. They
were really asking her: What is time? Her whole future
rested on her reply. Suddenly she was more frightened
than when she had stood unarmed and faced Basco
Fournier's sword. What did she know? What could she
show them about the Great Interval and how much she
had come to understand as her father patiently unlocked
secrets, first by teaching her how clocks and watches

functioned, then by carefully leading her to the higher wisdoms, where mechanisms meant nothing.

"Time has no second hand, no minute hand, no hour hand," she said impulsively. They waited. She fell silent. Then another thought came to her, and she spoke up: "If I stand still it won't pass me by, but if I leap ahead it will still catch me." Her second response was met by more silence, but she didn't know if that meant she was doing well or failing this crucial test. What was her deepest insight into the meaning of Time? She knew that it was pliable, amorphous, resilient, that she could plunge into it like a river and bob up or be swept along. Even now, faced with the heavy muteness of her interrogators, she felt it stretching like an elastic and slowing down. A metronome would have counted the beats steadily, but would not have been an accurate representation of the relative state of time in the room, where an eternity was being enacted in a quarter hour. Suddenly she found her voice.

"Everything depends on time," she said confidently. "Yet it is what we make it. We can shape it to our needs, bend it, even break it, but it remains intact, like the magician's cloth that can be torn into strips and appear anew as a seamless whole fabric. We can walk through rents in its warp and weave, and we can stitch it into a new cloth. We the Gnomonese are the masters of Time, and its most humble tailors. When we fashion a watch, it is in tribute to the innate beauty of the lord we serve. Time is all we have, it has us all in its thrall, and we are glad of it."

Suddenly Aivlys felt faint, as if it were not she who had been speaking but some voice from the ancient past, using her as a medium. She knew she had spoken well.

"You are a true watchmaker," said one of the men, unable to restrain his admiration for her pretty speech.

"Not yet," another voice cautioned. "We still must

vote. Up to the bells with you, Aivlys Platho, to await our decision." The figure with the stern voice directed her with a pointed finger toward the staircase to the bell tower. She assented with a nod of her head and ran quickly up the steps. The door creaked as she opened it, and found herself on a narrow catwalk between the hanging bells. A chair was set there but Aivlys was too excited to sit down. She ran her hands along the smooth, dull, pitted, gray-green metal surface of the bells and wondered how close it was to another quarter hour, and how loud the clanging would be if she were right here in their midst. Before that could happen, however, she was summoned to return to the meeting room below. Once again the men seated in the circle turned to face her. This time her father spoke for the group: "Your answers have pleased us. You are only the fifth woman to be offered admission in the four-hundred-year history of the Guild. What is your reply?"

"I accept."

"So be it." Her father sat down and another of the participants rose from the table and withdrew a carefully wrapped package from the folds of his robe.

"This is the symbol of our order. It represents all eternity in an instant. Show this in times of need. Many can identify it, even some who may surprise you, and those who do are bound and beholden to help you." It was a seal of bronze, embossed not with a watch but with an hourglass figure, laid on its side so that the sand was not flowing but rested at the bottom of the two ends of the tipped glass—a curious image: ∞

"I will." Aivlys took possession of the seal and pressed it to her heart momentarily, a girlish gesture that brought soft laughter from the group of men, who threw back their cowls and became ordinary human beings again. Besides her father and the clerk Henri Blouchette, whom she had recognized before, there was Basco Fournier, the toy shop owner, grinning and quizzical, and several watchmakers, men on whose knees she had bounced as a little girl—now she was their equal. They gathered around her to offer their congratulations. But before she let them embrace her with friendly hugs, she stopped them with upraised arms held out in front of her youthful body.

"Now," she said with a ferocity that startled them, "when do we catch my brother's killer?"

4

ENDIMIN'S PLAN WAS SIMPLE. BASCO
Fournier had suggested it to him as
they walked the hills above the Platho
farmhouse one morning.

"A man wants what he can see but
he can't reach," Basco said. "Aivlys
is a lovely young girl. She need only
make herself visible but unattainable
across the Impasse, and Beroth will
begin to desire her. When his desire
grows strong enough, he will cross.
When he enters Gnomon territory, he
is subject to our laws and we may le-
gally seize him."

"Will the Firoze honor such legal
niceties?"

"Whether they do or don't, we'll
have him. This Beroth is an important
figure in Firoze, a war hero, one of the
landed gentry. If we give him a fair
trial, show that we are a civilized people with respect for the law, they

should understand that we are only doing what is right and proper."

"You dream."

"Perhaps. But, Platho old fellow, if we don't dream, who will, for the world is full of men who sleep their way through life yet never dream. Now that Aivlys has proven herself, we ought to make use of her. She's certainly eager enough."

"Yes, I worry about that. Too much desire for revenge is a bitter wormwood that'll poison her heart."

The two men walked silently for a time. Finally Basco responded: "What you say is true. But I wish that there were more young men like your brave young lady in our land, and we might not've lived in fear of subjugation for so many years." The Gnomonese people knew that they were less militant than their cousins on the other side of the island, and so had maintained an uneasy neutrality in relations, a fine balancing act that had been sustainable only because of the formidable barrier posed by the Impasse and the difficult ocean currents that made access to Gnomon from Firoze by water a treacherous prospect.

"All right. I'll send her to the upper pastures with the flock, just as I did my son. But we must have 'round-the-clock watch on her. I am risking her life, but also mine, because I could never survive the loss of my other child."

Basco clapped a hand on Endimin's sagging shoulders. "I'll lead the reconnaissance myself. We won't lose her."

The plan was set in motion that very day. A neighboring farmer sent over a ram to replace Whitehead. The sheep, which had languished in their pen for several weeks, were delighted to be able to clop up the hillside once more. Maycome raced ahead and back, nipping at the hooves of the newly freed sheep, urging them upward unnecessarily, for they too could smell the high country in the fresh breeze that swept down the hillside.

Aivlys walked on her own. Her escort, made up of Basco Fournier and several young men from the town, followed at a discreet distance, even taking another path as if they were not part of the same shepherding party but another expedition gone off to hunt or fish. Endimin had drawn her a map of the fields where Runny had led the flock. From the uppermost corner of one of the pastures Aivlys could see the edge of the Impasse, and more important, she could be seen from there. She chose an outcropping where she would be highly visible and sat down to wait for her unwanted suitor. The day passed slowly and pleasantly. Aivlys had spent the past weeks cooped up in the repair shop in intense study. For her these hours were a welcome break from the tedium of focusing on the tiny machinations inside a watch or clock. Here in the highlands she could let her eyes roam far, out to the horizon where the indigo sky met the azure sea, or up to the peaks behind her, their rugged outlines framed against the deep blue heavens. Nothing happened the whole day. In the early evening she led the flock back down to the Platho barn. Perhaps Beroth had not visited his holdings along the Impasse that day, and even if he had come by, maybe he hadn't seen Aivlys, or maybe he suspected trickery. It was decided to give the plan a few days to work.

The first two days Aivlys lolled in a meadow while the energetic dog did all the work, but by the third day she was restless and weary of her role as the object of attention. She began to roam after Maycome as he raced around the sheep to keep them within the confines of the meadow. Occasionally one of the younger ewes would drift off in search of a sweeter patch of grass; then Maycome would chase her down and drive her back into the bunch with fierce yapping and by

snapping at her feet. On the afternoon of the third day
Aivlys followed Maycome up a small side canyon after a stray. The valley narrowed rather quickly to
steep, precipitous sides, and took several twists and
turns as it climbed toward the summit. Forgetting that
it would be difficult for her guardians to follow her,
Aivlys pursued Maycome at a trot in search of the lost
sheep. Soon she was wandering in a deep and dim
vale far from the pasture where the rest of the flock
was grazing. Suddenly the missing animal came racing back down the canyon past her, followed by
Maycome in close pursuit. Aivlys turned to follow
them and found her way blocked by the largest man
she'd ever seen. Her eyes flashed in anger, for she
was fairly sure from her father's description that she
was confronting her brother's alleged murderer, but
then she remembered the role she was supposed to
play, and lapsed into a coquettish smile and sweet,
tremulous voice.

"Hello," she said simply.

"I saw you from afar and wondered what you might
look like. I am not disappointed," the giant said to her.

"What's your name?" Aivlys asked him, and while
she felt him pressing closer to her she tried to step
back casually to give herself room to run if the need
arose.

"I am Beroth of Firoze. This is the first time I've visited your country since the the Impasse was broken, but
I'll have to make a habit of it, if all the creatures here
are as lovely as you." Beroth's attempt at flirtation fell
flat, but Aivlys tried gamely to encourage him, all the
while hoping that her protectors were somewhere
nearby.

"Yes, you must come to see our city someday."

"I will, if you'll take me there."

"Perhaps." *Sooner than you imagine,* Aivlys thought
as she tried to hide her loathing of this huge, hairy man.

She didn't like the way he was looking at her with his
narrow eyes under those shaggy eyebrows. If he had
touched her she would have screamed, but so far he
had only made her feel uncomfortable by standing
closer to her than she would have liked.

"What's your name?" he asked her.

"Aivlys."

"Aivlys what? I hear that you Gnomonese have two
names. In Firoze we make do with one."

"Aivlys Platho."

"Eh? Daughter of Endimin Platho?" Beroth roared.
"Your father is a tricky scoundrel who makes false ac-
cusations against me, then disappears, leaving me to defend my name against slander."

"And you are the beast who killed my brother!"
Aivlys shrieked, unable to contain her rage any longer.

"It's a lie. He slipped and fell, I tell you!" Beroth
grabbed for the girl, more in frustration than in lust, but
Aivlys slipped away from his encircling grasp and ran
down the hill. Beroth lumbered after her, careless of
delving deeper into a foreign land. It infuriated him that
this lovely young woman saw him as a "beast" and
wouldn't listen to his denials. He would make her sit
down and hear him, by the gods! With his wide strides
he closed the gap between them quickly, and was about
to snatch at her again when his feet went out from under
him and he felt his arms and legs becoming tangled up
in something. He bellowed and ripped at the snaring fabric, but this only caused him to become more enmeshed.
Blinded by the gauzy cloth, he could hear voices shouting.

"We've got him!" "Hold him now!" "Pull in on the
drawstrings!" "Sit on that leg!"

He couldn't see his captors. They swarmed over him,
wrapping him further with lines and cables. When
Beroth finally stopped struggling, he was completely
entangled in a web of net, ropes, and wire. His limbs

stuck out at oddly uncomfortable angles and his massive face showed signs of exhaustion and even a glimmer of fear.

"I suppose you're going to kill me now," he muttered through the binding. Endimin Platho stepped forward and peered at his captive.

"No. You can send to Firoze for a lawyer if you wish, or you can be represented by the public defender here in Gnomon. You'll receive the finest defense our system can offer—"

"After which I'll be beheaded."

"Even if you're guilty, we won't kill you, but you will serve a long sentence. If you're innocent, you'll be freed."

"I don't believe you. No one would be so stupid as to let their worst enemy go after capturing them. No, I'm resigned to death. Why don't you kill me now instead of acting out the farce of a trial?"

"Beroth, you still don't understand. We take our justice system seriously. By our custom, you're only a suspect. You'll have the right to call witnesses, present a defense, and prove your innocence."

"Will a Gnomonese jury find for me? If I must be tried, I want it to be in Firoze."

"You forget, I offered you that right. I came to Firoze to request your arrest. I was forced to escape from being imprisoned myself. By that action you have abrogated your right to trial in your own country." Endimin stood beside his daughter and watched as Beroth tried in vain to free himself from the trap the Gnomonese men had set for him. When he tired himself out completely, the men slung him from two poles and carried him down the mountain upside down like a carcass.

Word spread quickly in Gnomon. By the time the guard party trooped into the main square a crowd had gathered. Unlike the unruly masses in Firoze, however, this group of citizens did not throw stones or shout insults, but merely watched curiously as Beroth was trundled into a specially constructed outdoor cage (Gnomon had no real jail) to await his trial. Endimin, his accuser, was the first to protest, even before the prisoner himself, that this arrangement was unacceptable and that it would be necessary to house Beroth indoors.

"There must be no question that this man is being treated in the most dignified and respectful manner," Endimin told the court clerk, Henri Blouchette, who doubled as sheriff in those infrequent instances when one was required. Gnomon's fabled court system was in fact almost completely oriented to civil trials, matters of finance such as bankruptcies, and commerce disputes. Violent crime was extremely rare in Gnomon.

"Where can we put him, then?" Henri asked, because there really was no place that would be as secure as the pen of iron fencing that had been thrown together to hold Beroth.

"How about the bell tower? We could use the Guild room."

Members of the Watchmakers' Guild held an impromptu meeting while the assemblage in front of City Hall swelled and milled about and took turns peeking into the enclosure at the unhappy prisoner. The event took on some aspects of a holiday as fruit vendors and pastry sellers began to circulate, hawking their wares. The carnival atmosphere disturbed Endimin greatly —he didn't want it to get back to Firoze that Beroth was being treated like a spectacle. His urgency swayed the members of the Guild. A carpenter was sent up into the Tower to barricade the upper door and strengthen the lower entrance. In the interim, Endimin asked that the crowd be moved back a decent distance from the cell so that Beroth wouldn't feel like an object on display. Henri Blouchette shooed the citizens of Gnomon away ineffectually until the Guild members linked arms and walked forward, pushing the gawkers back. There were a few grumbles of complaint, but soon the novelty diminished and the onlookers dispersed. Within an hour the carpenter reported that the Guild room was secured and Beroth, still bound, was carried into City Hall. At the bottom of several flights of stairs the procession paused uncertainly. It would take a monumental effort to carry their charge all the way up to the Guild room.

"If we unbind your legs do you promise not to give us any trouble?" Endimin asked. Several young men surrounded the prisoner, but he dwarfed them in size and would have been able to put up a dangerous fight even with bound arms. But the fight had been taken out of Beroth by the long trek from the mountain, and he was still in shock at the very idea that he, a great warrior and veteran of numerous military actions, had been captured by a group of puny Gnomons.

"I agree. I have but one request."

"What is it?"

"Please notify my family that I'm here," he said despondently.

"Of course. We would have done so in any case."

"Then I'll cause you no trouble."

The leg ropes were removed from Beroth's thick lower limbs, but his arms remained fastened. He stretched awkwardly a couple of times to bring the circulation back to his feet, then as he had promised, he accompanied the guard party up the stairs without resistance. At the door he turned to them, a scowl on his dark face. Twigs and dirt still clung to hairs of his black beard from the struggle of his capture, giving him a wild countenance.

"You know of course this means war between our peoples. You would have been better off to let me go or kill me. Firoze will destroy Gnomon."

"That's bold talk for a man in chains," one of the

braver young guards blurted out, but Beroth's chilling words struck fear into the hearts of the elders of Gnomon. More than one wondered secretly if they might have been better off to leave well enough alone—all this trouble over a young boy of no consequence to anyone but his family. Endimin felt the mood of those around him and sought to reassure them by addressing Beroth sternly: "There's no need for war. You'll be tried. If you're innocent, you will be allowed to return home. If you're found guilty, there will be just punishment."

"So you told me, but will the army of Firoze wait for your decision? I doubt it."

"Close the door on him," Endimin said abruptly. "Bring him two meals a day, but don't let him out for any reason. Keep him bound at the wrists and spoon-feed him. And always send four men to attend to him."

"Yes, four, and even that might not be enough!" Beroth laughed, suddenly finding his courage. He tumbled into the center of the room and sat down cross-legged, stoically accepting his fate and ignoring his captors.

The next morning the elders dispatched a messenger across the Impasse with word of the action they had taken. In the early evening the messenger staggered back into Gnomon, where he was met by Henri Blouchette on the Courthouse steps. The man was severely beaten, and reported that he was lucky to have escaped with his life. Once again a crowd gathered, this time to hear the tale of his trip into Firoze.

"When I told them what we had done," he gasped, struggling for breath, "they strung me up and took turns whacking me with a stick until I was black and blue all over. I reminded them there was no reason to kill the bearer of bad news, but they only laughed and hit me some more."

"Did they send a message back?" he was asked.

"Not exactly."

"What do you mean?"

"They said I was the message, to look at me and see what would happen to Gnomon if we didn't let Beroth go." And at that the messenger collapsed and was carried to the Seamen's Infirmary for treatment.

Official protests and overt threats followed immediately from Firoze. At the Impasse, Gnomonese stonemasons erected stone walls hastily to re-create the once-inviolable boundary between the two nations; war seemed imminent. Talk in the coffeehouses and shops of Gnomon centered around this one subject only. Some expressed the sentiment that Beroth should be returned without delay, while others insisted that the rule of law must be defended, even at the cost of war. Few doubted the result of such a conflict. Gnomon had never been a military power; it had relied on careful diplomacy and its natural defenses of mountain and sea for protection. The erstwhile sheriff, Henri Blouchette, gathered a citizens' militia to practice in the city square, but most of its members were middle-aged functionaries like himself who huffed and puffed and were out of breath after only a few minutes of marching back and forth. The young men who had served as guards during the capture of Beroth were too few in number to make up for the preponderance of well-fed bellies and aging legs among the troops. Against a disciplined and vastly superior fighting force such as the Firozians, they would stand little chance. Only their magic might provide them with an element of surprise and tactical advantage, and this talent was limited to the few among the populace who were members of the Guild.

Endimin continued to train his daughter in the gray and mysterious arts of Altering Time, which they discussed in the watchmaker's shop and on walks through the hills above their house (though they no longer ventured high into the mountains for fear of meeting Firozians, but instead took the sheep to lower grazing pastures).

"All things can be predicted whose causes can be deduced, and all can be fathomed if we look to the true source of everything," he told her. "Study nature, essential, elemental nature. When a flower blooms to fullness, it will fade, the only question is when. The birds and insects know when a fruit will burst forth and offer its juices to them, why can't we? The answer is, we can. All things can be known, even the actions of that most erratic of animals, man."

Aivlys said nothing but looked at her father with awe. The meek, soft-spoken watchmaker was giving her a glimpse of wisdom she never knew he possessed, even after he had shown her first of the Guild magic spells.

"But the magic . . . ?" Aivlys asked.

"The spells are no more than entries into the obvious. There is only what is known and what is not known. To the ignorant man, the actions of the knowledgeable man are magical. But also, remember this, and remember it well: The overly sophisticated person will miss the magic in the mundane, the simple. Keep yourself open to everything. Open your eyes, your ears, your nose, your mouth, your skin, your mind. Try to take it all in. That, and that alone, is what will make you a good watchmaker, and give you the ability to play with Time."

"So the spells are real, then?" Aivlys hinted.

"Yes, the spells are real, there is magic. I contradict myself. But never mind, keep studying, and one day it will all be clear to you. Look up there, a rainbow!" Endimin cried out, as the sun struck moisture hanging in the valley air and splayed light into the refracted colors of the spectrum.

"How beautiuful!" Aivlys cried.

"There is your true magic!" Endimin reveled, and for

a moment the Platho family was able to forget about
their devastating loss and the shattering possibility of
war looming over them. Their happiness was short-
lived. When they returned to the farmhouse they found
Basco Fournier, Henri Blouchette, and several others
milling about in their front yard.

"Ah, there you are, Platho!" Fournier hailed him.
"Hurry it up, man!"

"What is it?" Endimin shouted back.

"We've received an ultimatum from Firoze. They
give us until noon tomorrow to return Beroth, or they
invade. We've come to ask you—"

"To give it up! Let us give him back or we all die!"
one man cried out.

Basco Fournier ignored him and repeated the first
part of his declaration: "We've come to ask you what
we should do. As the person with the greatest interest
in seeing Beroth tried, you may dictate to the Guild,
and therefore to all the citizens of Gnomon." Fournier
continued in a lower tone: "It's a heavy burden,
Platho. We've no business taking on the Firozians in
armed conflict, no matter how much in the right we
are."

"And what about my slain brother? Who'll stand up
for him?" Aivlys demanded. The crowd of men shuffled their feet nervously and said nothing. Endimin
strode to the porch of his home, followed by Aivlys,
who glared at the timid group around her with disdain.

With his daughter beside him, Endimin began to
speak, quietly at first: "There comes a time in the affairs of men when the most logical thing—the sensi-
ble, prudent thing—is not the best course of action.
There comes a time when it becomes necessary to
stand up to a stronger enemy, even if this means certain defeat."

"When? When is that time? When are you willing to

sacrifice our wives and children to gory war?" one of
the crowd objected.

"When life is no longer worth living. When your
principles are so compromised that to go on is a sham,
a rejection of everything you believe in. What does
Gnomon stand for? In the eyes of the world, it stands
for precision. Our watches and clocks are renowned on
many another island—cherished, prized, sought after,
for their accuracy, their worthiness, their craftsmanship.
But even more than that, we represent honesty—
products well made and sold at a fair price. And from
whence does this reputation stem? From our love of
justice. That is the foundation on which all our success
is built." Endimin's voice rose as he spoke with more
and more passion: "I tell you that if we give up this
man because of this threat, it will not mean only that
we have avoided war. It will mean that we no longer
serve as guardians of those values that have made us
great!"

"Fine sentiments, but sentiments mean nothing to a
dead man," one man responded.

"If you abandon your ideals you are as good as dead.
Also consider this: the Firoze have long been looking
for an excuse to enter our lands, even before the Impasse gave way. Do you think they'll stop eyeing our
country, our wealth, our women, because we give them
back this one man? Mark my words, if we bow before
them this time, their yokes will be on our necks in short
order."

Basco Fournier, who up to this point had kept silent,
suddenly stood up and marched to the porch steps.

"I'm with Platho. I say we make a stand at the Impasse to keep the barbarians from crossing even a single step into our territory!"

The sheriff, Henri Blouchette, then pledged his
young troops to the task, and the rest of the men fell in
behind, though there were still some worried looks

among the farmers, shopkeepers, and tradesmen that
made up the pacifistic population of Gnomon. What
could they do? Endimin was right: if they submitted
now it would only be worse for them in the future. No
one expected to defeat the Firoze, but maybe with luck,
the high ground, and a little magic, they might be able
to stave off a full-scale invasion.

A long file of Gnomonese set out for the high hills
the next morning in advance of the noon deadline. Some
were armed with swords, some with pikes and spears,
some with mere farming implements: pitchforks,
scythes, and rakes. The women and children of the city
lined the streets and wept as their husbands, brothers,
and sons marched off to their probable deaths. Beroth
laughed loudly from his cell in the Clocktower. He
couldn't believe the stupidity of the Gnomonese, who
were almost certainly marching to slaughter.

"Like your lambs!" he shouted so vociferously that
everyone in the main square could hear him ridiculing
them. "Like stupid sheep!"

They marched past Endimin's farm, where Aivlys
stood on the porch as if she hadn't moved since yesterday's tumultuous meeting. Seeing Endimin near the
head of the band, she realized suddenly that evening
could find her an orphan, without brother or father. Her
mother had died so long ago that she was only a vague
memory, but Runny still appeared in her dreams, laughing and playing with Maycome the sheepdog. Was she
now to suffer a final, terrible loss? Yet she held herself
from running and clutching at her father's sleeve and
begging him not to go because his firm step was all that
kept many others from breaking ranks also. He turned
his head slightly to look at her with grim face and set
jaw, sterner than she could ever remember seeing him.

Then they marched away, not singing as real armies
do, but silently trudging upward, climbing the greensward toward the barren peaks where they would find

the enemy waiting to move upon them with awful vengeance. Many of the men were city dwellers who had never been up here among the peaks that ran through the middle of the island. The natural barrier that for hundreds of years had been called the Impasse, because there was no known way across it, had collapsed at a point almost directly above Gnomon, but Endimin and his family were among the very few who had actually gone up to see where the breach had occurred. The urban folk were not used to the thin air and struggled with their footing as well. They clambered awkwardly over rocks and hugged the mountain's face when the trail grew steep, while experienced mountaineers like Endimin were able to leap spryly from boulder to boulder.

The expedition gathered to wait for stragglers at the rocky line where the sawtooth pinnacles of the mountain range had tumbled and lay broken and scattered in giant shards on the ground.

"If they are going to invade, they have to come through there," said Endimin, pointing to the lowest point, the fateful gap where an old ram and a young boy had gone to their deaths. "There are one or two other breaks in the line, but none that an army could pass through."

"Then here is where we hold them," said Henri Blouchette, who by virtue of being sheriff, and in the absence of a true military command structure, had become de facto leader of the Gnomonese forces, which could hardly be called an army.

The wind snapped at the meager Gnomonese pennons, which displayed the odd symbol of their trade: ∞, with its suggestion of endless looping as well as its reference to the tipped hourglass, gold on a field of green.

"I wonder if our swords will stand up to theirs," Basco wondered aloud.

"At least neither of us will resort to those new muskets. There is some honor among the Firozians."

Both the Gnomonese and the Firozians were aware that other islands were using newly invented muskets, killing machines that miniaturized and individualized the long-known capability of hurling projectiles from barrels using gunpowder. The Gnomonese people were too peaceful to introduce the efficient but cruel and deadly weapons, and the Firozians were so proud of their sword making they refused to succumb to the lure of those cowardly devices. As a result, personal feuds on both sides of the island were still settled by sword duel, and the specter of mass killing did not yet haunt the peoples of the island. A battle between the two peoples would be an ugly, messy affair, wtih terrible wounds, limbs hacked off, arteries severed and spurting blood, disembowelments, but at least it would be confined to the combatants, with none of the random massacre that had been seen to occur when the new weapons of mass destruction were employed. In this small but significant way the peoples of the island retained their dignity and showed a measure of civilized respect for each other's humanity.

Blouchette and Fournier devised a plan whereby the Firozians wouldn't be able to mass their troops and would have to send them through the gap in twos and threes. The Gnomonese were so far from their place of habitation that they had little to work with in the way of building materials or tools, but they did have a spirit of improvisation, driven by fear and desperation. Some finished the work Beroth had started of closing up the gaping hole, and set to work planting staves in the ground pointed end up to discourage the Firozians from leaping over the wall. Others laid animal traps and snares around to catch the unwary. A few wanted to venture into Firozian territory to do the same, but Endimin forbade them.

"We must show them that we have no evil motives, no devious ways. Despite how they feel about our seizure of one of their citizens, we are the wronged people in this conflict, therefore we must be more upright than our foes. I still hope to prevent a war with the Firozians. If they will only listen to reason—"

Endimin's speech was cut short by a shout from a lookout posted on a nearby peak.

"They come!"

In the distance one could hear martial music filling the air as the Firozian army marched to war in full regalia, with flags and pennants, accompanying fife-and-drum band and bugle corps at the head of a large column of men that stretched down the Firozian side of the mountain range and out of sight around a turn in the trail. The men from Gnomon were initially stunned by the size of the attacking force.

"There's more men in their army than in all of Gnomon, even if we brought up our grandfathers and grandchildren!" Basco Fournier declared.

"Fortunately they can't all perch here on the summit," Endimin noted.

"Yes," Henri Blouchette agreed, "we'll see how they do when they have to break up that handsome marching formation. Come on, boys, let's prepare a greeting for them."

Rocks and boulders were moved into place to hurl and roll down on the Firozians when they commenced their inevitable attack. The Gnomonese soldiers had barely completed their preparations when the first of the Firozian regiments came striding up the last switchback, wheeled to the right, and fanned out along the top of the ridge in a precise maneuver that impressed and intimidated the crouching Gnomonese. Their leader, a formidable-looking fellow with a gleaming sword-scabbard at his side and a grand metal helmet with the visor open, strode forward and hailed his enemy.

"I am General Sticer, commander of the forces of
Firoze. We know you're there, behind that flimsy wall.
Show yourselves. Come on, make it quick. This is your
last chance to surrender peaceably. Have you brought
Beroth?"

Endimin stood up. To the surprise of his compatriots,
he hopped down from the wall and crossed the rocky
ground between himself and the soldier from Firoze,
until they stood only a few feet apart. General Sticer of
the Firoze battalion towered over him, but Endimin
showed no fear. "Beroth remains in our custody,"
Endimin began, speaking slowly and patiently as if he
were talking to a recalcitrant child. "He is awaiting
trial. If he is found innocent—"

"Trial be damned!" the Firozian leader screamed, suddenly angry. "We do not honor your court of law. We
spit on it!" and at this he did indeed expectorate, dangerously close to Endimin's mountain-walking boots. "If
you don't have Beroth to hand over to us, there is nothing more to say. Prepare yourselves for battle."

Endimin was shocked by the man's rude and uncouth
behavior, but he refused to allow himself to be dismissed in such a fashion.

"Wait!" he cried. Something in his tone of voice
caught the attention of the Firozian soldier as he strut-
ted away. He clicked his heels, did an about-face in
military style, and waited expectantly for Endimin to
address him.

"In olden times these affairs were sometimes settled
by single warriors, one representing each side, rather
than involving entire armies. Is such a solution possible
in this case?" Endimin asked.

"You are challenging me, General Sticer, to a duel?"
the Firozian replied incredulously.

"Yes."

"It is customary to state your name when you issue
such a boldness."

"I am Endimin Platho of Gnomon. I'm not the leader of our little army, but I'm the person who's responsible for this conflict. It was my son who was killed." Endimin was careful not to say "by Beroth," because that hadn't been proved yet in a court of law.

There was a moment's pause. The Gnomonese men were stunned at Endimin's gesture, which was obviously meant to save them from near-certain annihilation. Finally the general responded: "Seek me out on the field of battle, then, Platho. I can't honor your request. That tradition holds when two armies of equal strength meet. Our sides are too unevenly matched."

"You are refusing me, then?"

"Yes. But I will say, I hadn't expected such resolve from you. You have my respect." Sticer touched the tip of his helmet with the forefingers of his right hand, slipped the visor down to cover his face, and returned to his line.

The Gnomonese forces *were* grossly mismatched—the Firozians would obviously wipe out the smaller, less well armed Gnomonese—it would be no contest, a terrible bloodletting that would serve no purpose other than to scar history with its ignominy. The Firozians moved slowly forward, while behind their wall the Gnomonese waited for a signal from Henri Blouchette to roll the first wicked-looking boulder down on their advancing foe. Just when it seemed that the battle was to be joined, a shout from a Gnomonese soldier broke the mounting tension:

"Look there!"

Despite their brazen contempt for their enemy, several of the Firozian soldiers turned their heads at the urgency in the crier's voice and stared where the Gnomonese lookout pointed. A fleet of gigantic ships had appeared on the horizon, and was pressing to make harbor in Firoze, led by a monstrous flagship. Black, huge, its deck looming many feet above the waterline unlike the low-slung canoes and flat-bottomed skows of the islanders, the lead vessel strained forward in its haste to reach Firoze. It was flying many square sails from its triple masts and also triangular sails fore and aft, the kind of rigging one might expect if it were still crossing a vast expanse of ocean, not entering a narrow harbor mouth. As it approached the entrance it suddenly tacked sharply sideways. From their vantage point high above the town, the soldiers of both sides watched as the man-o'-war opened the cannon ports on its hull and emitted a volley whose report reached them seconds later. Its accompanying ships lined up behind it to deliver more of the same.

"We're being invaded!" the Firozian commander shouted, and the entire troop of men ran pell-mell down the hill, leaving the Gnomonese men in stunned disbelief at having escaped certain death.

"Who could they be?" one of the soldiers wondered. "The Firozians are certainly afraid of them."

"Look at the size of that ship. Look at those cannons!" another soldier marveled. Even at those heights, their reverberating booms could be heard, and their black powder smoke, faintly acrid, was already drifting upward and enveloping the city of Firoze. Buildings could be seen ablaze, and a pall of denser smoke from their fires was mingling with the haze from the cannon fire.

"I hope they give them a good beating for us!" an enthusiastic recruit shouted.

"What makes you think they won't sail around to our harbor and ransack Gnomon when they finish with the Firozians?" an older soldier admonished his youthful brother in arms. "War is good for no one, except arms makers."

"And grave diggers," a nearby veteran added.

"Wouldn't our breakwater and the rough tides protect us, as they have from the Firozians all these years?"

"Ships like that can coast over the biggest waves and overcome the strongest ebbs and flows, but they won't try to drop anchor in our harbor—"

"They won't?"

"No, I'll wager that in their holds they carry landing craft that are larger than our largest vessels for launching attacks on protected harbors like ours. That's after they give us the kind of shelling that they're lambasting the Firozians with right now."

The ragtag Gnomonese troops stood around for a few minutes, watching as the plume of smoke from the burning buildings in Firoze mushroomed skyward.

"Let's hope the Firozians can fend them off," someone remarked.

"We should help them," Endimin proposed quietly. His words caused an immediate uproar.

"No!" "That's too much!" "After last night's noble speeches?!" "How can you even suggest such a thing, you who lost your son to their barbarity, who suffered injustice and indignity at their hands, whose pleading is the very reason we stand here today!"

With these and other imprecations the men of Gnomon protested Endimin's surprising words. Endimin listened with a resigned, implacable expression. When the din subsided, he spoke quietly.

"I more than any of you have cause to hate the Firozians. Yet it must be remembered, we are blood brothers to them."

Another howl of objections rose up. Endimin waited patiently until the mob's voice fell to a murmur, then continued.

"Like it or not, it's true, this island was once populated by a single people. Only when the Impasse was formed did we begin to diverge in our ways, our dress, our size, our temperament. Look closely at the Firozians, and what you see is a larger, coarser version of ourselves: blue eyes, square-jawed faces marked by prominent foreheads, long legs upon short torsos—there can be no doubt about it. If you want more proof, listen to our language; the centuries have caused us to grow apart in speech, yet we easily understand each other. Now, what about these invaders? We haven't seen them yet, but I have no doubt they are Vargans, with brown eyes, round faces, receding foreheads, short legs and long torsos, and they speak a tongue we can barely comprehend. In the greater sense they are our brothers, too, but in the lesser realm of this conflict, they are much more our enemies than the Firozians, with whom we have shared this island for hundreds of years."

Endimin paused to catch his breath after this impassioned speech and glanced at the serious faces around him. He could see that they had listened to him with their hearts, and that they understood, so he said little more, only this: "Were we to go down there now, the Firozians might think we were in concert with the Vargans, attacking them from behind. I propose we send a smaller delegation offering our assistance."

"Endimin is right," a veteran seconded his proposal. "From this high perch above the battle, we can see what's going on and report to the Firozians on the movement of their foe. If we provide them with good information, they'll recognize our honest intentions. If we descend en masse now, so soon after confrontation, they'd likely attack us."

"We'll leave a small detachment up here at the Impasse. The rest of the men can go home, there won't be any fighting and dying today, at least not for us." Vastly relieved, Henri Blouchette led the Gnomonese men down the mountain toward their wives and children. Endimin and Basco remained behind to organize a system of rotating replacements and runners to keep them informed of the goings-on in Firoze. After the details of the shifts were worked out, the two men sat down to enjoy a pipeful of tobacco together.

"Strange how things work out, isn't it?" Basco commented as he puffed on the soothing smoke.

"Yes. Here we were about to be butchered and now it's the Firozians who are getting it."

"Yes."

"That was a noble gesture you made, Endimin, offering to clash swords with the general directly."

"A calculated gamble, actually. As you know, it's much easier to work our spells on individuals than large groups. I didn't really think he'd accept. I wouldn't have done so, in his place. Why should he? He had all the odds in his favor."

"Still, everyone appreciated your offer. What do you know of the Vargans?

"Vargas is far to the south and east of us. Vargan ships are hardly ever sighted in these regions—none at all in our lifetime, until today, but I remembered my father talking about them, and when I saw the shape of their vessel I knew it had to be them."

"Can the Firozians withstand their assault?"

"Not for long, at least not without our help."

"So you really meant that?" Basco appraised his friend carefully.

"Indeed. Every word."

"Then you surprise me even more than you did the Firozian general."

"Mark my words, the Vargans will demand not merely Firozian swords and our clocks and watches, but fealty and subservience. It's in our best interests to unite with the people of Firoze, as quickly as possible, and throw out these invaders. When the battle below ends, you and I will walk into Firoze and see who rules the city, Vargans or Firozians."

Together they watched as boatload after boatload of

Vargan soldiers were sent into the water from the main
ship, which had been joined by a half dozen other
mighty sailing vessels, none as large as the first but still
impressively huge by Firoze or Gnomonese standards.
By dusk the outcome was no longer in doubt—the
Vargans were in control of the city. Half the town was
reduced to smoldering rubble. The Firozians, distracted
and caught unprepared by their conflict with the little
Gnomonese force, were unable to repel the waves of
landing craft.

"We'll travel under the white flag of truce," Endimin
decided. "The Firozians, and even the Vargans, will
honor that symbol."

"I hope you're right," Basco said with his quirky
smile playing at his lips.

They started down the trail, but had hardly traveled
more than a third of the way down the mountainside
when they came to an encampment of Firozian soldiers,
led by the same general who had confronted Endimin
so proudly a few hours before. Now his men were
bloodied and defeated, scattered among the rocks and
boulders of this desolate high place that bespoke terror
and despair. There was no band, no bugling; there were
no pennons or standards to be seen. The wounded were
moaning and crying out as field surgery was performed
on their mangled limbs. Soldiers lay listlessly on their
bedrolls, tormented by thoughts of their loved ones
down below in Firoze, and what harshness they might
be enduring at this moment. As soon as Endimin and
Basco entered the area they were seized and would
have been slain right then and there despite the truce
flag if General Sticer hadn't seen who it was and
shouted for his soldiers to halt. He limped over to them,
and the Gnomonese men observed that a bad gash on
his leg was still bleeding slowly despite the application
of a tourniquet.

"What do you want? Haven't you done enough damage today?"

"What do you mean?" Endimin asked innocently.

"Very clever."

"What's that?"

"Clever of you to lure us into battle, draw our army away from the city so that the Vargans could attack us with impunity! A brilliant distraction."

"We did no such thing. The timing of their attack was complete coincidence."

"You expect me to believe that?"

"We are not the enemy." Endimin then gave General Sticer the same speech he'd given to his Gnomonese cohorts—that the Firozian and Gnomonese people were more closely related and had more in common than outsiders, that they should work together to free themselves from the yoke that was certainly to be placed on them both, for as Endimin pointed out, the Vargans no doubt chose to attack the more difficult target first and leave the Gnomonese as easy prey for later, once they had secured the lee side of the island.

"And what about the matter of Beroth?" the general wanted to know.

"Nothing that has happened today changes that. Beroth must remain in custody and submit to our legal process. I tell you as I told him, if the jury finds him innocent, he will be set free."

At that moment one of the soldiers stood up and approached Endimin, a strange look on his face.

"Commander, with your permission, a word with the Gnomonese."

"What is it, Coker? Speak."

"I have information that may help to resolve the situation. I was there."

Endimin started in surprise. "What? Beroth never mentioned a witness."

"Nonetheless, I was there. We were hunting. We shot

your ram. The boy came, a plucky little fellow, too, and
when he saw what we'd done he reviled us, loudly and
ardently. Beroth was incensed, and stepped toward him,
but before he reached him the child fell backward into
a pit. It was an unfortunate accident."

"You would be willing to come to Gnomon and testify to this in court?"

"Isn't my word right here right now good enough?"

Endimin sighed. How hard it was to explain the rule
of law to a people who didn't appreciate its grandeur,
the aura of protection it afforded to every citizen. "I
could take a deposition, but it would be much more effective if you came with me. You could be your people's first emissary in our land, and you could bring
your friend Beroth back with you, for I have no doubt
the court will rule in his favor based on your testi-
mony."

Coker was skeptical but agreed to accompany
Endimin back to Gnomon. The general took Coker
aside to issue him a few orders, then returned to address Endimin: "I would like you to release me from
my obligation to cross swords with you."

Endimin smiled weakly. "I accept. No doubt you
have just saved my life. But I hope that our trust in
one another will lead to the saving of many more
Gnomonese and Firozian lives, and the return of our island to complete freedom. In the meantime, we'll act as
lookouts and report to you on the movement of Vargan
ships and men."

"Men, you call them. They are wild beasts, I tell you.
They finish off the wounded without a thought, and
give us no time to remove our dead from the field."
The general drew himself up, tried to muster the appearance of command and control. "We appreciate your
offer of assistance. We may be the only fighting force
left in Firoze, we can't be sure because it's too danger-

ous to venture down there now. We'll know tomorrow if any other troops escaped death or surrender."

There was no point in proceeding further. The Firozian general agreed to pass on the Gnomonese offer of help to any provisional or rebel government officials he could find. Coker packed up his duffel bag and strapped on a fine curved sword that would have been unwieldy for any Gnomonese but fit his proportions well, and set off up the hill with Endimin Platho and Basco Fournier.

5

THE TRIAL OF BEROTH WAS HELD IN THE largest courtroom in Gnomon City Hall, but it wasn't big enough to hold the overflowing crowd that gathered for the event. Despite the turmoil, the threat of war, and the invasion of Firoze by out-islanders, Beroth's day in court was a major attraction. The prisoner was once again bound in chains and brought down from the Clocktower. But much of the drama was provided by the presence of Coker, who was identified by gossip as the man who was present at the death of Runward Platho and would testify to the effect that the boy's death was accidental. Beroth had refused counsel so one had been appointed for him, but the lawyer had never been able to elicit any tactics for a defense from his sullen client. When Beroth saw Coker, he gave out a laugh that was a sardonic mixture of begrudging respect for the willingness on the part of the Gnomonese to hear his side and disdain for their weakness.

"Coker, you mighty fool, what are you doing on this side of the mountains? And why are you in uniform?" Beroth shouted to him over the hushed murmuring in the courtroom.

"Haven't you heard? The Vargans have invaded and taken Firoze."

"What?" Beroth's eyes bulged. He rattled his chains nastily and strained at their clasps but couldn't burst them. He fell back, panting from the effort, and stared at his hunting companion. Coker moved closer to the prisoner so they could talk without disrupting the pretrial preparations.

"I missed the biggest battle in our history, is that what you're telling me?"

"And the most bitter defeat," Coker informed him. "General Sticer's in the hills with a scant half of our army. The rest are in the stockade, the field hospital, or dead. Vargans patrol the streets of Firoze, arresting anyone who violates the curfew."

"You've got to get me out of here!" Beroth said, nearly weeping from frustration.

"That's what I'm here for. The little boy's father brought me back—"

"What?" Again Beroth couldn't hide his surprise.

"Yes. When he heard that I'd seen the whole thing he insisted that I come testify. He's also the man who's initiated the alliance between Firoze and Gnomon against the Vargans. . . ."

This news was so startling to Beroth that he could only shake his head and move his lips without speaking.

"He assures me that you'll be set free this very day. But the proceedings are about to begin, so I must take my seat."

Everything went as Endimin had promised the Firozians. Coker was called upon to give his account of the incident, and on hearing the evidence, the judge agreed that there was nothing he could do except free the defendant, though to his credit he did give Beroth a stern lecture. For his part, Beroth took the admonitions with surprising grace, as if he could hardly believe that he was going to escape the gallows so easily.

Aivlys was angry at her father and had refused to attend the trial. She couldn't understand why Endimin had made such an effort to save the one man she hated more than any other in the world. Endimin's considered defense of the nobility of the legal system did not sway his daughter's passionate heart. She sulked and fumed and spent the the day of the court case moping around the house. Endimin had forbidden her to climb the hills in case the Vargans came through the Impasse to attack Gnomon, though no one expected them to try that immediately. The lookouts atop the mountains reported that the remaining Firoze troops were harassing and sniping at the Vargans at every opportunity; the Firozians were fighting a classic guerrilla war from their redoubts in the hills.

Beroth and Coker were allowed to leave Gnomon on the morning following the trial. They agreed to communicate with the Gnomonese about the progress of the war and let them know when and if their assistance was needed. Beroth could not complain of his treatment by Gnomonese authorities—Endimin had seen to that by making sure that the prisoner was fed regularly, housed in a reasonable fashion (the Clocktower was austere but not unduly uncomfortable), and afforded all his legal rights. He remained bitter, however, that he had been forced into captivity against his will. To a Firozian, this was a supreme insult—death was much preferable to capture.

"At least you weren't subdued in single combat,"

Coker told him as they walked up the mountain path toward the Impasse.

"No, it took a woman's treachery to trick me," Beroth answered. "When they handed me back my sword I had to restrain it from leaping into the flesh of the man in whose keeping it had been entrusted. He did a good job of taking care of it, so I let him live. But wouldn't they be amazed to know that our swords have a life of their own."

"Yes, they're so clever with their time magic—if they only knew our secret, they wouldn't be so smug about it."

"Sword magic must remain the province of Firoze only. It's the one thing that may save us from the Vargans. They can make us manufacture swords for them, but we'll never teach them the unutterable mysteries of Imprinting."

"Agreed."

In their conversation the Firoze men discussed arcana known only to the greatest craftsmen and warriors of their race. Some (but not all, indeed only a select few) of the swords of Firoze were no ordinary pieces of metal. Like the clocks of Gnomon, they were at once more and no more than what they seemed. The Firozians used a form of rudimentary alchemy that strengthened their sword blades and endowed them with the personality of their owner; specifically, each sword Imprinted on the first person who held it after it came off the maker's anvil. Thus Beroth's sword was more than merely Beroth's sword; it was in some sense, a part of Beroth himself. Likewise, Coker's sword was imbued with Coker's unique qualities, his strengths and weaknesses, his likes and dislikes, his life-force and his foibles. A sword used by someone other than its owner could behave unpredictably. Sometimes that sword would balk at striking; sometimes it would even turn on the one who held it. More often, though, there would be subtle changes in the way it swung, or how sharply it cut, changes that would go unnoticed by all but the most sensitive swordsmen for whom they were created, that gave them that finite edge that could make the difference in combat between a successful strike and a near miss, between a fatal thrust and a glancing blow, in other words, the difference between victory and defeat, between life and death.

These swords did not have names, but would respond to their Imprinter's voices with a distinct and eerie wavering ring audible only to those who knew the secrets of Imprinting. They could be made to come like dogs at fetch, but Beroth had hesitated to use this capacity when locked in the Clocktower at Gnomon because it would have given away the immense power of sword magic to have let the Gnomonese see his blade flying through the air into his hand.

The relationship between a man and his Imprinted sword was like that between a faithful horse and its master, an unspoken union. When a man who owned such a sword was killed in battle, the Imprinted sword soon became a useless hunk of metal that rusted and pitted with astonishing quickness, depriving the victor of the spoils of war. An owner could bequeath his sword to a successor, either a descendant or a close ally, but the sword did not always take to its new owner. All this was known to the warriors of Firoze, to the blacksmiths who hammered the raw iron into steel, and to the members of the Swordmakers' Guild, who fitted swords with arm guards, finished their burnishing, and shaped and honed them into magnificent weapons. The Swordmakers' Guild was held in as high esteem in Firoze as the Watchmakers' Guild was in Gnomon.

All this was known to Beroth and Coker but they discussed it only briefly. Their thoughts were on their families and their country, now subjugated and oppressed by the invading Vargans. Beroth, as a highlander and a bachelor, was less immediately affected by the defeat. He lived alone in a rude dwelling high against the mountainside. Coker, on the other hand, was a city dweller and a married man. His wife and children would now be subject to Vargan rule. He had no way of knowing whether or not they had been harmed during the battle that led to the takeover of the city. His morose mood was lightened somewhat when he and Beroth crested the summit line, passing under the watchful gaze of a few Gnomonese guards, and descended into Firoze. Soon thereafter they were met in the woods by their comrades from the Firozian army. A great outcry of rejoicing followed—the despondent Firozian troops finally had something to cheer about.

"Our champion is back!" some of the men shouted, for Beroth was greatly revered as the most formidable warrior in the land, and even his capture by the Gnomonese had not diminished his stature.

"Now we'll show those Vargans what for!"

Beroth was shepherded with much back slapping and friendly jostling toward the center of the Firoze camp. He was led directly to General Sticer, the man whom Endimin had challenged on the field of honor.

"General—"

"I ought to have you hanged!" General Sticer exploded, the smoldering frustration of defeat finally bursting into flame on finding an object to wither with its blast. "Because of you we were unprepared and had our backs to the enemy. When they struck we were off chasing Gnomonese, a complete waste of time, and all on account of some foolishness on your part that caused the death of a young boy."

"It was an accident," Beroth protested mildly.

"I don't care!" Sticer yelled, his face was an inch from Beroth's face. "I hold you personally responsible for the deaths of one hundred sixty-three of my men. Until you redeem yourself, hopefully by dying valiantly at the head of our counterattack, you may consider yourself reduced in rank and stripped of all medals and honors previously awarded you."

"Yes, sir." Beroth, properly chastened, withdrew as quickly as he could from the still flickering rage of his commander. Though he was no longer part of the standing army, having served many times earlier in his life, he, like any able-bodied Firozian, could be impressed at any time on the whim of the army. Obviously he was now back in the service of his country. He shed his civilian clothes and borrowed a military outfit from Coker, several sizes smaller than himself, which looked as though it would burst at the seams when he put it on. He was ready right that minute to charge into Firoze and hurl himself at the Vargans in a glorious death struggle, but the rest of the Firozian force was still recovering from their humbling defeat. Beroth was reduced to roaming the encampment like a rabid dog, barking at the other soldiers, trying to rouse them for the coming engagement.

Halfway up the mountain, between Firoze and the encampment of the remains of the Firozian army, was a small town called Flailan, where the sword makers of Firoze had lived and worked for hundreds of years. The Vargans, content to hold the port city, had not extended their captured territory to include this village, which was held by a small contingent of soldiers under a commander named Magden. The workshops, forges, and kilns of the Firozian craftsmen remained untouched by the invasion.

On the third day after Beroth's trial, Endimin set out to meet General Sticer in Flailan for a discussion of their next moves. This time he took Aivlys with him. She dressed as if she were a young man and tucked her hair under a cap, but the effect only enhanced her lovely features. All Gnomon was jittery with the prospect that the Vargans would attack them next, but so far there had been no sightings along the coast on the Gnomonese side of the island. They passed through the army bivouac site without incident, though they were stopped and questioned at each end of the camp. The Firozians looked at Aivlys as if she must be a particularly puny and effeminate Gnomonese, but none realized she was a woman. As for Endimin, he had established himself in front of the whole army with his challenge to General Sticer, and the Firozian soldiers, having seen Endimin on friendly terms with their great general, were hesitant to give him any trouble. At the lower checkpoint a guide was assigned to accompany them to Flailan. They detoured off the main trail down into Firoze, scrambling up a side valley until they came out onto a main road leading from the city by the sea into the hills. From there it was an easy walk to Flailan. They were met by nervous sentries at the outskirts of town who made Endimin glad they had been provided with a protector. The guards had unsheathed their swords and were poised to strike at Endimin and Aivlys until their escort displayed safe-conduct passes.

"A little jumpy, aren't you?" the Firozian admonished the overzealous soldiers.

"Better edgy than being caught off guard and slaughtered by Vargans."

"This fellow and his aide," said the guide, referring to Endimin and Aivlys, "are honored guests of General Sticer. I'm to escort them to him. Please direct us."

One of the guards pointed to a ramshackle set of buildings a quarter of a mile down the road. They proceeded warily to the compound, where Commander Magden met them at the makeshift headquarters, a former storehouse converted to officers' quarters. "General Sticer sends his apologies. He has been called away for urgent meetings with the provisional government. He requests that you wait here until he returns. In the interim, I'm to show you around and answer any questions you might have." Magden glanced at Aivlys, surprised to see the form of a young woman here at the last outpost before the battlefront.

"My first question is, have the Vargans made any attempts to capture Flailan? Has there been any fighting here? Your lookouts seem worried."

Magden, a man with the same stocky build and thick appendages as Beroth, allowed himself a little smile.

"Not yet. We've captured one of them, although he claims he's not. Probably a spy, sent to inspect our fortifications. We're going to hang him in the morning, after we squeeze any information we can out of him."

"May I see him, before the torture begins?" Endimin asked pleasantly, though inwardly he was revolted by the idea of the interrogation the man would have to endure before death freed him. The Firozian press was an infamous device, designed to "squeeze" a man literally, as the Firozian officer had suggested, until his guts burst from the applied pressure. Few were able to hold back any secrets before they succumbed.

"Sure, why not? Now that we're allies, you ought to have your chance to play with the rat before we pounce. Bring the prisoner forward!"

A bedraggled-looking man was led out from a barn that had been hastily converted into a stockade. As he passed through the crowd he was pelted with garbage and stones, as Endimin had been on his first visit to Firoze. Endimin's heart went out to him, though he knew the man was the enemy.

"On your knees, Vargan!" Magden shouted while shoving him to the ground rudely. The prisoner, his hands bound behind his back, fell on his face, but rolled over and sat up, blood dripping from his nose.

"I'm not a Vargan, I told you. I'm an impressed seaman, the ship's navigator, and I was fleeing from the Vargan ship because I didn't want to serve them anymore, never did, in fact. I was waylaid in the port of

Bushcadie and brought aboard ship against my will, because I made the terrible mistake of bragging of my skill as an open-sea sailor."

Endimin stepped forward, wiped the blood from the man's face and stanched the flow with a strip of cloth he tore from his sleeve. He could see that the man was terrified of the Firozians, who had already roughed him up. At this the captive man smiled an odd, ingenuous smile and thanked Endimin silently for his ministrations. "And what talent is that, lad?" Endimin asked gently.

"I determine a ship's position without sighting in the stars, even on a cloudy day."

"And how do you do that?"

"With my Celestial Compass, which these brutes have seized from me and taken who knows where. I want to help you," the man said. "I know their strengths and weaknesses, the weaponry they carry, what kind and in what quantity, and more, I know their strategies. I can tell you how their admiralty thinks."

"First prove to us that you aren't one of them," the Firozian spat out.

Endimin was more patient. "Stand up. What is your name?"

"Hugh Boisset."

"And where are you from, Hugh?"

"From Bushcadie, I told you. It's a hundred thousand leagues from Vargas, not even in the same archipelago. We're a trading nation, like yourselves. The Vargans stop at our ports on their rounds. We're under their dominion, but that doesn't make them our blood relations."

The self-proclaimed navigator was a young man with thick blond hair parted on one side of his head so far that it made him look lopsided. He had a small nose (now bloody) and bushy eyebrows that didn't seem to go together, and his green eyes were wrong for his fair complexion. In short, he was an odd-looking fellow. His long legs made him look as if he were about to rush off even when he was standing perfectly still. Still, he had broad shoulders and a charming, disarming grin that somehow brought together the disparate elements of his features, the little nose and the heavy brows, into a reasonably handsome face.

If only he wore his hair properly, Aivlys thought as she stared at his dazzling smile, his symmetrical, even teeth contrasting with his uneven head of hair, and then she wondered why she cared about the stranger's looks.

"All right, back to the stockade with him. But don't squeeze him just yet," Magden ordered. "We may have need of his services."

"Wait," said Endimin. Magden scowled. He didn't like his orders countermanded, especially by a blasted little Gnomonese. "One more question. Did you invent this Celestial Compass, as you call it?"

"I did. I'm a tinker's son, and a tinkerer by nature. If I fiddle with something, it usually ends up working better than before it broke. I can't take full credit—an old sailor showed me the principle, but he was using baling wire and hemp for his device. Mine has brass and copper fittings and a true measure in hundredths of degrees."

"Ingenious. All right." Endimin nodded, and the man was hauled away roughly. Endimin turned to Magden. "Where is this young man's handiwork?"

"How in hell's furnace should I know?" Magden responded, still resentful of Endimin's intervention.

"Well, you'd better find out. That device could be the tool that saves Firoze and Gnomon from ending up under the Vargan thumb."

Magden didn't like being made a fool of in front of his officers, but he appreciated the thought behind the suggestion. If they were going to outwit the Vargans they were going to need every advantage they could muster. Quickly he gave orders for the missing instrument to be located and brought to him at once.

"While we're waiting, come take a look at our workshop. There are many things that should interest a craftsman such as yourself."

And indeed there were. A wide variety of half-made implements lay in profusion on the workbench: straight broadswords, curved sabers, daggers and short swords, and of course the famous Firozian brand, so called because it shone with high burnishing. They were in various stages of assembly. Some had their tangs exposed as they had not yet been fitted with handles. Others lacked the cross guard or were mere lengths of metal that had not yet had an edge applied. There were single- and double-edged swords, thin fencing foils and weighty rapiers meant to be wielded two-handed. They were almost all made of iron worked into steel, though on the wall hung a few relics of copper or bronze.

"There is as much variety in swords as there is in clocks and watches," Endimin commented. He could appreciate the craftsmanship involved in producing these weapons, though the skills were not as fine and delicate as those required for watchmaking, and the manufacturing techniques were grosser and less refined. Still the pride in workmanship was evident in the care with which the swords were made. There was one curious feature of the workshop. After assembly at the workbench, the finished swords were transferred to a windowless room to be kept under lock and key until their owners picked them up. Endimin asked his host about this practice.

"Uh . . . that's just custom, tradition," Magden stuttered, but Endimin could tell there was something more to it than that. As a test, he reached for one of the swords that was about to be moved from the end of the workbench. Magden sprang at him, shouting, "Don't touch that!"

"Magic, eh?" said Endimin coyly.

"None of your business," his host answered brusquely.

"What does it do? Do they harden especially well in the dark?"

"Sure, if that's what you want to believe."

"Or is there something special about when they're touched?"

"I'm sorry, you'll have to leave the workshop now," Magden ordered. Endimin was escorted from the premises, but before he left he caught a glimpse of a new purchaser being led with ceremony into the chamber where the finished swords were kept. Being a magician himself, he could almost guess the rest, how the swords bonded to their masters. Just at that moment a soldier arrived bearing Hugh Boisset's Celestial Compass, an intriguing-looking device that distracted Endimin's attention away from the rough implements of war to a highly tooled and intricate design that bore more than a passing resemblance to the products of Gnomonese skill. Endimin accepted the compass from the soldier and twirled it gently in his hands while he admired its lightness, sturdiness, and compactness.

"Look here," he pointed out to Aivlys, "how this bearing swivels where it attaches to the connecting rod. The man has a definite skill with the finer points of escapement mechanisms and toothed elements."

"Looks like an overcomplicated bedpan to me," Magden grumbled, but Endimin and Aivlys were lost in the intricacies of the hemispherically shaped contraption and scarcely noticed their host's impatience.

"May I take this with me to examine it at length?" Endimin asked.

"Take it," Magden spat. "It's of no value to us here in the hills." Magden stalked off to tend to other affairs.

"Such a fellow could be very useful to us, and not

merely for his skills in crafting this compass," Endimin told his daughter while they examined the invention.

"How so, Father?"

"As he said himself, he knows them, the enemy. But more than that, he's an outsider, he's someone who could dispassionately deliver the same message I've been trying to get across, that we, the Gnomonese, and the Firozians, need each other. I'm going to propose to the general when I see him that we free this man and enlist him in our service."

Aivlys was secretly thrilled to hear this news, but she hid her enthusiasm and busied herself with the compass. Touching it, she could almost feel the intelligence of the person who had made it, the sensitivity of the hands that had shaped and refined it. She vowed to study its form and functions as if it were a watch. Certain elements resembled a timepiece. The sky was marked off in minutes and seconds. A balance wheel kept track of the movements of the stars. A coiled spring ran the device. The machine *felt* like a clock—it seemed to be *in tune* with the universe, connected to the cosmic dance of the stars in some undefinable way, though it sat on the blanket next to Aivlys, silent and motionless. But she still wasn't sure exactly how it worked. She would have to interview the prisoner to find out how it charted the position of the ship it was on as it moved through the water. What strange computations could link sky, water, and wind, tie it all together with passing time, and tell a traveler where he stood on the wide water, with no reference point other than the rocking horizon? Aivlys saw that if she could comprehend this mystery she would enhance her understanding of her own people's conjuring powers.

Endimin too was fascinated with the compass, but more immediate was his desire to confirm what he suspected about the mystic relationship between Firozian swords and their owners. That evening, when Endimin

was alone with General Sticer (Aivlys had gone to
bed), he bluffed his way into a fuller knowledge of the
subject of Firozian sword magic by pretending that he
already knew about it. They had left Flailan and returned to the high camp where the rebellious forces
were still gathering strength for a counterattack. A great
bonfire was burning, because the Firozians were sure
enough now of their numbers that they believed the
Vargans wouldn't attempt a hill-climbing assault.
The flames were a beacon to other stragglers among the
Firozians to join them, and they did, by ones and twos,
coming out of the forest or descending from even
higher hideaways, regrouping and finding their units,
until a sizable army was once again assembled. Sticer
and Endimin sat a little ways off from the blaze, drinking tea and sharing some of Endimin's precious supply
of tobacco. It was a quiet scene, one that lent itself to
intimacy, and Endimin picked his moment during a lull
in the comfortable conversation to probe gently for
more information.

"So, Commander, the legendary Firozian sword
comes alive. How did you discover this potent magic?"

General Sticer looked at him sharply. "Give me the
name of the man who told you this—"

"And you'll have him executed on the spot."

"Yes."

"Fortunately, there is no name to convey; I figured
the thing out on my own. You see we Gnomonese also
have some tricks up our sleeves—it must be the native
charm of the island."

"Oh, we've heard of your Time spells, but we
thought we'd been able to conceal our own enchantments."

"So you have, so you have, Commander. Nor will
your confidences be broken by me. I merely wish to
hear confirmation from you of what I have already sur-
mised. The swords have a life of their own, then?"

"Not exactly. They have their owner's life." Sticer went on to explain the propensities of Imprinting in some detail, because he trusted Endimin and had grown fond of the little man's honesty and wit. Endimin listened with interest to the details of the process. The gruff, antagonistic Firozian grew expansive as he talked, while Endimin kept him supplied with sweetish tea and pungent tobacco.

"So you see, Platho, a man and his sword have two bodies but one soul. It's what makes us a great people, not merely another island tribe but a pillar among the races, and it makes our defeat at the hands of these sea-going scum that much more despicable."

"Ah, yes, the Vargans, well," Endimin stuttered slightly, because though he knew he shouldn't say anything good about the current conquerors, he couldn't help but think, *Yet they bested you, and your magic withal.*

As if reading his thoughts, General Sticer commented on the quality of the soldiers fighting on the Vargan side. "Oh, they wield their swords well enough, but there's no beauty in their cuts, only a crude ferociousness. You might think us boors and ruffians compared to your genteel people"—General Sticer surprised Endimin with his candor—"but compared to the Vargans we're veritable princes of courtesy and manner. They don't respect the basic rules of battle. They didn't allow us to clear the field of our wounded and dead. They refused an offer of a truce to discuss their intrusion. Worst of all, they take gruesome trophies from those they slay." Endimin was glad his daughter had retired early, so that she couldn't hear Sticer's vivid description of how the Vargans mutilated their victims for gory prizes.

"I personally repaid one of their swordsmen for perpetrating such an outrage, but he managed to wound me in the leg before I beheaded him. As a consequence I'll

probably walk with a limp for the rest of my life, but
it was worth the aggravation to avenge his desecration."

"Let me see your wound," Endimin said quietly.

"Are you sure? It's an ugly thing. Infection has set in
because we lack proper care here in the mountains, but
I don't think I'm going to lose it."

"Show me."

"Very well." General Sticer hoisted up his robe and
revealed a bloody bandage wrapped around his right
calf. Endimin splashed his hands with some of the left-
over tea and rubbed them together. Then he unwound
the blood-soaked dressing and stared at the open six-
inch gash.

"It's not healing well. Do you mind if I touch it?"

"Are you a doctor, too, Platho?" General Sticer asked
skeptically.

"A doctor, no, but I have some understanding of
medical affairs." Endimin was purposefully vague, because he intended to use a little Gnomonese magic on
his new friend. He began to rub the general's leg
slowly, above and below the cut, but this was only a
distraction. Under his breath Endimin repeated a simple
spell (one he hadn't taught to Aivlys) called Some Time
that caused time to pass *only on the general's leg!* It appeared that he was healing by touch, but actually the
leg was living an accelerated life of its own. Application of this same spell would cause premature babies to
develop rapidly after birth, or green fruit to ripen. There
were risks associated with such piecemeal playing with
time, but in the general's case Endimin saw that the
man was likely to lose the leg, or even his life, to the
gangrene that almost always developed in slicing cuts
such as the one he had received. After a few minutes of
(unnecessary) manipulation, Endimin examined the
wound again. The two sides of the opening had closed
up and formed a thin white line where scar tissue was
already beginning to form.

"That ought to be better," Endimin said, and General Sticer looked down, then stared at Endimin in amazement.

"How did you do that?" he asked.

"I'll tell you sometime," Endimin said coyly.

"I can lead my men again. You have no idea how much that means to me." Endimin feared the brave general was going to weep, so he laughed to change the mood, and reached for the tea.

"No!" said General Sticer. "For this we must have some Firozian plum wine to celebrate!" He snapped his fingers to summon an attendant, who soon brought them two glasses and a bottle. General Sticer poured Endimin's glass himself before allowing the attendant to fill his own.

"To the union of Gnomon and Firoze," he said boldly. "May our two peoples unite to drive out the Vargans!"

"To the union," Endimin agreed. They had taken no more than a sip when they became aware of a commotion down the road from the camp. Sentries rushed to the source of the sound, where they ran into the fleeing remnants of the troops who had been stationed in Flailan. A messenger at their head rushed to General Sticer and kneeled at his feet. The man was dripping blood from a head wound and seemed woozy, but he was determined to complete his duty without keeling over.

"Report!" Sticer barked.

"A night attack on Flailan, sir! Our contingent there was nearly wiped out!"

"Commander Magden?" Sticer asked.

"Killed, sir, but not before he slew a whole host of Vargans. They overwhelmed us."

Aivlys had awakened in the disorder, and stood sleepily by her father. When she realized what had happened she inquired about the prisoner Hugh Boisset.

"Ah! A hero! He's among the casualties. He grabbed a sword and fought beside Magden until they were both buried under the weight of the assault. We killed many more of them than they of us, because we held the high ground, but in the end their sheer numbers were too much for us."

"You see!" Endimin cried. "Here's a man, this Boisset, who fought for us even though the man he stood with had abused him."

"So, he's . . . dead?" Aivlys asked.

"I don't know," the messenger answered. "The last I saw of him he and Magden were going down under a sea of Vargan swords. Magden's body we found later. The prisoner, I don't know. The Vargans withdrew, but there were too few of us to remain in control of the town."

"'*Withdrew?*' That seems odd. Why should they invade and then not try to hold the ground they gained?"

"They were searching for something."

"What were they after?"

"We don't know. Once they penetrated our defenses they kept yelling, 'Where is it?' but we didn't know what it was they wanted. Not that we would have given it to them, in any case," the messenger assured the general.

"I know what it was," Endimin said quietly to General Sticer.

"All right, that's all." Sticer dismissed the messenger with orders that he be given the best treatment available from the camp physicians.

"What? What did they seek?"

"This." Endimin withdrew Hugh's Celestial Compass from the sack in which he had carried it up from Flailan.

"Is this thing really so valuable that they would expend a whole company of troops for it?" Sticer asked dubiously.

"It is if you're an admiral and this device can steer your fleet to its destination through storm and darkness."

"And now we may have lost the man who made it," Aivlys pointed out. General Sticer immediately issued orders for a large contingent of men to return to Flailan and search the village for wounded survivors among the dead.

"Magden was a good man," the general mused, "a little hard-hearted, but loyal and brave. I will miss him."

Endimin thought it best to say nothing, but he too pondered the meaning of the death of Commander Magden. It was poignantly ironic that the man had died trying to keep the enemy from capturing a piece of machinery that he had ridiculed, that wasn't even in the camp at the time of the attack, and whose creator he had imprisoned, brutalized, and possibly even tortured, yet who fought at his side to the end.

The troops who returned to Flailan found Hugh Boisset unconscious beneath a pile of Vargan bodies, his sword still in his hand. Next to him was his captor, Magden, with his throat slit and one arm nearly severed and dangling from the elbow by a single tendon. The slain warrior was carefully laid out on a stretcher and the two men were carried back to the upper camp. When Aivlys saw this sad procession entering the grounds she was sure that both men were dead, but the doctor quickly set her straight:

"Boisset took a whack on the helmet from a Vargan, but it must have been with the flat of the blade, because his head isn't split open. He'll have a terrible headache when he wakes up, but that's all."

Aivlys took charge of tending to him. She wiped away the blood (other men's blood) and grime of battle, and sponged his lips with water while Hugh groaned in troubled sleep. When he woke she was there.

"Who are you?" he said. "Have I risen to the realm of angels?"

"No, you're still on this earth," Aivlys said matter-of-factly. "You put up a good fight, but you lost."

"Oooohh, my head hurts." Hugh grimaced as he tried to raise himself up to a sitting position. "What's your name?"

"Aivlys Platho."

"And I'm—"

"I know. You're Hugh Boisset. And you're not a Vargan."

"No." Hugh tried to rub his head but it was too sore to touch. He smiled ruefully at Aivlys and lay back down. "Why are you taking care of me?"

"My father thinks you can help us defeat the Vargans," Aivlys told him.

"I can. I can do a lot of things," Hugh said. Aivlys wished he weren't so boastful, but she didn't say anything. She carefully said to him, "I saw how that Commander Magden treated you. Why did you stay to help him after he'd been so cruel to you?"

Hugh blinked and looked around as if he were waking up in the world for the first time. He took a deep breath and sighed. "Life is strange and wonderful, isn't it? Last night I was knee-deep in bodies in the middle of a bloody battle, and today I'm talking to a beautiful girl."

"Why did you stay?" Aivlys persisted as she dabbed at his bruised and swollen forehead with a warm, wet cloth.

"You might not like my answer. I stayed because I don't like to see an underdog beaten. I stayed because I like a good fight. And I stayed because I have nothing to lose."

This was the wrong thing to say to Aivlys, who ever since her brother's death had little sympathy for those who were careless with their lives. " 'Nothing to lose'?

This one precious life we're given is nothing to you? Oh, if I could trade your worthless soul for my lost brother's I'd do it, right now!" she said, and burst into tears, which so unnerved Hugh Boisset that he sat up, ignoring the pain and the spinning sensation, and tried to comfort Aivlys, but she pushed him away. Tearfully she told him about Runny, how his death had caused all the trouble between the Gnomonese and the Firozians, how the war had almost happened but then the Vargans had invaded. She hadn't accepted the verdict in favor of Beroth but had accompanied her father into Firoze because she didn't want to be separated from him if war should come to Gnomon.

"Our land has been at peace for six hundred years. Unlike the Firozians, we don't seek out trouble, we avoid it."

"That's not the way I live my life," Hugh said, without boasting. "There's more than one way to be in this world. If I'd lived like you I would never have left the sleepy little village where I came from, never have sailed the wide sea—"

"Never been imprisoned by the Vargans or tortured by the Firozians."

"True enough," Hugh admitted, "but I don't complain. My life would have been one of hard labor at my father's tinker's bench. I would have been old at thirty and dead at forty."

"Now you may die at twenty—"

"But I've already lived more life than many men of sixty, so you see, the equation works for me. Someday, perhaps, I'll settle down, but not until I've seen as much of the world as I possibly can."

The two young people were silent for a few minutes, contemplating each other's passionate defense of his or her way of life. Finally Aivlys spoke: "I hope you survive."

Hugh laughed. "I hope I do, too. If for no other rea-

son than curiosity. I'd love to come to Gnomon and see
the workshops there. I hear you do wonders with tools."

Now it was Aivlys's turn to laugh. "Oh yes, my father's a regular wizard." She wondered if Hugh had any
idea how close to the truth he was when he ascribed
magical qualities to Gnomonese watchmaking and
watchmakers. What an impetuous fellow. How bold and
daring he was, and yet for all his travels, how little he
seemed to understand of life. In her short time Aivlys
had learned that one can't take the world by force, that
patience is better than rashness, that Time, the soothing,
mellifluous song of the universe, would eventually
overcome and send to slumber even the most ambitious
of men. Hugh lay back down and soon fell asleep next
to his newfound friend, who watched over him late into
the night before drifting off herself.

6

AFTER TWO DAYS IT BECAME CLEAR TO General Sticer that he had neither the men nor the arms to mount a successful storming of Firoze to retake the city. Nor could they remain in the hills—there was simply not enough food or water to sustain this army for a protracted harassing action. He needed a place where his army could be fed and watered, where blacksmiths and armorers could set up shop, where he could plan strategy and recuperate from his wound (though his new ally Platho had certainly hastened the healing process by whatever clever manipulations he had done to the general's leg). In short, there was only one place on the island where he might accomplish all these goals—in Gnomon. He could mount a guard at the Impasse to ensure that the Vargans couldn't follow and at-

tack in force. The harbor at Gnomon was narrower and
more tricky to navigate; it was unlikely that the Vargans
could sail their big ships into it. They might still invade
by sending troops in longboats, but at least the army
would be spared the ordeal of cannon fire. No doubt
about it, in Gnomon his army could regain its bearings
and prepare for the counterattack. But how to achieve
this goal, that was the question. Should he strike boldly,
in the Firozian tradition, seizing by force what he
needed? The Gnomons certainly would offer little resistance; he'd already seen their pitiful army, which was
no match even for a reduced and battered Firozian brigade. But then he would be forced into the role of oc-
cupier. His displaced and disarrayed army would face
hostility and perhaps even the kind of subversive activity he knew the Firozian populace was inflicting on the
Vargans even now: poisoned food, misleading information. No, far better would be to reach some accommo-
dation with the Gnomonese. Hadn't Platho proposed
this very thing? Ah, but how would he feel about the
proposal when it meant a foreign army marching into
his homeland and camping out for weeks, perhaps
months? Still, it was the only answer. General Sticer
vowed to discuss this with the Gnomonese at the first
available opportunity. Imagine his surprise, then, when
Endimin appeared outside his tent that very morning to
propose that the Firozian army become guests of the
people of Gnomon!

"General," he said between sips of that sugary tea the
Gnomonese were so fond of that they even brought it to
war with them, "your army is in disarray. You have no
hope of waging a successful campaign against the
Vargans while your fighting force is in its current
shape. Come to Gnomon and enjoy our hospitality
while you refurbish and reinvigorate your troops."

"You would do this for us?" General Sticer asked
dryly. "What do you require in return?"

"That you help us defend Gnomon from the Vargans, and that our two lands unite in eternal peace."

"To the first I give my pledge. The second depends on the outcome of our struggle with the Vargans. It may be moot if we are both in chains."

"If we are ironed together then we would have even more reason to cooperate, but I don't think it will come to that. I have only one concern," Endimin said slowly, as if to accentuate the gravity of his apprehension. He stirred the coals beneath the morning campfire with a stick, hesitant to bring up the source of his anxiety. Finally he spoke: "Can you guarantee the good conduct of your troops, especially in regard to the womanhood of Gnomon?"

"I can promise you that any man who acts out of order will be disciplined severely. Soldiers are a rough lot, I'll grant you, and Beroth is one of the worst of them, but I think you'll find that men are men everywhere. Some are good, some are bad. All have the capacity to be both, at any time. If we provide them with good leadership, by example and by setting clear rules for conduct, they'll conduct themselves in exemplary fashion."

"That's the answer I wanted to hear, and it shows wisdom," Endimin responded. The two men shook hands firmly.

Endimin thought it wise to go on ahead of the army to prepare the citizens of Gnomon for the peaceful entrance of the Firozian army. He and Aivlys were joined by young Hugh Boisset. After his heroic stand in Flailan, Hugh was no longer a prisoner of the Firozians but instead was considered a hero by them. He expressed an interest in seeing the Gnomonese clockmakers' shops, and Endimin was enthused and Aivlys shyly pleased that he accompanied them. They climbed to the Impasse, where they met the posted lookouts from their own land, the first other Gnomonese they had seen in several days.

"Well, if it isn't Zanfer Thoughton," Endimin said jocularly to one of the soldiers, a bespectacled young-ster who looked hardly old enough to inhabit the uni-form he wore. "We've been wandering among giants for the past few days. Seeing a little fellow like you makes my heart warm."

Zanfer blushed but kept his eyes on the horizon. Aivlys admired his vigilance.

"What's to report?" Endimin asked.

"Some of the Vargan ships have moved off, sir. We fear they might be sailing around the island into posi-tion to attack Gnomon."

"Or they might be satisfied that they can do the job in Firoze with a smaller force," Endimin speculated. "In any case, we can rest easier about the Vargans try-ing to invade Gnomon. They can't sail into our harbor as they did in Firoze, and what's more, the considerable remains of the Firozian army are going to join us in de-fending the island on our side as well."

"What's that, sir? The Firozians are going to enter Gnomon?"

"Yes. When you see them coming, don't resist them. Welcome them."

"Welcome them, sir? After we almost went to war against them just a few days ago?"

"That's right. We've all learned a lot since then. We've learned that our little island is vulnerable, and that unless we cooperate with all who share our lovely land, we shall lose it."

Zanfer, who had braved high winds during the day and extreme low temperatures for three nights running, removed his glasses, rubbed his windburned face, and blinked his strained eyes as he tried to comprehend this change. His recent enemies, who had been transformed into allies, were now going to march straight into his homeland without a fight.

"When are they coming, sir?"

"In a few hours. In the interim, you and the others might spend some time opening up the wall so that more of their army can pass through abreast."

"Sir, we just finished repairing the wall."

"Well, that's the way of things in the army, Soldier Thoughton. Build a wall, tear it down. Dig a ditch, fill it up. Fortunately we haven't had need for such senseless activities in Gnomon for a very long time. We're rusty at it. The Firozians can show us a thing or two there."

"I'll be sure to take notes, sir," Zanfer Thoughton replied, so earnestly that Hugh Boisset broke into a laugh.

"You do that, good soldier!"

"And who are you?" Zanfer asked, a little bit insulted by Hugh's joshing tone. "Are you a Firozian, or a Vargan, or what?"

"I'm a Bushcadian, if you must put a label on me. I'm a son of the sea, and a piratical fellow. I'm one of your new allies." Hugh finished his speech by dancing a little sailor's jig while humming a sea shanty.

"Oh." Simplehearted Zanfer didn't know what to make of the odd-looking dandy who cavorted before him. Even Aivlys had to giggle at the spectacle of the serious, innocent guard eyeing the irrepressible Hugh Boisset askance.

"Come now, Zanfer, don't look at him so strangely, he's only playing the fool for your amusement," said Endimin.

"I can see that, sir, and he does it well."

Hugh winced at Thoughton's dry rejoinder. The three travelers left Zanfer and the other watchmen and began the descent into Gnomon. Hugh remarked immediately how much more inviting was the greensward of Gnomon's hillsides than the barren rocky slopes of Firoze.

Everywhere the ground was laced with mountain flowers in bloom, red penstemon and purple pinkroot, mountain lilies and lavish ne'er-do-wells. In some places whole swales were ablaze with orange glazia and yellow mustard. Below them the farms and villages of Gnomon spread out peacefully, and beyond them the capital city ringed a shallow bay that was drenched in sunlight. A single thought ran through Hugh Boisset's head: that it would be a shame to see this paradise destroyed by the ravages of war.

"Your country is lovely," he said to Aivlys as he tried to help her over a ledge; she resisted his aid and clambered gracefully down on her own. "I wonder what it will be like to have several thousand Firozian troops descend upon it."

Endimin didn't hear Hugh's remark, but Aivlys, who had been informed of the plan by her father, felt a sudden pang in her heart as she realized what it might mean—hundreds, thousands of men like Beroth, whom she would never forgive despite what the court had decided, hardened soldiers, not raw recruits like young Zanfer, wandering the streets of her beloved land, leering at the women, threatening the men. She wondered at the wisdom of her father's actions. Yet, throughout this crisis, Endimin had shown himself to be an astute judge of situations as they arose, with that uniquely Gnomonese characteristic of exquisite timing, knowing when to be bold, as when he had marched right into Firoze to demand a trial for Beroth, and when to give way, to yield, as when he had realized that Runny's death, despite appearances, really was a tragic accident. She decided that once again she would have to trust Endimin's instincts, which so far had not failed him.

"Do you know any spells, Hugh?" Aivlys asked her new friend.

"Spells, ha! Don't believe in 'em. I trust only what I can see, hear, smell, touch, and taste."

Aivlys was about to say "That's stupid!" and perhaps to give Hugh a small demonstration of her considerable powers, when she remembered the oath she had taken when she became a member of the Guild, which included a caution never to reveal the secrets of the Gnomonese white magic arts to non-believers. She contented herself with an offhand remark—"You've got a lot to learn"—which Hugh missed because he was suddenly distracted. The first of a line of Vargan warships had rounded the coast at the promontory known as Shepherd's Bluff.

"Look there!" he shouted. In an instant all three of them—Hugh, Aivlys, and Endimin—had broken into a run, dashing downhill as fast as they dared. Things were happening faster than Endimin had hoped—it was now a race against time as to whether the Firozian army would arrive quickly enough to make a stand against the Vargan invaders. When they reached the city they found the place in chaos: people running every which way, the bells in the Clocktower clanging madly, skittish animals roaming the streets.

"Stop those bells!" Endimin shouted to no one in particular, for who could hear him over the wildly insistent ringing that was responsible for much of the pandemonium in the streets.

"Aivlys, go home and secure our house—padlock the animals in the barn and shutter the workshop! Hugh, come with me!" Endimin ordered. Aivlys was disappointed but unwilling to disobey her father's orders. She ran off.

Hugh followed Endimin to the main square, where they found Henri Blouchette trying to organize a resistance force from among the panicked and half-crazed citizenry. After so many years of peace, the idea of imminent war was more than some could bear sensibly.

"Platho! Thank the gods you're here. We're being invaded from two sides!"

"What are you talking about?"

"The Vargans are at our shores, and the Firozians, those cowards, are ambushing us from behind!"

"Nonsense!" Endimin let his impatience show for just an instant, which he immediately regretted, because he knew that the poor clerk and sometime sheriff was doing the best he could.

"But they signaled us from the mountains that the Firozians are coming through the Impasse," Henri said meekly.

"As allies, Sheriff Blouchette. As allies!" The message from the watchmen on the summit must have gotten garbled as it was passed down to the town by means of coded signals.

"Really?"

"Yes. Now get your men and bring them all down to the waterfront. Where are they likely to land, Boisset?"

"Well, first off, they won't land right away," Hugh told them. "For starters they'll promenade back and forth across the harbor mouth, checking for chains—"

"Chains?" Henri Blouchette asked.

"Yes, some nations have learned to stretch huge iron chains across their port entrances, that can be raised and lowered to allow ships in or bar their way."

"Well, we have none. But those big vessels might run aground inside our breakwater."

"Exactly. That's the other thing they look for. If they find the depths too shallow, then they'll bombard from farther out and send in landing parties in double-ended longboats they carry on board for such purposes."

"How can we delay them until the Firozians arrive?" Endimin asked.

"Well, for one thing, you could request a meeting under truce, as if you intended to surrender without a fight. They'd like nothing better."

"Let it be done. Who among you has a small boat we can use?" One of the fishermen-turned-soldiers stepped forward. Endimin sent him off to prepare his craft for the short voyage out to the Vargan warships.

"Hugh!" Endimin shouted. "Go to the Clocktower and tell whoever's pulling those bell ropes to stop right now. Cut the ropes if you have to! Then come right back here. No—then go get Aivlys; she should be here, too."

Endimin did some quick calculations. The first Firozian troops would have crossed the pass by now, but it would take at least two and a half hours for the vanguard to reach Gnomon, and the rest of the day for troops to be deployed in any kind of effective defense against a longboat landing. Still, if they could only stave off the Vargans until then, they would have a good chance of repelling an attack. For one thing, the long shallow beach of Gnomon would force the invaders to wade slowly for many yards through the water, making them easy targets, unlike the deep-water port of Firoze, where the ships were able to sail right up to dockside. There was only one place in Gnomon where ships could approach land in that manner, and it was through a narrow channel easily defendable and not accessible to the heavy, deep-drafted Vargan vessels. The town itself was also more spread out and less densely populated than Firoze, which would make shelling by cannon, though devastating, less effective. And then there were the Gnomonese spells—but which ones to use, and when to use them? Aivlys had already shown herself to be intuitively advanced in her understanding of Gnomonese magic. As long as there was no actual fighting, Endimin wanted her to be present. She represented the next generation of Gnomonese wizardry, but she still needed tutoring, and Endimin had done about as much as he thought he could with her. Then he remembered—there was someone else from whom Aivlys might profit!

"You there!" he shouted at a small boy who was

playing along the dock; oblivious to the great drama
that was unfolding around him, he was tossing stale
bread to a flock of seabirds who circled and screeched
above his head. The youth came running over dutifully,
as the birds descended, squabbling amongst each other,
to pick up the scraps. "Do you know the house of
Zentina Wraight?"

"Yes, sir," came the polite reply.

"Go fetch her for me! Tell her Endimin Platho wants
to see her at the beach below Shepherd's Bluff."

"But she's a wisth!" the boy answered anxiously,
whistling though a missing tooth.

"She won't hurt you. Just give her the message.
Here, here's a penny for your trouble." Endimin dug
into his pocket and produced a copper coin, remembering briefly that he had done the same for a youngster in
Firoze, and quietly remarking how boys were the same
everywhere. The little fellow scampered off. Confident
that his message would be delivered, Endimin turned
his attention to the preparations for the perilous trip to
meet the Vargans, though he found it hard to concen-
trate because of the constant jangling in his brain from
those confounded bells! Just when he thought the incessant noise was going to drive him mad, the bells ceased
with a final clang as if they had all rung together once.
Hugh must've scared the wits out of the bell ringer,
Endimin thought, allowing himself a small smile in the
midst of his travails. *Now, if we can only outwit the
Vargans.*

Hugh had sprinted the full length of the town to the
Clocktower. He burst into the room where the bell
ropes dangled, expecting to find a crazed Gnomonese
tugging madly at them, but instead saw only the ropes
jumping and squirming as the bells swung high above.
He leaped to the staircase and climbed the several
flights as quickly as his legs would carry him, passing
through the room where Aivlys had been inducted into

the Guild and where Beroth had been held captive, then up a final twisting set of stairs that led to the bell chamber itself. The noise had grown steadily louder and was nearly overpowering when he finally entered the upper tower, where, to his surprise, he found—no one! The bells were ringing of their own volition, or so it seemed. Hugh was momentarily at a loss—how could he stop the racket? Just then he felt a hand on his shoulder—he whirled, in the same motion withdrawing his short dagger, to find Aivlys!

"I can stop them," she said, and she spread her hands (for effect only; it didn't matter how she held them, but she wanted to impress Hugh) and repeated the words of the enchantment known as Quiet Time: *"Settle down, Wrack and Riot. Turn inward, be Quiet."*

Suddenly there was stillness, a bit unnatural, as if a blanket had been thrown over all the sounds of the day. The bells ceased.

"Someone must have cast a spell on them and forgotten to remove it," said Aivlys to Hugh, who was looking at her wide-eyed.

"Uh, if you say so," Hugh mumbled. "Come on, your father wants us down at the dock. Say, why did you show up here just now, anyway?" Hugh asked with a hint of suspicion in his voice. They began to retrace their steps down the inside of the tower.

"Why do you think? I couldn't stand the bells anymore," Aivlys said with a laugh. Sometimes she didn't understand herself, or life. Here was Gnomon on the eve of a terrible invasion, yet she felt more lighthearted than at any time since her brother had died. At least now she had a sense of purpose; her father had made her feel useful and needed, and her new friend Hugh was looking at her with an increased respect.

Hugh rubbed his temples. The world of sound still seemed fuzzy to him, as if there were cottony plugs in his ears. He couldn't hear the sound of his own booted footfalls on the wooden steps. Aivlys noticed his concern and sought to reassure him.

"Don't worry, it'll wear off in a minute or two," Aivlys told him. She was right. Slowly sound came back to him, the clatter of hooves, the occasional shout, the sigh of the breeze, somehow separate and distinct, not yet merging into the constant background buzz of existence. It was as if he were hearing everything for the first time, as if an impediment had been removed and he was suddenly perceiving the world as it was meant to be heard. He could almost have fallen down and kissed the ground, the noises were so sweet.

"Aivlys, I'm ... having a strange experience," he said, trying lamely to articulate the sensations.

"It will pass," she said matter-of-factly.

"I don't want it to," he rejoined.

"Well, it will. Let's hurry now." They had reached the ground floor, where the bell ropes hung still and silent. Aivlys broke into a trot. They skirted the main hall and the courtroom where Beroth had been tried, and passed through a side door into the street, where another wave of joyous din and clamor struck Hugh's newly opened ears. It astonished him that this girl could make the pealing end, douse the whole spectrum of sound, then bring it back by sweet degrees, filling his head with wonder.

"Will you come on?" Aivlys shouted impatiently to him as he dawdled along, savoring each new tone: the rustling of paper shuffling in the hands of a passing merchant, the rough grating squeak of an unoiled door swinging open, the strident, explosive clang of a nearby blacksmith's hammer striking anvil. Even Aivlys's harsh command was music, pure music; especially her voice, that lovely smoothness of youth. Hugh rushed to catch up to Aivlys as her slim figure disappeared around the corner toward the docks. As he raced along he heard shouted rumors: "The Vargans are about to land." "They have landed!" "The Firozians are attacking us, too."

But Hugh could see that none of this was true. By the time he reached the docks the sailor who had been commissioned to prepare his boat was ready for them to step aboard. Seagulls screeched overhead, sending shivers of delight down Hugh's back. The lapping of the waves against the side of the boat, the clanking of the halyard against the mast, the soft slap of the canvas sail in the breeze all triggered emotions within Hugh, feelings he never knew he was capable of or interested in, all engendered by that sudden stopping and starting of sound that Aivlys had engineered by . . . by what? Magic? Enchantment? It must be. Yet he had never believed in such things before today. He shook his head as if to clear his mind of cobwebs and set his eyes upon the Vargan flagship *Regina*, looming large in the water dead ahead.

"I spent many an unpleasant day on those decks, or worse, below them," he told Aivlys.

"What's their leader like?" Endimin wanted to know.

"A gruff and impatient sort, the kind you don't want to cross or make wait," Hugh answered.

"Oh, I don't know," Endimin replied calmly. "Sometimes people like that enjoy being put off, it gives them something on which to graft and grow their anger." They soon found themselves in the shadow of the immense ship, bigger by tenfold than any the Gnomonese people had ever seen. The sides of the vessel seemed impossibly high; the truce party wondered how they were to get aboard, until a rope ladder came whistling down at them, dangling out of their reach until the boat owner seized it with a gaff hook. It was a difficult climb up the swaying hemp to the solid planking of the deck where Admiral Francisco met them, surrounded by his officers and aides and a contingent of battle-hardened soldier marines who towered over the Gno-

monese and approximately matched the height of the
Firozians and the gangly Hugh Boisset. Francisco fixed
his eyes on the peripatetic navigator.

"I see you've changed sides, Boisset," he said, with
a less-than-friendly stare. Francisco was stocky, with a
chest like a wine cask, a thick black beard, and stumpy
legs. He was shorter than most of his soldiers, but still
taller than the Gnomons, and his bearing made him
seem taller than his actual size.

"He would never have joined you if you hadn't kidnapped him," Aivlys said hotly, without waiting to be
introduced.

Admiral Francisco laughed. "Is that what he told
you? The truth of the matter is that he volunteered,
braying of his skills as a navigator, and was only imprisoned after he ran aground one of our finest vessels,
in the mouth of the harbor no less, and succeeded in
ruining our port of entry for several weeks during the
height of the trading season. That's what got him into
trouble, not our seamen's impress, though I don't deny
we take on men against their will on occasion, when we
need to. That's the prerogative of strength."

Aivlys was no longer listening to the admiral; she
was looking at Hugh, who blushed under her gaze and
shrugged his shoulders bashfully to confirm the gist of
the admiral's story.

"Yes, our precipitous friend here is quite the braggart
and boaster. Sometimes he can make his claims stand
up, as with his fine nautical navigation machine. Other
times they fall flat. Boisset is a dashing, voluble, and
persuasive fellow, but not without his faults. Don't
think too badly of him, young miss," Admiral Francisco
said with a sneer. "All young men are given to hyper-
bole. It's part of their nature, especially when the aim
is to impress women."

Admiral Francisco abruptly turned his back on the
truce party and stared out at the sea. He said nothing

for a long time, while the members of the peace delegation fidgeted and glanced at each other. Finally he addressed them, still with his eyes on the open sea beyond the harbor.

"I am many sailing days from my homeland. In my conquest of the other side of this island, I've used up the time allotted to me for this mission. If I set sail within the week, I can still return within the appointed time. If I am delayed by even so much as a day beyond that, they will take my command from me. So you see, I am a desperate man."

He turned back to face them. "I can't tolerate any feeble resistance. I am issuing you an ultimatum—lay down your arms or face retribution the likes of which this island has never known."

Endimin coughed politely. "It is customary in our dealings to offer our trading partners a little repast before serious negotiations begin. I've taken the liberty of bringing on board some of our local tea and our excellent baked goods. Won't you sit with us and break bread before we enter the painful business of our capitulation?"

"If you insist."

"Aside from your former hostage, you don't even know our names," said Endimin. He launched into lengthy and almost absurdly detailed biographies of the various personages who had accompanied him, while Aivlys laboriously spread out a luncheon on the deck of the *Regina* and Admiral Francisco tapped his foot impatiently and glanced at his timepiece, which Endimin noted with satisfaction was an inferior imitation of a Gnomonese design.

Admiral Francisco was a cautious man. After Aivlys had set out the plates he had them repositioned—"How do we know the food isn't poisoned?"—and waited until each of the visitors had taken a bite and swallowed

before unenthusiastically nibbling and sipping at the offering.

"Well?" he demanded finally, after Endimin had ex-
temporized as long as possible.

"Well," Endimin began, but just then he heard the
faint sounds of music drifting on the breeze, martial
music, the sound of drums and horns, the proud, stirring
airs of Firoze. The army had arrived! "Well," Endimin
said, "we've decided not to give in. Our allies, the
Firozians—"

"Your allies?" Admiral Francisco exploded. "Captured Firozian soldiers told me what they think of your
people, that you are effete, prissy, given to too much
talking and playing with toys, far less warlike than
themselves, who at least put up a fight. Now they are
your allies?"

"Look for yourself," Endimin said with satisfaction.
The Firozian army was arraying itself smartly, with
crisp precision, along the shore. Francisco realized he
had been outwitted by this unlikely entourage who had
lulled him into delaying his final assault, and that the
moment had now slipped by him.

"Only my respect for the white flag of truce prevents
me from slitting your throats this minute," Admiral
Francisco raged. "Put them on their little boat and cut
them loose," he told his officers. "Begin the first bombardment as soon as their prow touches shore."

"You may throw cannonballs at us, you may burn our
buildings and destroy our city, but you will not conquer
us," said Endimin. "We have Time on our side."

"We shall see," said Admiral Francisco haughtily,
and with that he wheeled and disappeared belowdecks.
The members of the truce party were unceremoniously
shoved into their boat and set adrift before they were
ready, nearly causing the vessel to capsize. Once they
righted themselves and took their seats, the owner made
ready to hoist the canvas, but Hugh put his arm on the

man's shoulder and turned to Endimin with a grin on his face.

"Let's bait him a little more," he proposed. "Francisco said he wouldn't fire until we landed. Let's take our time." They raised sail with infinite pains, then tacked broadly back and forth across the channel in a zigzag journey that gave the Firozian army and the citizens of Gnomon an extra few minutes to prepare for the imminent rain of grapeshot and lead balls.

They were just about to reach the shore when a thudding roar from behind them signaled that they had tried Admiral Francisco's patience to the full. The first volley passed over their heads; they watched in horror as it descended upon the wooden houses of Gnomon, tossing up timbers and shards of brick in a column of smoke that almost immediately threatened to engulf the entire city in flames. The little boat was tied off at the dock and everyone aboard scrambled ashore just as a second round of cannonballs whistled over their heads and discharged more destruction onto the unprepared city.

"Hugh, find Basco Fournier and make sure the volunteers are organized to fight the fires. Aivlys, come with me. We've got to locate General Sticer. I don't think the Vargans will try to land right away. Maybe we can use his troops to save the city from burning."

"What does this Fournier fellow look like?" Hugh asked, reasonably enough, but a nearby explosion forced them to duck their heads and scatter, and when Hugh looked up again the two of them were well down the line of the docks, dodging and zigzagging in and out among the abandoned nets and mooring ropes, the traps and trappings of the fishing fleet.

And now they were all plunged into the horrors of war—the streets running with blood, women and children with frenzied eyes wandering aimlessly, animals and men racing in frantic gallop toward unknown des-

tinations. The disciplined troops of the Firozian army
moved in groups from one position to another, strange
islands of unity, these blocks of men marching in order
amid a land that was suddenly torn asunder with as
much force as an earthquake, except the devastation
came from above instead of below, and was the work of
men and not nature. Choking black smoke soon hung
over Gnomon as it had over Firoze, these twin cities, so
different and yet so much alike, now both shattered by
the crushing blows of seaborne artillery, a method of
warfare never before employed against them.

The Firozians dug in and held their positions despite
the intense cannonade. The Vargan ships continued to
circle and fire, but had not yet made any attempt to
send in troops. Nor were they likely to do so, now that
the Firozians held the assault positions. Endimin's delaying tactics had worked brilliantly: the Vargans had
lost both the element of surprise and the psychological
edge of terror. The artillery barrage was fearsome,
daunting, but not as threatening as if an actual battle
between invaders and defenders were being waged.

For the first time, Aivlys felt fear, yet somewhere
within her was also a strange calmness, as if she were
where she was supposed to be, next to her father, as
they alternately ran furiously and threw themselves
down on the ground to escape the next blast. Run, then
fall, run, then fall. It was a curious way to progress, she
thought, the third or fourth time they found themselves
stretched out beneath a sheltering wall or crouched
against a column. Finally they were forced to hunker
down behind an overturned rowboat. Aivlys turned to
Endimin and hugged him tightly.

"Yes, my daughter, it's all right, you've been very
brave," Endimin whispered, and Aivlys couldn't really
hear him because of the continuing barrage, but read
his lips and found comfort in his words.

"It's not that, Father. I'm not afraid for myself, but I worry, what will become of Gnomon?"

"Gnomon will find peace again, dear daughter. Perhaps not today or tomorrow, but soon. I promise you. Let's rest here awhile."

Hugh, meanwhile, had set out to look for a man whose name was his only clue. He stopped people in the street to ask if they knew where Fournier could be found, but received only blank looks or shrugs of the shoulders. He wandered farther from the water, back toward the center of town until he encountered a large crowd trying desperately to quench a fire in a warehouse that had taken a direct hit from a Vargan sixteen-pounder. He pitched in by organizing the mob in a bucket brigade, shouting commands as if he were an authority, something that came to him easily from his days as navigator aboard the Vargan vessel.

"What's in there?" he shouted to the man next to him in line, as they handed full buckets forward and pitched empty buckets back at a feverish rate.

"It's the civic museum. That building contains some of Gnomon's most precious relics," the man responded. "Clocks and watches from the earliest days. Real antiques. One of a kind. Irreplaceable."

But the fire had gotten the upper hand and the building, made of wood and furnished with plush draperies that burned quickly, was soon on the verge of destruction.

"Stand back, everyone!" Hugh shouted. He ran back and forth, pushing the firefighters away from the structure just as the roof collapsed, showering him in a hail of embers and cinders. His face blackened and his clothes singed, Hugh stood stunned for a minute, then regained his senses and began to give orders again.

"All right, on to the next one, and this time start the brigade right away!"

He had just turned to continue his search for Basco
Fournier when there before his eyes, sauntering down
the street as if she hadn't a care in the world, was a
striking-looking old woman dressed in black, with a
small umbrella over her head to protect her from the
sun (though in this hour it also provided some [perhaps
illusory] cover from burning embers and shell frag-
ments). Her nose was hooked and her wrinkled face
was covered with warts, but somehow, they were *at-
tractive* warts. Hugh heard the unmistakable sound of a
twelve-pounder whistling in, and saw that it was going
to land in the street directly where the apparition in
black was walking. He rushed toward her and virtually
tackled her, flinging the two of them to the ground
under a nearby bush. The cannonball struck the empty
street harmlessly, dug a crater, and threw up a shower
of dirt that pelted them.

"What are you doing? Are you crazy?" Hugh scolded
the woman, who responded, "What do you mean, grab-
bing an old woman? You might have broken my brittle
bones!"

"You wouldn't have any bones if that lead ball had
hit you!" Hugh yelled.

"I had my parasol up, didn't you see that?" the
woman replied nonsensically, or so it seemed to Hugh
as they both rose and dusted themselves off.

"Who are you?"

"Who are you?" the old lady snapped back. "You
must be an off-islander. You're too big to be Gnomonese and not big enough to be Firozian. Just who and
what are you?"

"Endimin—" Hugh began to explain, but the quirky
oldster lashed out at him as soon as she heard the name.

"Yes, yes, he summoned me, what for I don't know.
Why he would want a poor, frail old woman like me
out on such a terrible day as this I can't imagine."

"I don't think he knew it was going to be like this," Hugh said charitably.

"Don't defend him. He doesn't need it."

"Are you Basco Fournier?" Hugh asked with a sudden inspiration.

"That's a man's name, can't you tell? Are ye daft? My name is Zentina Wraight, and there's your Basco Fournier right over there." She pointed out Basco, who was charging down the street at the head of a group of volunteers, hauling the city's single pump-wagon by hand toward another burning building. "Now, where can I find Platho?"

"Last I saw him he was searching for the Firozian commander along the waterfront."

"Gnomon in flames, ships of another nation attacking us from offshore, the Firozian army marching through —on our side, no less—what is the world coming to?" Zentina asked, but without waiting for an answer and without ever learning Hugh's name she continued on, parasol held high. Hugh watched her go, then ran up to Basco Fournier, who, very much like himself a few moments ago, was directing the efforts of a group of men against wind-fanned flames.

"Fournier!"

"Yes?"

"Hugh Boisset. Endimin rescued me from the Firozians. I've been helping him. He sent me to see that you're doing . . . what you're doing."

"Ah yes, one of the returning lookouts mentioned you. Well, then, you can report to Platho that the firemen are at their job; though at this rate we'll never be able to keep up with it, we might be able to prevent the whole city from burning to the ground. How does it look on the waterfront? Are we going to be invaded?" Fournier asked, cocking an eyebrow and keeping one eye on the flame-smothering operation.

"Not today. The Firozians are making a good show of force, even though some of them are still trickling in from the mountains."

Hugh and Fournier sized each other up, and decided immediately that they liked each other. Among his many talents, Endimin Platho was a good judge of men; somehow he had foreseen that these two, the head-strong young navigator and the perpetually bemused toy shop owner, would form an alliance.

"So," said Hugh, "what else can we do besides put out fires?"

"We're going to need to rally the people in this city. None of them have ever experienced anything like this. And we're going to need a go-between, a liaison for contact among the Firozians and Gnomonese for there are sure to be misunderstandings, conflicts."

"That would be my role, I'd guess, at least until the actual invasion comes, then I'll want to be where the fighting is."

"Ah, the brashness of youth," Basco murmured, looking around him at the carnage, homes aflame, cob-bled streets torn apart, wounded citizens being dragged or carried to and fro, "always in such a hurry to get themselves killed."

"Oh, I don't want to die, I just want to be where the action is."

"And I want there to be no action, other than a return to the sweet peace we enjoyed on this island for so many years. I've heard you're quite the fancier of me-chanical devices. Come, I'll show you my toy shop, if it still stands."

They hurried down the lane, past the tea shop and into a side alley. From a distance Basco Fournier could see that his little store was already a smoking ruin. He held back his emotions as he approached the spot, but couldn't prevent a sob from escaping his lips as he fell on his hands and knees to scrabble among the twisted figures of melted lead toy soldiers blown into the street by the force of the explosion that had destroyed his life's work. Hugh picked at the wreckage, finding whimsical items in shambles: charred puppets and dolls, smoking half-burned balls of leather stuffed with feathers that gave off noxious fumes, scraps of paper that represented the pathetic remains of children's books.

Hugh helped Fournier to his feet. "Come, my friend, there's nothing to salvage here."

"Nothing, indeed. The boys and girls of Gnomon will not be playing at toy soldiers for many a day, I fear. They have the real ones to entertain them." Dispirited, Fournier trudged away from the pile of debris that had once been the pride of his existence. Hugh followed behind him.

Zentina Wraight's appearance on the pier caused quite a stir among the Firozian soldiers, who gazed in amazement from their quickly dug trenches as this black-clad spirit strolled unconcernedly through the incoming downpour of hot angry metal, calling out Endimin Platho's name periodically. They shouted at her to get down, take cover, but she ignored them as she had ignored Hugh, and none of the Firozians was willing to leave his shelter to rescue her. Their amazement turned to shock and disbelief when a fourteen-pound cannonball came crashing out of the sky, scored a direct hit on the top of her umbrella, and bounced off! Zentina Wraight kept walking as if nothing had happened. Her wrist, holding the handle of the protective shield, did not bend even a little. The slow-moving ball rolled off the pier and dropped into the sea with a plop and a sizzle.

"Oh, furious gods!" one of the Firozians shouted. "What witchery is this?"

Zentina took no notice of the astonished howls coming from the emplacements of the Firozians, she was still searching for the man who had summoned her from her isolation, Endimin Platho. What could he want of her, especially at this time, when she should be at home, protecting her precious collection of—but there he was up ahead, waving frantically to her, the old fool. Surely he knew that she was safe beneath her parasol? After all, he had been there when she had first demonstrated Time's Shield. It was a simple matter, really— nothing could touch you if you weren't there when it arrived. Her umbrella wasn't there, therefore, nothing could penetrate it. How could it? It wasn't there. It was just ahead or just behind, never in the moment. Zentina remembered dimly how it had been explained to her: it was like the bow wave that breaks the water ahead of a boat's prow, like the—but for the gods' goodness, why was Endimin signaling so vociferously? She was closer now, and his voice reached her between volleys of thunder from the cannons.

"Zentina, come quickly, I need your help!"

Zentina hastened to reach him, but she was old and hobbled by arthritis, and couldn't move very quickly. As she approached she saw the reason for his urgency: Aivlys lay unconscious on the ground at his feet, hidden behind a stack of barrels where they had sought cover from the incessant cannon fire. Her smock was bloodied, and she seemed to be having difficulty breathing. Endimin was on his knees, holding her hand helplessly. When Zentina Wraight arrived he looked up at her in anguish.

"I've already lost one child, I just can't bear to lose another," Endimin pleaded, his voice shaking.

"What happened? Was she struck by a ball?" Zentina asked, fearing the response, because if lead entered a victim's body, infection and death often followed, no matter how slight the wound.

"No, thank the gods, but a section of the warehouse behind us came down"—Endimin indicated the pile of rubble with one hand—"and we were caught under it. I'm afraid she's broken some ribs, and I don't know if there are any internal injuries."

Zentina closed her parasol and knelt down. With gentle, practiced movements she ran her hands along the girl's supine form, checking the extent of the damage. There were a few abrasions and a cracked rib that caused Aivlys to moan when Zentina pressed on it lightly, but no serious punctures or hemorrhaging that she could discern. Still, there was no need to take any further risk. "We must bring her to my house," she said firmly, as if expecting resistance from Endimin.

"Yes, fine!" Endimin almost shouted. "I sent for you because I wanted you to take Aivlys and give her some additional training, but now I need you to help her recover—"

"That's why she must be moved to my house."

"I'll carry her," Endimin offered.

"No, that would involved too much jarring and shaking. We'll fly."

"Ah, I had almost forgotten, you really are a witch," Endimin said with a smile. Aivlys stirred and opened her eyes. When she saw her father smiling above her, she relaxed and closed her eyes again.

"Hand her to me," said Zentina, who suddenly seemed taller than she had appeared before. Endimin looked down knowingly and saw Zentina Wraight hovering a few inches off the ground. He lifted Aivlys's inert form and carefully placed her in Zentina's outstretched arms, then hung her parasol over one crooked arm. The old woman was surprisingly strong, especially for one who was no longer rooted on earth. As soon as she accepted Aivlys, she began to move off, and one who wasn't looking carefully might think that she was merely exceptionally elegant and smooth of stride as she glided along, never soaring but not touching down, either. She headed back through town toward her home in the hills, her magical parasol providing all the protection she and Aivlys needed to pass untouched through the still-falling rain of metal.

7

AIVLYS AWOKE TO A HORRIBLE ODOR, acrid and rancid and bitter all at once, that filled her nostrils and almost made her retch.

"Drink this," a voice commanded her, and she opened her eyes to see Zentina Wraight's wart-covered face inches from her own, the elderly woman's beady eyes peering into her sleep-glazed orbs. The witch was holding a wooden cup of the noxious-smelling stuff under Aivlys's nose with one hand and tilting Aivlys's head up toward the vile mixture with the other. Aivlys took a tentative sip, and though the drink was foul, it didn't taste nearly as bad as it smelled. She gagged slightly but managed to take down about two-thirds of the liquid before pulling her head back in disgust. She felt dizzy and weak as Zentina laid her back in the

bed, into which she sunk as though it were a pile of
leaves. A musty down comforter covered her, and she
felt pleasantly achy, as if she had been exercising rather
than lying here for who knows how long. Aivlys started
to ask about her father and the war, but Zentina shushed
her with a wave of a bony hand.

"Gnomon remains free of foreign invaders, if you
don't count these Firozian soldiers, who lie about indo-
lently, or sneak around stealing chickens and goats and
wineskins."

"What day is it?" Aivlys asked dreamily, for she
had the sensation that much time had passed since she
had last been awake, but Zentina Wraight wouldn't answer her question, and instead pulled some tattered
drapes shut across dust-covered windows and ordered her
back to sleep. The last thing Aivlys remembered was the
old woman cackling as she closed the doors behind her.

Some time later Aivlys stirred again, in darkness.
This time she was alone. She struggled out of the
deeply sunken bed and tottered to a window on wobbly
legs. When she drew back the ragged cloth she saw
faint shadows stretching across a filthy, disheveled
barnyard crowded with scrawny chickens and sickly-
looking goats and sheep. Endimin would never allow
his animals to live under these conditions, Aivlys
thought with a shudder. She couldn't tell if it was early
morning or late afternoon until she heard the cock crow
his exultant herald of dawn. At the rooster's call the
sleepy world began to stir. The chickens woke from
their dozing and began to peck lazily at the dusty earth.
Goats and sheep that had been asleep on their knees
rose unsteadily and stretched. Light came creeping over
the distant hills.

Aivlys thought that as soon as she saw Zentina
Wraight she would ask her, "Why is your farm so
poorly kept up?" but then the old woman came into
view, dragging a sack of cracked corn behind her, toss-

ing handfuls to the scrabbling fowl, and the answer was obvious: She was alone, and the many chores of farmwork had overwhelmed her. Aivlys dressed hurriedly, noting with surprise that the sharp pain in her ribs was gone, replaced by a tenderness, and only occasionally gave her a twinge of discomfort. How many days had she slept? What was going on in Gnomon? From the front yard she would be able to see the rooftops of the city below, if there were any homes still standing with roofs on them, she thought ruefully. But first she hastened to catch up to Zentina, who was pumping feebly at the well in the center of the barnyard for water to fill the trough for the sheep.

"Let me help you," Aivlys said while she tried to take the water bucket from Zentina's right hand. The old woman turned around without relinquishing her hold on the pump handle or the bucket. A little water sloshed on the ground and was quickly absorbed by dust.

"Well, if it isn't sleepyhead," she laughed, a dry, throaty laugh that would have sent shivers up Aivlys's spine if she didn't know that Zentina Wraight was a harmless old witch. "I thought you were going to dream your life away in there."

"How long did I sleep?"

"Only a day and a night, precious one. That's nothing. Some of my spells would cause you to slumber for years."

"I'm better now," Aivlys said. "I want to help you."

"You're here to learn magic, not to muck stalls or sweep barnyards."

"I can do both," Aivlys insisted. With an energy that surprised her (but not Zentina, apparently, who looked on with satisfaction that her home brew had exhibited its restorative powers so quickly) Aivlys began to rearrange and tidy up the yard. While she worked, Zentina brewed some tea and brought it in a lumpy mug to the active young girl, who took a sip and found it delightfully spicy. A couple of corn muffins satisfied her appetite, and she continued to work, scraping the ground with a rake, then splashing water on dusty windows and long-neglected corners of the barn. By the end of the morning she had cleaned the area of old hay and spread a new flooring of fresh straw. After a short break for lunch and a quick nap, she continued to clean and rearrange the barn and yard, while Zentina Wraight looked on approvingly and occasionally. By the end of the day she had transformed the dirty, dusty place into a neat, smaller version of the Platho farm.

"What did you put in that tea you gave me?" Aivlys asked when she finally put down the cleaning tools and sat on the polished steps of the back porch with her new mentor. "I slept for days, then woke up with fantastic energy. What was it?"

"The elixir of life, my dear," Zentina said with a crinkly smile.

"Will you teach me how to cook up such remedies?"

"That and much else, dearie. Tomorrow we start your lessons. Tonight we rest and talk. I want to hear what you know already, for I understand from your father that you are quite adept at certain forms of Gnomonese Time magic already."

"Father is a good teacher," Aivlys agreed.

"Yes, he was one of my best pupils, too."

"You taught my father?" Aivlys opened her eyes wide with surprise.

"Yes, him and many others, but they all had one attribute that held them back—they were men. You are my first female student, and you shall be the best, and learn the most, for when it comes to magic only a woman can understand the deepest mysteries."

"Why is that?"

"Because we suffer more, and are closer to our hearts

than men. Because we give birth, and birth is the progenitor of magic."

So began Aivlys's initiation into the innermost circle of Gnomonese mysticism. The lessons were much different from those conducted by her father Endimin and Basco Fournier. There were no masculine testings with weapons or in mock combat. The first class of the day was cooking! Zentina Wraight's pantry was stocked with the most amazing proliferation of jars, boxes, and bags, containing all manner of spices, dried plants, herbs, ground-up powders, pastes, crushed leaves, dried flowers. There were bowls full of whole miniature starfish, glass beakers of cloudy, murky liquids, and slim capped vials, all stacked and overflowing the counter space in no discernible order, yet Zentina seemed to know what was in each and in what combination to use them for different purposes. Some were salves, some were pills, some were not to be ingested at all, but simply worn in cloth sacks around the neck, or mumbled over and then cast away. There was a whole wall of tiny drawers with brass fittings for labels, each encoded with symbols and pictures that made no sense to Aivlys but were a complete index for Zentina.

"What's this one?" Aivlys asked, pointing to a drawer marked by a picture of a dog howling at the moon. "It must have something to do with Time magic, phases of the moon, and all that."

"Not at all. That's for curing the lover's lament."

"What?"

Zentina eyed Aivlys carefully. "I don't think you're old enough for that one yet," she decided.

"I'm almost eighteen, and I'm a member of the Watchmakers' Guild," Aivlys protested, but Zentina passed on to the next row of drawers down and pulled one open.

"This is far more interesting than love potions," she winked. "This one, properly administered, will daze and confuse any man or woman who gets a whiff of it. They will lose their sense of Time, and for as long as they are in range of its scent they'll be delirious. Here, try some." At that, Zentina took a pinch of the powder and blew it gently into the air. All at once Aivlys was suffused with a sense of peace and security. She had all the Time in the world. There was nothing to worry about, no war in Gnomon, no bombs, no fires, no explosions, no hurting and killing, only a drifting sensation—she was floating in a timeless ocean, deep beneath the waves. Only when Zentina opened the window and blew away the fragrance and gently shook Aivlys by the shoulders did she return to the present time, slowly, as if she were rising to the surface after sleeping underwater.

"Goodness, that one was stronger than I intended," said Zentina. "I'll have to change the recipe."

"It was very pleasant," said Aivlys dreamily.

"Yes, but imagine what damage I could have done to you if you were the enemy and I had reduced you to that immobile state."

"Yes. I wouldn't have resisted at all, even if you were going to slit my throat."

"Exactly. Come, we're going to war."

Aivlys looked at Zentina with a stunned expression. "What are you talking about?"

"I don't intend to sit here in my farmhouse while the Vargans ruin Gnomon. Now, let's go make some mischief on these outsiders."

"What about my classes?"

"We'll start with some on-the-job training. Come. I've an idea that may delay the Vargans from attempting any more mayhem for a while. Or it may so enrage them that they make a critical mistake."

Aivlys was hesitant to leave the farmhouse, where she had begun to feel safe after the terrifying events of the day she was wounded, but to her relief, Zentina did

not head down toward the ruined city, but instead took
her by the hand and started up a path that led toward
the hills behind the farm and the city proper. As she
walked, Zentina often stopped to collect grasses and
flowers, placing them in a many-pocketed satchel she
carried for that purpose. It seemed that the makings of
magic were everywhere, everywhere and in everything.
Aivlys asked Zentina, and the old witch answered:
"Yes, there is magic in each leaf, each root, each
breath. It travels on the rays of the sun. It surrounds us,
it enters us, passes through us. Only those who are the
most wise know that it *is* us."

Aivlys wanted to ask exactly what Zentina meant by
this, but the crone hurried on ahead, muttering to herself. They were on a hillside to the south of the Platho
farm, one that faced the bay where the Vargan ships lay
waiting for the invasion signal that so far had not come
from the flagship *Regina*. From up here the devastation
in Gnomon was painfully clear. There was hardly a
street that didn't have a house destroyed. In some areas
whole blocks were nothing but smoldering piles of rubble. The Clocktower remained standing, but was pock-
marked by places where cannonballs had torn through
it, and Aivlys doubted that the structure was safe to enter, judging by the fact that the clocks themselves had
stopped at 3:23 in the afternoon on the day of the attack. It goes without saying that Gnomonese prided
themselves on the accuracy of their clocks and
watches—if there had been any way for a repair crew
to ascend to the main mechanism and restart those
clocks, it would have been done.

"What can we do up here?" Aivlys asked Zentina.

"Oh, there's much magic this high up. Did you know
that there are Gnomonese in the hills who never come
to town? They're even smaller than we are, having
stayed apart these many years. If you meet them, don't

be afraid, but don't linger too long with them, either: they like to detain their visitors—forever!"

"How?"

"They dance their guests into a trance, carry them off to their hideaways, and no one ever sees them again."

"Oooohhh!" The very thought made Aivlys shiver.

"But those are elves of the mountains, far higher than where we are now. Come, we can send the foreigners a message, and at the same time demonstrate our powers to them. Sit, watch, and learn," Zentina commanded. With her back to Aivlys, Zentina began to wave her arms above her head in odd ways, while chanting some unintelligible syllables in a cracked, singsong voice. It was all very mysterious and slightly comical. Finally Zentina cast a powder to the winds and sat down next to Aivlys.

"Watch now!" she said triumphantly. The powder did not disperse, as one might have expected in the breezy high air, but instead began to swell and coalesce into cloudlike puffs of purple color, swirling and rising and expanding until there were several of them aligned in the upper air. As soon as they were positioned, they began to transform themselves into shapes, at first not discernible but soon becoming clearer as they condensed and their edges sharpened—they were letters! Zentina was writing a message to the Vargans in the sky. The shapes defined themselves with increased density, until they clearly spelled out two words: GO HOME!

Aivlys laughed at the craziness of Zentina's plan—who could believe that such a simple trick would make the Vargans raise anchor and sail away, but as she thought about it she realized that it was a valuable demonstration of Gnomonese will, and a hint at their hidden powers might make the invaders think twice about trying to land in force.

When the message appeared over the hills above Gnomon, Endimin and Hugh were supervising a crew of Gnomonese volunteers working on salvaging equipment from one of the warehouses damaged in the initial bombardment. The Vargan guns had been silent for a day now, yet the invasion had not begun.

"That's some of Zentina Wraight's doing, mark my words," said Endimin. "The people of Gnomon won't be alarmed, but we ought to warn the Firozians so they don't think it's directed at them."

"You people have some funny ideas about things," Hugh said.

"Why do you suppose the Vargans haven't made their move?"

"Perhaps they've trained their spyglasses on the Firozian emplacements and they don't like what they see. That's the only explanation I can think of," Hugh answered. "If they really wanted to come in here they could, but it would be a horrendous battle, and both sides would suffer terrible casualties."

"We Gnomonese would surrender before we allowed that to happen."

"You would?" Hugh sounded surprised.

"Certainly," said Endimin. "We would want to spare ourselves, the Firozians, and the Vargans that loss of life."

"Even if it meant giving up your freedom?" Hugh pressed his question.

"Yes. But it hasn't come to that yet. Come, let's finish up here and run over to Firozian headquarters before they take offense at Zentina's writing in the sky."

A disturbing sight greeted them when they arrived at the small cluster of tents that represented Firozian army headquarters, set up in the street behind the first row of warehouses along the waterfront. A makeshift gallows had been constructed. As Hugh and Endimin turned onto the street, a soldier was being led up the steps to the hanging rope. Endimin rushed ahead. He found

General Sticer about to give the order to commence the execution.

"Stop! What's this?"

"This man was found looting one of your homes. I'm hanging him. I thought you would be pleased."

"We do not have capital punishment in our country. Please, bring him down from there."

"Military justice demands—"

"General! This is Gnomon. You must abide by our concept of the law, which does not include the taking of life."

After a tense moment, the general conceded the point. "All right, one hundred lashes, then. If he survives that—"

Endimin interrupted the general again. "Nor do we allow physical abuse. If you must punish him, lock him away somewhere."

"Platho, you are undermining my authority," the general said sternly, but in a low voice, as his troops looked on impassively, but with obvious interest. No one had ever confronted the general before, not even Beroth, who acted like a meek lamb when the general tongue-lashed him. "If I don't administer some public punishment, military discipline will suffer."

"Then do what we do," Endimin proposed. "Force him to endure some public humiliation. Shame him. We often find that after such treatment even incarceration is unnecessary. May I suggest?" he asked, and he whispered in the general's ear.

"Very well, then." General Sticer called over his orderly and issued a few terse commands.

The guilty soldier, bloodlessly white-faced after his near escape from the noose, was ordered to dismantle the ghastly gibbet himself. This took only a few minutes, as the soldiers who had been called to witness the carrying out of the sentence poked fun at the unfortunate with catcalls and jeers. Next he was told to use the same lumber to set up a booth, behind which he was made to stand. Finally, the orderly brought out a placard on which had been written the words: I'M A THIEF in large letters. This was hung about the convict's neck, and then he was ordered to sing out the same phrase so that all could hear him.

"I'm a thief," he murmured.

"Louder," one of the amused soldiers shouted.

"I'm a *thief*!"

"Louder!" came a chorus of voices and laughter from the soldiery.

"I'm a thief! I'm a thief! I'm a thief!" the now thoroughly shamefaced man cried out, as his fellow troops whistled and cheered in derision.

"Very good," said General Sticer. "Keep that up until nightfall, then into the stockade with you."

Endimin's punishment proved exceptionally effective. All afternoon the abashed criminal's voice rang out, until he sounded hoarse and raspy, but his fellows wouldn't let him stop, they kept coming around and shouting in his face for him to keep it up and cry louder. By the end of the day the man was repentant and humbled. Firozian justice required that he serve some time in jail (if he wasn't going to be hanged) but it was superfluous and unnecessary—the man would not steal again. Moreover, it had set an example—no other Firozian wanted to suffer the same public degradation.

Evening found Hugh, the general, Endimin, and a few of the general's officers in the headquarters tent sharing a laugh over the day's events, including the public punishment and the strange affair of the cloud letters.

"I have to admit," said the general, "that at first I thought the missive was addressed to us. Couldn't she have specified 'Vargans Go Home!'?"

"You have to know the woman, General," Endimin replied. "She's blunt. She doesn't waste her words. Besides, she probably does want to see you all leave."

"And we too wish only to return to our homes. Please tell her that. But until we find some way to outwit or overcome these hostile foreigners, I'm afraid you're stuck with us."

Hugh had been quiet during the evening, his cheerful face unusually somber. Finally he spoke up: "I've been thinking . . . it has troubled me why the Vargans haven't attacked. They usually press their advantage when they find one, and with all due respect to the general and the Firozian troops, they could have overrun us by now"—some of the officers began to protest but the general silenced them with a look and bade Hugh to continue—"though it certainly would have been plenty costly to them, the loss of life never deterred them before. And Francisco himself told us he's under time pressure to get the job done."

"So why haven't they tested us?" the general asked.

"That's what I've been asking myself," Hugh said. "The only answer I can come up with is this: they want the island."

"We know that, but—"

"You misunderstand me—they don't want to be rulers here, they want it all to themselves. They want you all to leave. They are trying to break your will so you will pack up and go, abandon Gnomon and Firoze to the people of Vargas."

"Leave Firoze?" the general nearly shouted.

"Leave Gnomon?" Endimin asked, as if the idea were too staggering to comprehend in a single thought.

"Yes. Vargas is a beautiful place, but harsh and dry. When the Vargans saw Firoze, they were intrigued, but when they rounded the island and discovered the comparative lushness of Gnomon, they were captivated. I believe they want to force you off so that they can move here themselves. I believe you are under siege. My guess is that Francisco has sent back for an even larger invasion flotilla to join him and finish you off for good, or send you into exile. That is what he is waiting for. Unless we rout him before his reinforcements arrive, his plan will succeed."

"Outrageous! Preposterous!" the general fumed, but at the bottom of it he could see the wisdom of Hugh's analysis. His opposite, Admiral Francisco, was taking a calculated risk. If his gambit failed, he would lose his command, and possibly his life, but if he succeeded in finding a new homeland for his people he would be a national hero. But that he would choose this, General Sticer's country, for his conquest—no, it was too much, he would never allow it to happen. He and his men would die before they would abandon Firoze. Still, the seriousness of the situation impressed itself on the general's mind. They were no longer fighting merely to avoid being subjugated, they were now fighting for the very existence of their nations. He saw even more clearly than before the wisdom of Endimin Platho, who had insisted that only by collaborating could the two peoples retain their sovereignty. Now even more than their sovereignty was at stake. On those rare occasions that the general had been called upon to travel to other islands, he had always carried a pouch full of Firozian dirt in his pocket, so that if he lost his life he could be buried at least symbolically in his native soil. The thought of being driven off the island forever tormented him and galvanized him at the same time.

He stood up. "Officers, guests in my tent, or rather, my distinguished hosts. Our young friend Hugh Boisset has undoubtedly analyzed the situation correctly. The situation is desperate. We cannot wait until the Vargans supplement their fleet with additional ships and men. We must counterattack, and soon. In the morning I want a report from every officer under my command on the state of readiness of their troops."

In the flickering candlelight the general looked as if he had suddenly aged—his gray-black beard appeared yellowish and his eyes were deeply sunken, yet they burned with an intensity his officers had not seen in a long time. Each of them pondered the frightening prospect of a sea battle with the Vargans, whose ships were vastly superior in size, gunnery, and munitions to anything the Firozians or Gnomonese could set upon the water. It would be a fight of giants against comparative dwarves. Yet sometimes that was an advantage; sometimes the huge and clumsy could be outmaneuvered by the small and quick of step. This was their only hope—to manipulate the lumbering Vargan ships into strategic errors where the more agile Firozian vessels could attack them without facing the enemy's heavier guns. At Hugh's suggestion, they postponed any action for a day, because he thought he saw a change of weather in the offing, and with his sailor's intuition he knew that wind changes would favor their side.

That same day confirmation of Hugh's theory was received from the Vargan commander. Apparently he had found Zentina's message so insulting that he couldn't resist a response, which revealed his plans and allowed the Firozian-Gnomonese alliance to strategize with greater confidence. Still, it was a shock to read the Order of Relocation, as it was titled. An official-looking document, it was delivered by arrogant Vargans in a quick and unfriendly visit under the flag of truce.

"Read this and make your peace with it, and prepare," said the haughty Vargan officer who presented it to General Sticer and Endimin at dockside, without even stepping off the small boat that brought him. The parchment bore the Vargan seal, an outstretched talon grasping a bolt of lightning. Endimin read it quickly and passed it to General Sticer, who read it aloud to his officers:

" 'Be it herewith proclaimed that the Empire of Vargas does annex and forever incorporate this island unto itself. The current residents'—"

"We are not residents, this island is our blood and bones!" a hot-tempered Firozian commander cried out.

". . . 'are ordered to make preparations for removal from this island to the land of Quentilique'—"

"That barren patch of sand?" another Firozian shouted.

". . . 'at the soonest possible moment. By order of Her Majesty, the empress, this day' . . . and so forth . . ." General Sticer concluded his reading with a grimace as if he had just swallowed something disgusting and indigestible.

"They want to exile us to a waterless sandbar where we would surely all die within a generation," Endimin said, summing up the Vargan edict bluntly, almost in the manner that General Sticer would have done.

"This will not happen," General Sticer swore. A quiet conviction spread from man to man in the gathering. The order concluded with a demand for it to be posted prominently in the city square of Gnomon, and advised that another copy had been delivered to the residents of Firoze. General Sticer ripped up the proclamation and threw it into the water, where the tattered pieces scattered on the waves. A curious gull dived to see if they were edible and flew off, squawking its disappointment. "No doubt our brethren in Firoze have done the same with theirs," he said. "The only question now remaining is how we fight them."

"If it clouds over tomorrow, as I think it will, I propose a night attack on their outer ships," said Hugh.

"That would leave their biggest and strongest ships untouched," General Sticer pointed out.

"Yes, but if we can't attack them all at once, this is only to show that we have no intention of giving in."

"Permit me to ask, General, why do we let this outsider have a say in our battle plans?" one of the officers asked.

"He was at the side of our enemy, Admiral Francisco, during the long sail from Vargas to Firoze. He knows them. So far he has been correct in his estimates of our foe's actions. He fought valiantly beside the late Commander Magden, or have you forgotten? Why shouldn't I trust him?"

Hugh stood quietly while the general defended him. Then he stepped forward. "It's true that for you this fight is for your land, for your very existence. But I too have strong feelings against the Vargans. They kidnapped me, they beat me (of course *you* beat me too, but no matter), they tried to steal my navigating invention. Give me the chance and I'll prove a worthy ally."

There was a momentary silence. One of the officers stepped forward.

"Tell us your plan," he said.

"Well," said Hugh, trying not to let his relief show, "here's how it is. The Vargans are using their lighter, more maneuverable vessels, their corvettes, as a picket line, while they kept the frigates and barkentines within this perimeter. Against the big cannons of the three- and five-masted ships we have no chance, but we might be able to capture one or two of their smaller ships and use them to harass the rest of the guard-watch. Lure them out, that's what we have to do."

"Let it be done," General Sticer ordered. "We Firozians have little experience in naval warfare, but when it comes to close-in, hand-to-hand combat, we are a formidable opponent. Your task, Hugh, is to create conditions that favor our fighting style."

"The attack I have in mind will do just that." The officers and Hugh marched inside the headquarters tent and gathered around a table to draw up their plans.

8

A GRAY PALLOR COVERED DAWN'S FACE the next morning, and the sky grew darker as the wind rose and a stream of thunderheads descended on the coast of Gnomon. From shore the Firozian lookouts could see the Vargans reefing in the mainsails and hauling down some of the lesser sail from their ships to keep them from heeling over as they made their stately circles in the picket. The larger ships remained at anchor in the center of the harbor, confident that there was no possibility of attack from the non-existent Gnomonese navy. From the first day they had prevented the boats of the Gnomonese fishing fleet from leaving port as part of their plan to conduct a siege. With the weather and darkness as cover, Hugh hoped to break the blockade. He instructed the fishermen and sailors of Gnomon to work surreptitiously during the day to prepare for an evening raid. Most of the boats had been abandoned since the opening salvo of the Vargan barrage. They needed to be bailed, refitted, and in some cases repaired from damage caused by stray cannon fire. As unobtrusively as possible, Endimin sent work crews out to make sure that each boat was seaworthy. The Firozian troops remained in their positions so as not to raise suspicion from the Vargans, who were undoubtedly monitoring activity in the town from the crow's nests of their ships. At noon a thunder-and-lightning storm struck, providing further camouflage for the repair teams, but also increasing the difficulty of their task as the light boats rocked violently in the squall. Hugh scuttled back and forth, keeping low and hiding behind pier posts at every opportunity, as he urged the workers to make ready every available boat. The Gnomonese sailors and Firozian soldiers were certain to be outnumbered in any encounter, but the more men they could send into the fray, the better were their chances. A successful boarding required the element of surprise but also the advantage of initial strength, to overwhelm the defenders before they could organize a resistance.

By nightfall preparations were complete. The Vargan edict had called for evacuation of the island "at the soonest possible moment"; Hugh theorized that even if the Vargans had observed the activity at the docks they might have thought it was in conjunction with the order to prepare for exile.

"We may have been aided by their arrogance—if they think we'll comply with their pronouncements without putting up a fight," said Hugh to one of the Firozian officers as they watched the fighters gather in a warehouse to hear their final instructions. It was still raining, and the warehouse, whose roof had been blown away during the bombardment, offered little protection from the elements but did conceal the troops from the

Vargans. The officer, a young firebrand named Rathman who had been chosen by General Sticer for his raw courage, moved his sword up and down by its pommel inside its sheath, as if he were ready to draw it right then and there.

"At last we have a chance to take some revenge for the capture of our lands." Rathman's eyes blazed and his breath came in quick gulps, even though they still had miles of water to cross before engaging the enemy. He was tall like Beroth but lacked Beroth's girth and beard. Hugh found him likable in a rough sort of way, honest and determined.

"Please remind your men to keep their swords from clanking and to muffle any other sound. We've wrapped everything metal on the boats in cloth, but sound travels so clearly across water that they're likely to hear something, unless this wind keeps shrieking, as I hope it will." With that the signal was given to board the boats. There were a dozen craft in the unlikely flotilla, unarmed fishing trawlers with single masts, whose holds were meant to transport fish, not men. Usually these boats were manned by a crew of four, one to steer, one to sail, and two to haul nets and do the other work of fishing expeditions, but tonight Hugh crammed twenty into each vessel, so that the attack force numbered more than two hundred. They set out for the Vargan perimeter in the face of a raging gale, but the Gnomonese men were experienced at sailing in this sort of weather and were able to hold course despite the blustery conditions. Some of the Firozian soldiers quickly became seasick, but they managed to hold their nausea, and when the boats fell off on the port tack to come up behind the first Vargan ship, the pounding and pitching became somewhat less pronounced.

The storm covered their approach perfectly. The Vargans had called down their crow's-nest lookout because of the rain and wind, and the deck watch was huddled under a mast, and not venturing close to the rail. Ladders attached to grappling hooks were tossed onto the rear poop deck behind the main afterdeck, and Commander Rathman led the first boarding party up the swaying ropes. Five boats were able to unload their soldiers before they were discovered, and the force of one hundred men was more than enough to handle the sleepy, surprised crew of the ship, almost without a fight. Rathman prevented the ship's captain from signaling to the next ship in the line. Gnomonese sailors took over the sailing duties, and though they were unused to handling such a comparatively large vessel, the principles were the same, though on a larger scale, and they quickly figured out how to hoist and lower sail and steer, and were able to keep the boat in line while the rest of the boats sped ahead to attempt the same maneuver on the next ship.

The courageous attackers were able to repeat their success on a second Vargan ship, boarding and overpowering the guard before any effective resistance could be mounted against them. At their third attempt, a sharp-eyed Vargan saw that the ship behind was no longer flying its signal lamp and sounded an alarm just as the first Firozian soldiers reached the ship's main platform. The Vargan crew came pouring out of their quarters belowdecks. A full-scale battle ensued. Many of the Firozians were caught on the ladder between the fishing boat and the deck, and clung to the sides of the ship, desperately trying to board and join the fight. The Firozians on deck could do no more than maintain a stalemate, neither seizing control nor being pushed off the ship. In the confused fighting a fire broke out, smoking heavily in the continuing downpour. The other line ships began signaling to each other, and activity could be seen on the main battleships within the protective ring. The burning ship began to list heavily, and men from both sides jumped into the water to avoid a fiery death. The smaller boats picked up as many men from both sides as they could manage, there being extra room now that some of the boarding parties were occupying the two captured vessels. From his station aboard the first seized ship, Hugh sounded the retreat call, and the two captured ships broke away from the circle and raced toward shore, with the smaller Gnomonese vessels in their wake like a gaggle of baby geese following their parents.

Hugh, on the deck of the lead ship, wanted desperately to save one or both of his prizes, but he realized that in the open sea he would soon be broadsided by cannon fire and sunk. Thinking quickly, he chose the only option available to him.

"Beach them!" he cried, and sent a signal for the second ship to follow him onto the rocks near the pier. Both ships came crashing onto shore with an agonized rending sound and the crunching of timbers as the hulls stove in on the Vargan vessels. The Gnomonese sailors anchored their boats more prudently, and everyone rushed to the site of the wrecks. The raiders clambered off the now-useless ships. Both had remained relatively upright, side by side, their bows on shore, their backs broken and their sterns sagging into the water. A great cheer rose from the throats of the Firozian soldiers who had not been sent out to sea but had waited and watched from afar.

"At last we've drawn some blood!" one shouted.

"Hang the dogs!" another yelled as the dazed and shaken Vargans were led toward a temporary stockade that had been made out of a converted warehouse.

General Sticer, who had not permitted himself the luxury of accompanying the troops on this daring raid, approached Hugh. "Well done, navigator."

"Not really. I wish I could have saved these two for our use," he said, pointing to the Vargan ships with their crumpled hulls, "but there was nowhere to sail them that we wouldn't have been easy targets for the Vargan guns. This is only the first skirmish," Hugh cautioned. "Tomorrow the Vargans will try to extract their own revenge."

"Are these two rendered useless?" the General asked.

"We can strip them for weapons and timber, but I don't think they'll ever sail again," Hugh replied.

"Ah, you don't know what wonders the Gnomonese carpenters can perform," a passing sailor commented. "If we could have them for a week we could patch them up, even those huge center beams."

"A land of optimists!" said Hugh with a smile. "All right, let's haul their carcasses away from the water so the men of Gnomon can show us more of their magic, this time with carpentry tools!"

A team of men was assembled. Some of the rocks were cleared away and a path of logs was laid down to provide a rolling platform for the dead hulks that moments ago had been sailing ships. It was not a night for such work, but there was no alternative. If the Vargans saw the vessels on shore in the morning they would know what had happened, but if the islanders could hide their booty, they could perhaps fix up the two ships and put them to use against the Vargans in another surprise. Endimin Platho appeared and watched the work crews grunting and straining with an odd look on his face. There was a spell that would assist them in this effort, but he hesitated to use it. *Let them show their mettle tonight,* he thought. *There will be another time for Time Flies.* It took most of the night to drag the two ships off the rocky shore and out of sight behind the one standing wall of a destroyed warehouse, that had been shored up with timbers. By dawn the wind had shifted again and the sun emerged through a broken cloud cover. The Vargan fleet had reconfigured itself. Hugh gazed at the new arrangement from his position on shore, trying to fathom the meaning of the new deployment. They were up to something, he knew that.

"What news do you hear from Firoze?" he asked General Sticer. Both of them had stayed up the entire night to supervise the hauling out of the two Vargan ships, and both men looked haggard, especially Hugh, who had played such a large role in the raid. The general had his lips clamped down on a pipe, which he removed to provide an answer.

"Not much. The people are suffering under the occupation, but with our army in Gnomon, there is little resistance. Why do you ask?"

"The Vargans have split their fleet. The *Regina* is still out there but two of the big frigates are gone. It's possible that as punishment for our actions last night they may strike again at Firoze."

"But there are no military targets left in Firoze," the general replied.

"No," said Hugh.

"I see." The general suddenly understood the import of Hugh's speculations.

"Is there anything we can do?" Hugh asked.

"Our people will take it as best they can."

"Send a small contingent of observers," Hugh suggested.

"No. They would only throw themselves away in hopeless fighting, and we need every man here. Our messengers will bring us the news."

During the morning a faint, distant rumbling could be heard, as if thunder from the recently passed storm was casting an echo from far out at sea, but Hugh and General Sticer and a few others knew what it was. Later that afternoon a runner arrived from the other side of the island. Word quickly spread through the Firozian encampment and the city of Gnomon. The Vargans had temporarily evacuated, and then shelled the city of Firoze indiscriminately, striking civilian targets. A hospital had been struck, and a school. There were many casualties, especially among infants and women—a massacre. A few old men had attempted to sail out in their fishing vessels to stop the attack—their boats had been sunk, and unlike last evening, when the Gnomonese picked up all survivors from the burning guard ship, Firozian and Vargan alike, in the Vargan attack the survivors were left to drown. Firozian soldiers gnashed their teeth and shouted curses at the portion of the Vargan fleet that still lay at anchor beyond their reach. A clamor arose for another night strike, but General Sticer knew that this time the Vargans would be prepared, that no more surprises of that sort were possible. Momentarily at a loss, the general retreated to his tent to brood over the bitter news from Firoze.

9

AIVLYS CRUSHED ANOTHER PETAL INTO the mixing bowl and marveled at the spicy sweet fragrance emitted by the seemingly ordinary flower, hardly more than a weed with a knotty blossom atop a thin fibrous stalk. She was deep into her studies, and Zentina was pushing her hard to memorize whole dusty volumes of recipes and spells. She had been made to understand by Zentina that she was no ordinary young girl, and that even after her ascension into the Watchmakers' Guild, she was far from finished with her training. As they stood at the counter of Zentina's workshop, surrounded by her alchemical tools, the old woman harangued her protégé with a mixture of encouragement and reprimand: "Don't you understand, you are the hope of Gnomon—no, not so much burrberry leaf, just a pinch, and always stir in the same direction, clockwise, don't you see, all Time recipes go clockwise, except those that are meant to turn back the clock. Ah, dear girl, if you don't pay more attention you'll never learn a thing."

Aivlys *was* paying attention, she was studying with all her concentration and the most dedicated attitude she could muster, but there was just so much to take in, and (if Zentina's dire warnings were to be believed) so little time left to learn it all before she would be asked to step in and save her people. It was a terrible responsibility, especially for one so young, who had only recently lost her brother (ah, was it only a few weeks, his memory was still fresh and her heart still ached at the loss) and whose father was somewhere below in the decimated city, awaiting the next act of Vargan butchery.

"Couldn't we take a break now, Zentina, my head is spinning, I think I must have breathed in some of that lichen dust for the Drowse spell."

"All right, then, lazy child. Fetch us some lemons from the tree outside and we'll make ourselves some juice."

Secretly Zentina was quite pleased with Aivlys's progress; given the girl's sweet nature, she couldn't be as hard a taskmistress as she would have liked to have been. Aivlys had applied herself dutifully to the learnings, and in addition she had brightened the farmhouse with wildflowers and she had cleaned and straightened up both the barn and the house, which Zentina in her old age had let lapse into a state of comfortable shabbiness. *What do I care if the farm is a pigsty,* she thought, *but it is nice to be able to see through the windows again* (the dust had piled so thick that the world had taken on a permanent dimness indoors). Her pupil had a natural facility for spells, and a memory that assimilated long and convoluted strings of nonsense syllables easily. *A born witch.* Zentina chortled at the thought, though she would never have told the girl that—one must keep up appearances, so that there was no slacking off, no indulgence. Still, a little lemonade sweetened with honey from the apiary would do them both good, and perhaps a spell of sitting on the back porch watching the clouds dance their way across the hills.

She was so tired; how long had she lived? She couldn't even say now, hundreds of years, surely. She remembered when Gnomon was a small town, barely more than a hamlet, with no port and no industry, only a dusty unpaved square where farmers exchanged vegetables and bartered tools. She remembered when the business with the clocks was only a cottage industry for the local farmers to supplement their agricultural earnings, before they discovered the power of (in) Time. Even then she had been a witch, and before then, when Aivlys's great-great-grea—grea—(how many greats?) grandfather had first asked her why the hands of her clocks didn't seem to obey the same laws as everyone else's. Oh yes, she had seen so much, known so much, done so much, and then they had forgotten her, left her with a barn full of goats and chickens while their watch-and-clock business boomed and only a few of the men, the Guild, remembered from whence it had all sprung, and the Platho family kept her memory alive, kept her alive, and now when it was all falling down around their ears they had come back to her, and she was helping them and giving all her stored-up knowledge to the next one, the next keeper.

"Miss Wraight . . . Miss Wraight—"

"Don't shout, child."

"Here's some lemonade. You must have dozed off, you were dreaming."

"No, I wasn't," Zentina said crossly, but then she remembered, and softened a little. "Very good lemonade, just the right amount of honey, dear. We'll just sit here a minute. You go around to the front and see if there's any activity in the city."

"Yes, Miss Wraight."

She was fading, passing out of existence, entering the Timeless place from whence she and all other creatures came. Was this all there was to it? Just to slip off like this, so easily, without a care in the world, now that her Time was up? But wait, there was so much more she needed to tell the girl, where was she, ah, but she felt so light, it was so good to ease out of the wrinkled, warty, creaky body that she had inhabited for so many long years. The girl would know to keep on reading, practicing, mixing potions and reciting the ancient words. All was well. In the final moments of her long, long life she had found someone to receive the sacred teachings. Yes, she could die peacefully, floating away on the river of Time. At the very last second Zentina Wraight remembered to shut her eyes so as not to frighten Aivlys with her final piercing look at Eternity.

Aivlys came back around the corner of the house to report that the city looked peaceful, but something was not right, she felt it immediately. The old woman was so still, so distant. The black cat that always jumped into Zentina's lap when she occupied the porch chair was nowhere to be seen. Aivlys's knees shook, but she maintained her balance and crept slowly forward to verify what she already knew. There could be no doubt— Zentina Wraight was dead. Aivlys's first thought was to run down the hill for help, but then she realized that was not what Zentina would have wanted, not after so many years of solitude up here, to have a bunch of strangers troop into her house, commenting on the strangeness and age and decay of everything. No, she, Aivlys, would live here now. She would wrap the body in a winding cloth, with the spices and unguents that Zentina had described to her for such occasions, and bury her among the wildflowers she loved so. Then

Aivlys would continue her studies, as Zentina would
have wanted.

The next day Endimin arrived to find his daughter
plowing a section of land behind the farm, in the har-
ness herself and pulling a blade behind her. The place
was much different from the ramshackle affair Endimin
remembered. It reminded him of his own home—neat,
clean, and cheery looking. He hailed his daughter with
a shout. She cast off the reins of the plow and ran to
her father's arms. "Zentina is gone!" she cried, and
suddenly she realized how much she had kept inside
herself during the past twenty-four hours. She had dug
a grave for Zentina and transported the body laboriously up the hill on a makeshift sled. Alone she had
conducted a ceremony of burial and laid the body in the
grave and covered it over with the fresh-turned earth.
All this she told her father between sobs as she kept her
head pressed against his comforting shoulder.

"Come, show me," he said quietly, marveling at his
daughter's strength and resilience. They climbed toward
a dell hidden behind the first hill above the farm. As
they crested the hill, Aivlys gasped in disbelief and then
pleasure. At the site of the grave, and spreading out in
a wide irregular ring around it, was a carpet of wildflowers in profusion, a rainbowlike splash of colors. "I
didn't do this," Aivlys said, but her father knew and
said nothing. They sat down above the plot and took in
the bouquet of fragrances emanating from the ring of
blossoms. "I've learned so much. If only she had lived
to teach me more, if only I had time enough to learn it
all," Aivlys whispered, for the place seemed holy and
worthy of the reverence of hushed voices.

"Unfortunately you don't, my dear child," Endimin
told her. "We need all the help we can, especially of the
type you can provide. A final Vargan assault is expected at any moment. You may not know that their intention is to force us off the island so that they can

move their people here, and it appears they will commit any atrocity in pursuit of their goal." He described Hugh's successful raid and the savage Vargan retribution.

"Who will take care of the farm? I was just starting to fix it up and tend to some of the repairs poor old Miss Wraight wasn't able to do."

"If we don't hold back the Vargans the whole country will fall to ruin," Endimin said. "We'll drive the livestock down into town and sell it, and crate up the fowl, too. The rest we'll simply have to board up and hope we can return in better times. Take what you need from her other stores, the herbs and such—you are her heir and successor."

"I know."

Endimin wanted to ask his daughter what she had learned, test her knowledge and her power, but Aivlys was no longer the adolescent he had left in Zentina's care. In just a few days she had matured, to the point that he felt intuitively that she now knew more of Gnomonese magic than he did. Zentina had always said that the deepest wisdom rested in the feminine, and now he was sure of that. He glanced at Aivlys with a mixture of admiration and curiosity—what had transpired between the two sorceresses in the fastness of their retreat? And now, after so many years of isolation, Zentina Wraight had found a pupil, then passed away before she could confer her most precious secrets.

That night Endimin and Aivlys returned to the Platho farmhouse, which had been spared any damage because it was far from the city, so aside from being a little dusty, the house was intact. A neighbor had been providing food and water for the animals in their absence. Aivlys rummaged in the kitchen and found enough dried grains and legumes for a simple meal, and she and her father slept in their own beds for the first time in a long while. Aivlys slept fitfully. Several times she had the impression that someone was calling out to her, but when she awoke she heard nothing. Finally she drifted into a deeper sleep, where Zentina Wraight appeared to her, dressed in a gown woven from garlands of flowers.

"We must continue our lessons now, my dear."

"But you are dead," Aivlys heard herself say.

"Yes, I've become a field of flowers, but flowers can talk, too, if you listen carefully enough. Now, where were we, ah yes, the Fourth Spell of Sanctuary." (Indeed, that was the one Aivlys had been practicing just before she asked Zentina if they could take rest.) The lesson continued in the dream state, until near dawn, when Aivlys shook herself awake with a start.

"Oh my," she said, and rushed to tell Endimin of her lengthy and detailed visitation, and found him already seated at the kitchen table drinking a mug of hot tea.

"Write it all down so you don't forget, daughter."

"Oh, but it's just as clear to me as if she had been right here in the room."

"So," Endimin paused. "It seems that your teacher hasn't abandoned you, after all. This is good news. But proceed carefully."

"Proceed? I only slept, Father."

"Well, then, sleep carefully. No doubt Zentina will watch over you, but remember that in the dream state you, your body, is still in this world. Don't let the gap between the two worlds grow so wide that you can't return."

Aivlys was puzzled by this advice but there was no time to ponder its deeper meaning, for just then they were jarred by the sound of huge explosions in the city. They rushed out the front door together to see if another attack had commenced. A plume of smoke was rising from the port area. Was this the prelude to the Vargan invasion? The day before, General Sticer, head of the government in exile, had insisted that the battle

be moved away from the city of Gnomon if possible, to
spare its citizenry the suffering that had been inflicted
on Firoze. He had developed a plan to lure the invaders
away from the main port by a flanking maneuver, and
if possible to hold the high ground to the south of the
city and draw the opposition into a mountain pass
where even with inferior numbers his troops might win
the day. Endimin was thankful that the general was so
concerned, but doubtful that the Vargans would fall for
the trap. The port was the obvious prize—take it and
you effectively have seized Gnomon. Why would the
enemy chase after the Firozian army if they abandoned
their waterfront positions? Now, as he and Aivlys hurried down the path toward Gnomon, he saw that Hugh's
worst fears had been realized. A whole second fleet had
arrived to swell the size of the Vargan flotilla. The explosions they had heard were merely a welcoming fusil-
lade of salute from the *Regina*. The harbor was dense
with masts, like a floating forest, and one could almost
have walked across the sea on the decks crowded together in the relatively small inlet. From Endimin's
vantage point, the quickly rising walls of the coastline
to either side of the mouth of the sound were the one
saving grace of Gnomon harbor. There was only one
place to land; consequently only a limited number of
landing ships could unload their cargo at any one time.
When the invasion came, it would be difficult for the
Vargans to take advantage of their numerical superiority, especially if General Sticer could somehow lead
them out of Gnomon and into the nearby hills in pursuit
of his army. But sooner or later the sheer numbers of
the Vargans were almost certain to overwhelm the be-
leaguered defenders. The situation looked very grim indeed.

Once again the leaders of the resistance convened in
General Sticer's tent. Hugh was there, along with Commander Rathman, Endimin, Aivlys, and the general

himself with several aides-de-camp. Despite all their
warlike trappings, their weapons, armor and shields,
their fierce demeanor, the Firozians could not hide a
gloomy sense of impending doom. They had already
been driven from their own country, and now were
faced with the prospect of being swept into the sea.
Like cornered animals, they were more dangerous, and
would fight with the unbridled abandon of those who
had nothing to lose, but would that be enough to overcome the numerical superiority of the Vargans? There
was some desultory talk of the best ways to engage the
Vargans, and whether the attack would come today or
tomorrow, but the meeting lacked spirit. General Sticer,
usually not a man to stand for indecisiveness among his
men, sat unmoving on his camp stool, studying the
faces of his officers as if trying to read their minds, but
said nothing.

Endimin spoke up in an attempt to change the mood
of the gathering: "My daughter has been studying
magic, perhaps she . . ." but Commander Rathman did
not want to hear any foolishness from Gnomon women.

"No more magic, now we must rely on our swords.
They've always saved us in the past, surely they'll do
so again."

"Not swords only," said Hugh, who had been quiet
up to this time. "The craftsmen of Gnomon have
teamed up with some of your Firozian smithies to manufacture a few useful items with some of the material
we salvaged from the beached guard ships. After the
meeting we'll give you a demonstration," he said mysteriously.

"Very well." General Sticer seemed impatient, as if
the battle had already begun. "For the rest, I agree with
Commander Rathman. The time for trickery is past.
Our fine Firozian steel must be put to the test. Small armies, well positioned and highly motivated, have won
great victories in the past. Today it is our turn to chal-

lenge ourselves. It's not the enemy who represents our greatest foe, it's our own minds, our fears and our uncertainties. If we believe that we will win, it may happen despite our deficiencies. If we have no confidence, we will most certainly lose, indeed we have already lost. I once told my former superior officer, the late great General Roydan, at a sword-fighting exhibition, that I could tell which swordsman would be the victor before each bout began, simply by observing their faces as they touched swords. I was, that day, unfailingly accurate. Today as I look at you I see great resolve, great determination. Don't let that courage fail you. The Vargans are ambitious land grabbers—we are fighting for our homeland. Now, let's see what the combined talents of the Firoze and Gnomon craftspeople have produced." He nodded to Hugh, who led the group out of the tent and behind the Firozian encampment to a clearing occupied by a line of mounds the shape of small haystacks, each with a set of proud workmen standing at attention next to it. With a young man's flair and flourish Hugh threw back the burlap covering on the nearest pile, at the same time signaling the workmen to do the same. The dramatic flourish revealed a row of burnished cannons, each mounted on wheels so that they could be hauled to shooting sites with ease. Next to each weapon stood a stack of cannonballs on a pallet, also ready to be transported.

"Very impressive," General Sticer commented, though at heart he had a soldier's distaste for such weapons, which were used by the ungallant who could not face man-to-man combat. "These are the first such devices ever to be produced on this island. I don't know that I consider it progress, but it certainly is a necessity, given the weaponry of our opponents. Have you tested them yet?"

"No, sir, I thought we'd hold them back as a surprise. They'll work, I'm confident. In fact, I think they'll be more accurate than the Vargan cannons, given the precision with which they were cast by your excellent foundry workers, and the advancements the Gnomonese have added in the way of sights for them."

"Sights?" the general inquired.

"Yes, sir. A means of calculating the range and angle of arc to hit a target. Not unlike a watch in its fulcrum-and-lever functioning. Our cannon may be accurate to within seven or eight yards, whereas the Vargans can only hope to hit within a hundred-yard perimeter, as we have seen."

"All right. Down here they're useless. Send a crew on ahead with them and mount them on the bluff overlooking the harbor. If we can convince the Vargans to follow us, wait 'til we enter the pass, then shell them, unmercifully." General Sticer turned his attention to other matters. There was no doubt in his mind that the Vargan attack could begin at any moment. He ranged up and down the lines, personally exhorting the troops, inspecting the preparations for the battle, and constantly peering out toward the sea from where the Vargans would come. *At least there's no surprise there,* he thought. Despite Endimin's magic healing, the general walked with a slight limp from the sword wound he had received in the first encounter with the Vargans in Firoze, but this didn't deter him from checking each and every particular of the field on which his troops would fight their most desperate engagement. The Gnomonese had buried spikes point up in the sand where the invaders would land, and had laid plans for other harassing actions on the open stretch of beach. Their small boats would all weigh anchor and scatter at the first sign of an invasion, to be hidden in coves and inlets up and down the coast in the event they might prove useful again. Hugh's crews had not had time to make the captured guard ships seaworthy; they had concentrated instead on the manufacture of the cannons, but now a team of carpenters were swarming over the two vessels, trying frantically to put them into service before the onslaught began.

Hugh sent the cannons on ahead, making sure that they were disguised as hayricks, and stayed behind to see if the ships could be launched in time to sail against the Vargans. That would be a suicide mission, surely, but in time of war some men must make the sacrifice so that others may gain the final victory. Hugh fully expected to be at the helm of one of the two ships if they could be made serviceable. Now, though, there was little he could do other than to supervise the work crews as they sawed away shattered beams and replaced stove-in timbers. One of the ships had suffered less damage than the other when Hugh had run them aground, so was being given more attention as being more likely to be made seaworthy in a shorter amount of time than its crippled sister. He was aloft in the tangled rigging of the *Salazar*, trying to make sense of the jumble of intertwined ropes, when Aivlys found him.

"Hullo up there!" she shouted. "Come down and have some lunch."

"What are you offering? Fried bats' wings? Toad sweetbreads?" he teased her.

"Nothing so exotic. Goat-cheese sandwiches with tomatoes and cold milk."

"Why don't you jump on your broomstick and fly up here?" he called from his high perch, where he could almost touch the exposed roof beams of the nearby warehouse wall.

"No, come down, I want to talk to you," she shouted back, though she could have done just what he said. Hugh and Aivlys had known each other only a few days, yet already a bond of affection had grown between them. Like everything in war, their friendship had developed at an accelerated pace. Each time they saw each other it was sweet and meaningful, and each time they parted they knew they might never see one another again. A few stolen kisses were all they had shared, but both knew in their hearts that they were in love, though most of the time they hid their romance behind a jesting, teasing manner. Now, with the biggest battle of the short war about to explode around them, both felt the need to drop pretense and express their affection directly. But there was so little time left. Aivlys watched nervously as Hugh flung himself down the hemp ropes that held the sails aloft from their masts. He swung from one yardarm to another like a seasoned performer, showing off a little.

"Hey, you! Stop that!" Aivlys yelled, bringing smiles to the faces of the workers watching his precipitous descent. Finally Hugh leaped from the propped-up bow of the *Salazar* and landed in a heap at her feet. A round of good-natured applause and heckling accompanied his performance. The two young people hurried off to an isolated corner of the warehouse, where they sat down facing each other. Aivlys spread out the simple lunch she'd brought and they ate wordlessly for a few minutes, each wondering what the other was thinking but neither willing to break the almost magic spell of silent companionship. At last Aivlys asked Hugh when he thought the action would begin.

"Hard to say. They've certainly got enough ships and men out there, but this Admiral Francisco is a tricky, cautious fellow. He might make us sweat for another day or so, or he might come in strong this afternoon. In any case, Gnomon is as good as his, the best we can hope for is a retreat into the hills.

"Then they'll hold both Gnomon and Firoze."

"Yes, but that's not what they want. They want you gone, shipped out so that the island is empty, free for them to colonize with their own people. That's Francisco's dilemma. If he drives us into the hills then he'll have to deal with the constant irritant of our continued presence, even if all we can do is harass his troops at night. But if he waits, we might build up enough defenses to keep him from making a successful landing. If I were him I'd—"

Hugh's next words were drowned by the roar of guns. The container of milk tipped over and left a wet white stain on the dusty ground. The couple spontaneously grabbed each other and clung together while the building shook around them and the sky once again grew dark with smoke. Aivlys wondered how there were enough buildings left in Gnomon to start another fire, with so many of them already burned and destroyed. With her head pressed on Hugh's chest she waited for a break in the constant pounding so that she could whisper something to Hugh, but none came, so she said the words anyway, not knowing if he could hear her, but he wrapped his arms even tighter around her and she knew that he understood.

Then Hugh broke away and raced toward the *Salazar*. "Come on," he shouted to the workmen who were cowering beneath the vessel. "Let's launch her!"

"She's not ready, Boisset. She's got no ballast, we unloaded it all to haul her up here. She'd balk and pitch in the slightest swells."

"I don't care, she's all we've got. Here, we'll throw in all this debris to give her some hull weight. Aivlys, find your father, tell him I want two of those cannon back for the *Salazar*."

"I want to sail with you," Aivlys pleaded, but Hugh knew that he was unlikely to come back from this voyage, and wouldn't let her near the ship for fear she'd stow away. Almost roughly he pushed her toward the door.

"Find your father," he repeated. "Stay with him. I'll catch up to you. The *Salazar* has one final voyage to make."

"What do you mean?" Aivlys said, her lower lip

quivering, for she feared she knew the answer, that her heroic but reckless love would try something bold and dangerous to stave off the Vargans. Hugh wouldn't answer her but kept shoving her out so insistently that she grew angry and broke from his grasp, kissed him once on the cheek and ran off.

Hugh turned to the workers who had been watching with astonishment the lovers' quarrel under the thunder of the guns. "All right, men, you know what comes next. Bring me the explosives."

Aivlys ran through the streets of Gnomon, heedless of the detonations all around her. She reached the hill at the southern edge of town where she should have found the train of wagons hauling the cannon, but they must have halted to take cover during the bombardment because she couldn't see them anywhere up the path. From here she could look out over the bay, where she saw that the Vargan fleet had changed its alignment and was preparing to off-load its soldiers onto landing craft for the first wave of the invasion. Suddenly Aivlys felt dizzy. The image of Zentina Wraight appeared before her, and at the same time she had a premonition, a sense, a vision, of the Vargans rounding the southern point and landing on a narrow beach there to try to cut off the Firozian army before it could retreat into the hills. And she knew what she must do. She turned and ran back toward the city. On her way she passed through the chaotic streets where Firozian soldiers were rushing to line up for the shore defense while Gnomonese citizens fled toward the outskirts of the city, where the shelling couldn't reach them.

Hugh was busy loading the last of a supply of unstable charge powder onto the *Salazar* when Aivlys came around the corner shouting his name: "Hugh! Hugh! The Vargans are going to surround us. I know what to do!"

"I thought I told you—" Hugh began, but he was really so happy to see her he couldn't bring himself to be too severe with her. In a rushing flood of words Aivlys explained her daydream, the appearance of her mentor Zentina the witch, and the future scene she had witnessed in her mind's eye.

"Yes, of course they would anticipate our movements. But how can we stop them?"

"The *Salazar*?" Aivlys asked.

"Is a floating bomb," said Hugh. "Yes, if we sank her in the mouth of the channel we could stop them from landing there!" He grabbed Aivlys and kissed her again, passionately. "Come on, then, there's no time to lose. If they don't sink us on the way around the point we'll beat them there for sure and stall their strategy. Francisco'll have to back off, because he doesn't want to risk an attack he can't finish. But—"

"What is it, Hugh?"

"One shot and we'll all go up like dust. And we're an easy target. I don't even know if she'll float, much less sail, and if she does"—Hugh pointed to the still-tangled web of rope that hung from the masts of the *Salazar*—"I don't know how we'll control her. But never mind, we'll do it somehow. Now you go—"

"No!" said Aivlys firmly. "I can help. I can hide us, for a few minutes."

"The whole ship?"

"Wait and see."

"All right then." The false wall that hid the *Salazar* was pushed away and the rolling logs made ready for the launch. The Vargan attack had continued unabated, with the result that the sun was once again shadowed by clouds of black smoke, which lent a temporary cover to the activity by the shore. Hugh insisted on being the only man aboard when the launch was attempted. The *Salazar* was heaved and shoved down its plank causeway until sheer gravity sent it plunging toward the water, where it crashed in a gigantic splash and righted itself and sat there bobbing like an ungainly duckling. For a moment Hugh was nowhere to be seen. Had he been flung into the water or hurled to the deck? Then his spritely form appeared at the wheel of the ship, where he began a mad struggle to keep the ship from immediately dashing itself on the rocks again. One man cannot sail such a huge vessel. Gnomonese sailors, the same men who had worked as carpenters for days on end, barely sleeping, and had just exerted themselves to the full to push the ship into the water, now leaped into the freezing sea to swim to Hugh's aid. They scrambled up ropes hung over the side of the ship and sprang into action, pulling on sheets and lines, heaving themselves against the unwieldy rudder, rushing here and there on deck to do whatever was necessary to keep the *Salazar* from repeating its shore crash. Slowly, ever so slowly, the ship hove to and came about. Aivlys too had flung herself into the waves, and struggled to climb the rope. Her thin arms were not strong enough to hoist herself, but a couple of sailors helped her aboard. She wisely stood clear of the frantic activity on deck, and Hugh didn't even know she had joined him until he found her at his side.

"*What?!* How did you get up here? Are you practicing more witchcraft?" Hugh exclaimed. Aivlys held up her rope-burned hands in silent response. Hugh took them in his and caressed them gently. "Here," he said, "put this on them," and he tore a strip of cloth from his sleeve to wrap her hands, but she drew them back.

"No, they'll heal up," she said, for she had in mind some healing salves she had taken from Zentina's stores that would mend the broken skin quickly.

Beroth was among the warriors who jumped onto the *Salazar* as it rocked in the estuary. Ever since his release from the Gnomon jail and the tongue-lashing he received from General Sticer over his conduct, Beroth had thrown himself into every dangerous situation that came his way, and sought out risks when they weren't readily available. He had accompanied Hugh in the night raid. He had stormed up and down the Firozian lines during each bombardment, alternately shaking his fists and waving his sword in frustration, shouting curses at the Vargan cannoneers, calling them cowards and shameless butchers. Now, as the *Salazar* began its fated last journey, Beroth muscled his way aboard, even throwing off another soldier who stood in his way. He assumed that Hugh was going to make a heroic, futile charge at the flagship of the Vargan forces, the *Regina*. When the ship began to curl away from the main fleet, he ran up to the navigator, who was still wrestling with the steering of the unwieldy and half-demasted ship.

"Where are you sailing?" Beroth shouted. "Aren't you going to attack those devils?"

"All in good time, Beroth," Hugh said; at the same time he noticed Aivlys cringing and shrinking away from the bearded giant. "Don't be afraid of him, Aivlys. Beroth's got only one thing on his mind right now, how to die properly."

Beroth glared at Hugh and then smiled a grim, hateful smile that required no accompanying language.

"In answer to your question, Beroth, no, we are not going to attack the *Regina*. We are going to take this shipful of explosives and blow ourselves to eternity on the reef at Headland Cove, where the Vargans are going to try to flank the Firozian army to prevent our retreat into the hills."

"Good!" Beroth grunted, and he ran off toward the bow to assist the crew, which was trying to untangle the lines to the flying jib.

"We aren't really going to blow ourselves up, are we?" Aivlys asked.

"Not if I can help it. We may let Beroth light the fuse, though," Hugh joked, trying to ease the tension. Just then the first volley sounded from the Vargan fleet,

which had spotted the *Salazar* and had dispatched three
gunships to sink her. They were still beyond range and
their cannonballs fell harmlessly into the sea, but Hugh
knew that these were mere sighting shots to calculate
range, and he yelled to the crew, "Prepare to come
about!"

"Aye aye," came the lusty call back, followed a minute later by Hugh's shouted command, "Coming
about!" as he spun the wheel to force the rudder over
and place the ship on a new line of sail. Aivlys, who
had not done much sailing, was caught unprepared by
the sudden shift in the tilt of the deck and found herself
rolling dangerously toward the rail. Hugh caught her
just before she tumbled overboard. "No sea legs, eh,
missy?" he said. "Can't lose you to the fishes just now,
we need your help. Those guns will be within striking
distance in about three minutes, and they'll make short
work of us. Especially if one of their shots hits the
powder magazine. If you have some magic, use it now."

"Bring me a bowl of fresh water."

"Uh, Aivlys, there may not be any fresh water on
this vessel. Remember, she was in dry dock until a few
minutes ago. I'll check the galley, but there's probably
nothing in storage, and even if there is, it's likely to be
stale Vargan water. Can't you use salt water? We've got
plenty of that!"

"No!" A look of panic came over Aivlys's face. The
spell she had thought of to conceal the ship from the
Vargans required no extraordinary spices, herbs, brews
or potions, merely a simple glass of water, but without
it, she could do nothing. Now she knew she was being
tested—she looked around for Zentina's image to come
floating to her rescue, but the spirit of the old woman
stayed maddeningly absent. The Vargan fleet sent another volley their way, and this one dropped within fifty
yards of their position, making great splashes and sending up spouts of angry white water. *Think,* Aivlys said

to herself. *What else? Oh, that terrible feeling, when Time turns against you, when the seconds slip away and tragedy looms.* Here she was, sitting on a powder keg, about to be torn to pieces in a huge explosion, and Aivlys could think of nothing that would help herself, Hugh, or the valiant crew that had risked their lives to save others. Then, as if she were practicing the first spell she had ever learned, Slow Time, although she wasn't, she watched the fatal ball come hurtling in. The Vargans had found the range. A single cannon shot tumbled through space, like a black sun starkly outlined against the sky, traveling so slowly it looked as if a boy had lobbed a ball at play. In a few seconds it would tear through the deck of the *Salazar*, seeking and finding the volatile munitions Hugh had filled her with, and that would be the end of them all.

"Wait!" Aivlys yelled, jumping up and stretching her hands toward heaven. "Out of Time!" she cried, and the *Salazar* vanished. It simply wasn't there. For a few minutes the Vargan fleet sailed over the spot where it should have been, but the ship had disappeared. Several minutes later it reappeared, rocking at anchor in Headland Cove. Aivlys was most surprised of all, because the spell she had used was the one she had thought required water to perform—yet there had been no water. A phrase of Zentina Wraight's had come into her mind just before she attempted the trick—"All this stuff and such," Zentina had said one day, waving her hands at the elaborate panoply of her pantry, "is just so much puffery," Zentina had said. "If you're a true witch, a true magician, you don't need such things, your mind alone will suffice!" And it was true. Without recourse to the liquid that the spell called for, Aivlys had been able to hide the *Salazar* in a fine mist, a mist over the eyes of the Vargans and the crew members of the *Salazar*, not over the waters of Gnomon, while the ship continued to sail in a dimension Out of Time. The men

of the *Salazar* were a little groggy, as if they had succumbed to a light sleep, yet they had continued to work
the ship as if it were still in the physical world, the
world of wind and sun and powerful blue water.

"We must have outrun them," Hugh said nonsensically, for he knew that the ship he commanded could
never have beat a Vargan cruiser to Headland Cove in
a match race.

"No, silly, I—" Aivlys said, and then hesitated, because she didn't want to undermine the confidence of
her handsome young lover. "Yes, and a fine bit of sailing it was. Now, how are we going to get off the ship
before you smash it to smithereens?"

"A good question. We can set a timer on the fuse,
but it would be better if we could set off the explosion
exactly when we wanted to, and not a predesignated
time."

"I will stay," said Beroth, who had been standing by,
shaking his hairy head to clear the cobwebs of Aivlys's
subtle spell.

"It would be sure death to be on this ship when that
magazine blew."

"I've been through worse," Beroth answered curtly,
without bragging. "I choose to stay. Take the witch and
be gone. I'll know when to do it."

Hugh looked in the face of his rival and saw only determination and a weary resignation. He could not deny
that by staying aboard Beroth would provide Hugh with
the best possible timing for the feat.

"All right, then, let's make for shore. Lash together
some of this planking and we might be able to ride a
raft onto the combers."

Aivlys was a bit wan from her exertions. Hugh, on
the other hand, had recovered quickly from the effects
of the temporary dislocation; he had to lead her off the
ship and onto the crude floating platform the sailors
made to transport them to the shore. As they departed

she glanced at Beroth, but he was busy with the preparations for setting off the explosion and did not meet her look. *How strange,* she thought. *I hate him so much yet he's going to help save Gnomon.* Suddenly she knew what she must do.

"Wait!" she cried, and she leaped from the raft, which had almost cast off, back up the ladder to the deck of the *Salazar.*

"Where are you going?" Hugh shouted.

"I'll be right back."

"Hold your position," Hugh ordered the man at the primitive makeshift helm of the raft's rudder, which was barely more than a pole thrust into the water.

Aivlys approached Beroth, who had thought himself alone on the ship and was almost at the point of giving way to unmanly sobs. "Here," she said, handing him a small crystal drawn from her supplies. "Take this, and when the time comes, say 'Small Time' twice."

"Will this trinket save my life?" Beroth asked dubiously.

"Perhaps."

The hoary giant nodded his thanks and turned back to the task at hand. Aivlys ran back to the ladder and climbed down onto the raft. They had barely passed from beneath the shadow of the *Salazar* when the first of the Vargan fleet rounded the point of the cove.

"Row, you sons of Gnomon! We've got to make shore before we set off the powder or we'll be drowned in the backwash." A race was on, between the mighty ships of the Vargan fleet, and the lone raft containing Hugh, Aivlys, and a dozen or so brave Gnomonese sailors. The Vargans, intent on regaining the *Salazar,* paid scant attention to the small craft as it churned through the rough waves at the edge of the island. Half a mile offshore the *Salazar* lay at anchor, to all appearances abandoned, between the points of the curving shoreline, at the very spot where the ships would have to pass to enter the calmer, deeper waters of the cove, from which they could launch the landing boats of troops that would deflect and turn back any Firozian/Gnomon retreat toward the hills. The *Regina* hung back while the *Castille* and the *Prendo* circled the *Salazar* cautiously. There was no sign of life aboard the guard ship. Finally the two warships bracketed the smaller vessel and a boarding party was ordered aboard. They had scarcely set foot upon the deck of the *Salazar* when a tremendous explosion lifted the ship clear out of the water and broke it in two pieces. A huge waterspout mingling with a smoke cloud rose into the air, the water falling back to create a massive wave that surged toward the nearby Vargan warships, but the smoke rising higher in the sky was a dark signal for the Vargan fleet. The *Salazar* settled to the bottom exactly as planned by Hugh, the wreckage creating a dangerous obstacle that prevented easy access to the shoreline. The *Castille* sailed around the disaster, picking up survivors from the boarding party, but one lone figure was spotted swimming toward shore. The enraged Vargans let loose a volley of cannon shots but the intrepid swimmer dived repeatedly and managed to avoid the balls that fell all around him.

10

WHEN BEROTH EMERGED FROM THE WA-
ter, a murmur of amazement gave
way to a roar of laughter. Otherwise
uninjured, he was now the size of a
Gnomon man, at least a foot and a
half shorter than his original height!
Yet there was a denseness, a condensed compactness about him that
suggested fantastic strength. The
laughter ceased when Beroth approached the line of men, his face
black with anger. Apparently he was
aware of what had happened to him,
because he ran up to Aivlys immediately and screamed at her, "You
accursed witch! I'll be the laughing-
stock of my people!"

"I doubt it," Aivlys answered.
"Here, test your power. You've lost
none of it."

In frustration Beroth turned and
struck a nearby tree with his bare

hand. It split in twain. He stepped back in surprise and looked at his fist, which showed not even a scratch, so dense and tight was his skin.

"Now perhaps some pretty Gnomonese woman won't find you so oppressively huge to look at," Hugh suggested. Still fuming, Beroth stomped off. There could be no denying that if you knew him before you might find it hilarious to see his shrunken form, but woe to him that laughed to his face. And it was true that he was more handsome, less ungainly than in his former proportions.

"You've certainly taken the air out of his sails," said Hugh.

"He'll get used to it," Aivlys told him. "Besides, there's no going back. That's a one-way spell."

"You saved his life. He should be grateful."

"If we beat the Vargans he'll grow to like his new form. Or perhaps that's a bad choice of words. He'll find it useful. And you're right, the Gnomonese girls will like him better, at least his looks."

There was no time to dwell on the peculiar fate of Beroth the ex-giant, because the *Castille* and the *Prendo* had commenced shelling the beach.

"Fall back! Our job here is done. They can blow the sand around all they want, they'll never be able to bring those big ships in close enough to disgorge landing craft with men on them."

"What now, Hugh?" said Aivlys, who was enjoying herself despite the imminent danger. Her spells had worked wonders, her hands had healed (mysteriously, even to her, during Out of Time), and she was with Hugh again, safe on shore.

"Now we wait to see how the battle goes, we've done our share for now. We'll probably end up retreating into the hills, but now at last we'll be able to make a run for them without being outflanked and surrounded."

"Not Beroth, apparently," Aivlys noted, for the now diminutive warrior was spotted on the ridge above them, marching back toward the town of Gnomon to join the forces fighting there. Out to sea, the two Vargan ships sailed back and forth like frustrated beasts, unable to claw their way through the barrier of the sunken *Salazar*, and fired off an occasional round to show their displeasure. From time to time they hoisted flags to signal to the *Regina*, farther out and positioned where it could maintain contact with both these two ships and the rest of the Vargan fleet, which was busy attacking the city of Gnomon proper, around the point. Hugh could read the messages and was able to keep the group informed of the progress of the battle. The news was not good. The Vargans had landed and were already occupying the pier and port area. The Firozians had fallen back into the city and were fighting house to house. The citizens of Gnomon, those that remained after the week of shelling, had begun a disorderly evacuation. It was apparent that soon the Firozians would be forced into retreat. Their path would take them over the knoll at the upper end of Headland Cove and down into the bay, past their current redoubt and into the hills behind. Gnomon would fall that afternoon, and cease to be a free city for the first time in its long existence. Aivlys wondered where her father was, down there amid the chaotic turmoil of war, and a tremor of fear passed through her, but then she realized that her psychic senses had been so sharpened by Zentina Wraight that if anything had happened to Endimin she would have felt it, and she rested a little easier.

"Let's climb the hill. We can watch the battle from up there," Aivlys suggested. "And I know a place," she said, but then she stopped suddenly, as if lost in thought.

"What kind of place?" Hugh asked her.

"A beautiful place, a place that war shouldn't touch," she said.

"Well, it will. Let me round up the crew, and we'll move. Those Vargan gunners are going to find us sooner or later."

Aivlys had regretted her words immediately, but she knew that once they were spoken she could never call them back. Atop the hill stood the remains of an ancient monastery, a stone building with thick walls that would make a fine defensive structure, until the cannons of soldiers tore it down. Her father used to take her there when she was little, and her memories of the locale were of a dreamy, secluded ruin, romantic and idyllic. She didn't want to bring a troop of rough sailors to this paradise. She would have liked to go there alone, or at most with Hugh. Moreover, she knew that if this little group occupied it, other soldiers were sure to follow, and then war would make its appearance, with its fire and destruction. The ruin would be ruined anew, and the isolated splendor of the place would be lost. Still, there was no denying that the monastery stood at a strategic spot, straddling the ridge between Gnomon and Headland Cove. She would have to lead them there. The crenelated parapets of the abbey would provide a perfect vantage point for surveillance, which is undoubtedly why the site was chosen in the first place, back in the days before the founding of Gnomon, when the monks had to defend themselves from earlier invaders. Still farther to the south rose the sloping end of the mountain range that separated Firoze from Gnomon, which tailed down to a sheer cliff guarded by turbulent waters punctuated by the peaks of treacherous submerged rocks. If there was an escape route, it was straight up into the maze of canyons and valleys that hid under the cloud-wreathed mountaintops of Firoze.

Hugh returned with the band of seamen, who had been collecting what they could salvage from the wreck

of the *Salazar* as it washed ashore. Among the items
were a chest of sailor's clothes, a couple of cutlasses, of
the Vargan style, with curved blades wide at the base
and narrow at the point, and elaborate wrist guards of
filigreed silver, and, amazingly, a barrel of dry gunpowder that hadn't gone up in the explosion. Hugh awarded
one of the swords to each of the two sailors who had
helped him control the ship in the first uncertain moments when it seemed that the *Salazar* would end up on
the rocks. Its demise had been delayed by only a few
moments, but that may have made all the difference in
the outcome of the ongoing battle, he told them.

"The actions of one or two can affect the fate of
thousands," Hugh pronounced as he handed the men
their rewards. Aivlys thought he sounded like her father. *Perhaps that's the tone that all leaders adopt,* she
speculated. It made her feel comfortable that the care-
free navigator, who had previously seemed immature,
reminded her of Endimin. *The war must be changing
him, as it is us all,* she thought. Indeed he seemed more
subdued, more serious, his shoulders slightly bent with
the weight of responsibility for these men, and for her.
She decided that it would be all right to bring him to
the monastery site. They could share a simple lunch and
perhaps rest for a few precious moments before the hor-
rific action began again.

"Come on," she said, "I'll lead the way." Some of
the Gnomonese sailors, whose eyes and lives had always been on the sea, had never been to this part of the
island, but Aivlys, a farm girl, a hill girl, had wandered
all over the land, and knew every path, every landmark.
That's why Runny crossed the Impasse, she thought, *to
explore new places.* She and her brother had often
played up here while their father napped in the shade of
the cool, leaf-covered walls. Now she led a group of
near strangers to her childhood playground. By the time
they reached the spot, the group was dusty and sweaty.

A well had continued to supply fresh water from an underground spring even in the many years since the monks had left their hilltop retreat. A sign on the quaint peaked roof of the well stated that any passerby was free to avail himself of the cool, soft water, which came as a welcome relief to the weary hikers. After the excitement of the morning, the serene silence of the abandoned sanctuary was startling, almost disturbing, but the rumble of the Vargan guns and the distant confused din of the fighting in Gnomon reminded them that they weren't likely to enjoy this respite long.

Hugh sent one of the men up into the crumbling tower with his spyglass to see what he could of the conflict. The man shouted down his observations: "The town is in flames again. It looks like the Firozians are already backing up the hill toward us, but they're still a good four miles from the point. The Vargans have landed in force and are in possession of the Clocktower."

And at those words he paused, for even a simple sailor knew the effect they would have on the rest of his Gnomonese compatriots. The Clocktower was a symbol of Gnomonese independence. The city might burn, but as long as the tower remained in Gnomonese hands the people felt they were safe. Now that last vestige of liberty was taken from them. There was nothing that Hugh, Aivlys, and the sailors could do now except wait for the battle to come to them. Hugh sent two more men to the other standing corners of the building and ordered the remainder of the group to take rest in the overgrown, untended grassy plot of the former abbey garden. It was a delightful setting, cool, shaded, protected from the wind. A few hardy apple trees were in blossom, though no gardener had pruned them for many years, and later in the season the fruit would fall uneaten except by children come to play. Hugh and Aivlys leaned against one of these old souls; the rest of the band gathered nearby, as if loath to separate, but the young lovers didn't mind. Hugh brought them into the circle by starting up an easy conversation.

"You know what I admire most about the Firozians," said Hugh.

"Their swords?" one sailor ventured.

"No, their whetstones. They have the finest pumice sharpening stones I've ever seen. There's a whole industry there they've never tapped, I'll wager. Only soldiers can use their weapons, but housewives, farmers, merchants, everyone needs a good whetstone. I'll bet the lee side of that volcano is a veritable treasure trove of stones for whetting."

"It's true."

"If only the world were as peaceful as it seems right here, and our only worry were how to buy Firozian lava stones to sharpen our kitchen knives," said Aivlys.

"That time may come again. The Vargans won't be here forever."

"You don't believe they can drive us off the island, then?" an older fisherman asked. His name was Emile Dorger. The ferocity of the Vargans had frightened him. His wife Franca had been killed in the fire that followed the shelling, and his home burned. He no longer thought of Gnomon as a rock of safety to return to from the uncertainties of the ocean. If you saw him rolling down the street with his bandy legs and his swaying sailor's gait he might strike you as a comical figure, like something out of the song and literature of Gnomon, the classic man-o'-the-sea, but now, squatted on the grass in this sheltered garden, he was just another ordinary human with common concerns that touched them all.

"No, Dorger, I don't think they can. Your bravery today and the damage we've done to their hopes of pinning us down here in the cove are two reasons why I think they'll have a long, hard fight of it, and eventually give in. Their supply lines are too long. They're strung out from here to Vargas, a good eighteen days' sail in favorable winds. That's too much. They've lost their chance at a quick victory, and unless they have some other way of wiping us all out quickly, we can hide and fight from the hills until they despair of ever seizing total control, then they'll leave."

"I hope to the gods you're right, navigator." A murmur of assent came from the weary sailors, some of whom had by now flopped onto their backs to catch some needed sleep. One of the men pulled out a small pitch pipe and began playing softly, and was surprised when Aivlys joined in with a clear, light voice that was like a puff of breeze among the apple blossoms. It was a sailor's ditty, but it captured the mood of all those gathered there in the abandoned garden:

Oh I've been away for many a day
Sailing the great glassy ocean,
Now making port in old Gnomon Bay
Coming home to my lass of devotion.

So draw me an ale and fix me some broth,
Sit on my lap and show me your smile,
Give me a kiss and I'll pledge my troth
And hey, I might even stay for a while!

Hey! he might even stay, says he
Sing the girls of Gnomon, all laughing
So very honored and grateful are we
That we'll dance for a kiss or for nothing!

The sailors were silent for a few minutes after the song ended, thinking of wives and girlfriends back in Gnomon. Dorger sobbed quietly for the woman he would never see again. Then Hugh spoke up.

"Aivlys, this monastery looks more like a fort—it's

square, with defensive walls and high towers. Are you sure it was a religious site?"

"It has a name—MainSpring—because of the freshwater well up there and of course a reference to our preoccupation with Time. These monks were the ones who first began our investigations into the Mysteries of the Hours. Those were dangerous times, before Gnomon was fully established as a city-state, but the men and women who lived here were definitely a religious order. My recent teacher, Zentina Wraight—"

"The witch—"

"You can call her that if you want, but she wasn't one, really."

"But the spells, and the warts . . . ," Hugh teased her.

"Anyone may have warts, even you, and I'll give you some if you're not careful," Aivlys rejoined. "What I was going to tell you is that Zentina lived here as a child when the monastery was still functioning."

"What? Impossible! She'd have to have been several hundred years old, by the looks of the ruins here."

"Yes."

"You mean, she was that old?"

"Yes."

"Then she was a witch—no ordinary mortal lives that long."

"Ah, Hugh, you forget, our Time is not your time."

"Ah yes, and how long are you going to live?"

"I don't know," Aivlys said simply. She had never considered the possibility. "If we don't fare any better against the Vargans I might not live long at all. I doubt that I could survive anywhere except Gnomon. Its dust is my bones, its water my blood. Take them away from me and I'll shrivel up and die."

"Not if I can help it," Hugh declared. He stood up suddenly. "What was that?"

"I didn't hear anything."

"Listen!" In the distance a muffled roar could be

heard. Hugh interpreted it. "The Vargans have broken through! Come on, we'll have to get ready. First the Firozians will come, retreating, in an orderly fashion, I hope, and then the Vargans. We need to prepare so that as soon as the Firozians have passed, we can surprise the Vargans."

"What can the dozen of us do? We don't even have any weapons," one of the sailors lamented.

"Ah, but we have the powder. We can give them a good dose of their own." Hugh had hauled up the cask of black powder on his back. Now he set about preparing to use it. He ventured down the trail a few score yards until he found a place where the hillside above sloped sharply and the ground was loose and gravelly. Then he set charges in the ground and strung them together with some hemp string. His plan was obvious, to cause a landslide that would bury the trail, and some of the advancing Vargans, and slow their pursuit of the fleeing Firozian army. There was only one problem with his plan: one person would have to stay behind to light the fuse that would detonate the charges. As always, Hugh volunteered to take the risk himself. He was challenged by two Gnomonese men for the honor. One of them was Dorger, the old sailor who'd lost his wife.

"I'll stay," he said quietly. "Not much for me to live for now. And anyway, they're going to have to catch me first, an' these old legs can still shinny up a mast."

"All right, Dorger. After the last of the Firozians pass, wait for the advance scouts of the Vargans. Let them go by, too, and stay hidden, they'll be on the lookout for booby traps. When the main guard comes, let the first few by, then ignite the charges, and be well above the blast or you'll get swept down on them with the rest of the hillside."

"Aye, aye, navigator."

Hugh shook Dorger's hand briskly, then returned to the garden, where Aivlys and the others were waiting.

"The rest of us should deploy around the monastery walls. Make sure the Firozians know where to go. Aivlys, the trail continues up the mountain from here, doesn't it?"

"Yes. Out the back gate and on up."

"Good. We don't want to create another siege here. The idea is that this will be a blockade point once the Vargans dig out from the obstruction we're going to create below. But once the whole Firozian army has passed through here we want to pull out as quickly as possible."

"There are ghosts here," Aivlys said quietly to Hugh, so that the sailors wouldn't hear her. "They'll fight for us, too."

Hugh took her by the arm and led her off to the side. "What are you talking about?"

"The old ones, the monks, they're still here, a little."

"What do you mean, 'here a little'?"

"I've been talking to them."

"Aivlys, this is no time for idle dreaming."

Aivlys shrugged. "They want to help. They have plans to surprise the Vargans, too."

"Great." Hugh was suddenly impatient. "I know you have some magic spells, but to expect me to believe that monks hundreds of years dead can fight against flesh-and-blood Vargans is too much."

"You'll see," Aivlys said dreamily, but Hugh was already dashing around frantically trying to prepare for the maneuver he saw as necessary: to rush the Firozians and any accompanying Gnomonese through the abbey while delaying the Vargans as long as possible from taking the same route. The sounds of war were upon them now: the fierce, excited shouts of the fighters; the moans and shrieks of the wounded; the thud of feet running and bodies crashing through the underbrush. The first of the Firozians burst through the trees into the clearing in front of the monastery and stopped, startled to find a building in front of them, so high up in the forest.

"This way, this way!" Hugh shouted, and he used the first group to set up the line of defense and sent those following through the gate and into the fortress, where the Gnomonese sailors handed them a drink of cool water and sent them on their way out the back. Many wanted to linger there, behind the illusory safety of the high walls, especially those exhausted or wounded, but Hugh knew that they would never be able to hold the Vargans here, that to stay was to risk almost sure capture or death. A long stream of Firozians passed through, received the momentary refreshment from the well, and pushed upward into the higher forest. At last the stragglers appeared, some bleeding, others gasping for breath or panicked and rigid with fear that the Vargans were about to overtake them.

"Come on, come on!" Hugh screamed in an effort to rouse them. From her vantage point behind a parapet within the monastery, Aivlys watched the gangly navigator turn into a hero before her eyes. He was fearless, careless of his life, and a good leader, sure of himself and concerned for the fate of the men under his command, for he had taken over this little fort and made it his own. General Sticer, surrounded by a loyal guard, came at the last, once again soaking wet with the sweat of exertion and covered with grime, as Hugh had seen him in the last battle.

"Their advance party is less than a hundred yards behind us," he told Hugh as he grasped the navigator's outstretched hand. "Were you able to blockade the bay?"

"Yes, General, and"—just then the ground rocked from the explosion down the trail, and a rumbling could be heard as the loosened hillside slid away—"and the trail, too!" Hugh grinned.

"Well done, Boisset."

"Have some water, General, but don't tarry here. The trail continues out the other side."

"Too bad we aren't more well supplied. This fortress looks nearly impregnable."

"Yes, but today it would be a death trap."

"I agree. Well, let's move, no need to defend the place now."

"We'll be right behind you. I want to see if the man I left down there to set the charges makes it back."

General Sticer gave Hugh a funny look. "Not likely, is it, man? Don't risk your own life for one already lost."

"I won't. Anyway, the young Gnomonese woman seems to think we have supernatural allies here."

"We'll need them. The Vargans made quick work of us once they landed." General Sticer sounded disappointed in the performance of his troops, but Hugh suspected that they had fought as well as they possibly could, given the disadvantages they faced.

"How are the townspeople faring?" Hugh asked.

"Most of them fled before the fighting began. I think they'll be all right. They took their livestock with them and headed into the hills, and the Vargans seemed more concerned with following us than rounding up the citizenry."

"All right, then, push on. We'll see you up the trail."

Dorger didn't return from his mission. Hugh and Aivlys sent the rest of the sailors on up to follow the Firozians while they stayed behind. Aivlys had to plead her special purpose before Hugh relented reluctantly and allowed her to remain with him, because he feared the arrival of the Vargans at any moment, but the afternoon lengthened and they did not come. Hugh sus-

pected that their scouts were combing every inch of the
trail between the landslide and the monastery, searching
for more traps. It was nearly twilight before the vanguard of the Vargan column made its appearance. They
assembled at the edge of the clearing, expecting a challenge from the fort, but receiving none, they grew em-
boldened. From their ranks they sent captured Dorger
forward on wobbly legs. Before Hugh could rush to his
aid, a savage-looking Vargan warrior strode out behind
the old sailor and slew him cruelly with two sword
thrusts, in full view of Hugh and Aivlys, who sup-
pressed a shriek and clutched Hugh in agony.

"Islanders!" a Vargan commander shouted. "Give
yourselves up. Don't make us storm this redoubt, or
you will pay as this one has paid. Lay down your arms
and come forward."

"They still have no idea the Firozian army isn't
holed up here," said Hugh with grim satisfaction. "If
only we could make them think so for a few hours,
we'd give the Firozians a chance to dig in somewhere
favorable up above, and give ourselves time to get
away, too. I wish I had more powder. I should have
saved some."

"We have allies," Aivlys said. She drew away from
Hugh, ran down the stairs from the parapet, and began
to dance alone in the garden. Hugh feared that the
sight of poor Dorger being slain had unhinged her
mind. He was about to run after her when suddenly
the woods were filled with the sounds of a confident,
strong, lusty-voiced army, singing as they marched.
They seemed to be everywhere, their high-spirited
voices echoing through the darkened trees. In the
dusky light their shadows towered as tall as the trees
themselves. Whole lines of them marched across his
vision. The Vargans were thrown into a panic. The last
thing they had expected was a counterattack. Without

waiting for the unseen army to make its appearance, they stampeded toward the rear, giving up the ground they had so laboriously gained over the last few hours. The strident commands of their officers were to no avail, the Vargan infantry was in now full disordered retreat, terrorized by the advance of the ghost army. For it was a ghost army—no soldiers were ever actually seen by Hugh, the frightened Vargans, or even by Aivlys, who had summoned them, or had answered their summons; it was never clear which to Hugh. They filled the air with their monkish voices, alternately chanting, praying, and shouting, their formless forms gesticulating in shades thrown against the walls of the monastery in gigantic relief, but none ever appeared to stand before him.

As soon as Aivlys stopped dancing, the spirit soldiers began to recede, the noise of their battle songs subsiding and their shadowy images wavering and fading into the lush stillness and darkness of the forest night. Hugh ventured out of the monastery and retrieved Dorger's bloody form. He wrapped the corpse in a blanket and carried it back inside. Aivlys was lying on the ground in the garden, spent from the exertions of summoning her kindred spirits from the past. Hugh hurriedly dug a grave in the soft, fragrant earth of the garden, because he wanted to bury the sailor before Aivlys could see what the Vargans had done to his ravaged body. He picked a spot overlooking the moonlit sea of Headland Cove. As he was shoveling the last dirt on the newly dug plot, Aivlys roused herself and wandered over, still faint and exhausted. Hugh helped her to place a dogwood blossom on the fresh-turned earth.

"He would have preferred a watery grave," Hugh said quietly, "but he can see the ocean he loved."

"No, he would have liked to be beside his wife,"

Aivlys said. "At least they share the Gnomonese soil."

They stood quietly together for a solemn moment. Hugh thought he could still hear the drums of the spectral regiment somewhere in the distance, haunting the Vargan army as it fled.

11

"I'LL NEVER DOUBT YOU AGAIN," SAID Hugh, thinking of the eerie spectacle he had just witnessed.

"They didn't respond to me," Aivlys whispered.

"What do you mean? I saw you dancing, and the next minute the night sky was inhabited by these banshees—"

"It wasn't me," Aivlys insisted.

"Who, then?"

"It was Dorger they came for. I was only the messenger. If the Vargans hadn't killed Dorger, the old ones who live here might not have showed themselves. But when his soul rose up to greet them they came forward."

"Ah . . . ," said Hugh, not knowing what to say. The world was so much more complicated than he had ever imagined, this son of a tinker, this former cabin boy turned navigator

who now found himself on an island where time was
not Time, and a young girl knew the mysteries of
magic. If he had stayed around 'til the next day one
more surprise would have greeted him, a full-flowering
dogwood tree sprung up where he and Aivlys had
placed a single blossom that evening, but instead they
abandoned the monastery and trudged wearily up the
trail. Before leaving, they locked the gates and left candles burning in the windows to make it appear as if the
place were still inhabited (by ghosts or humans, let the
Vargans figure out which). A brilliant full moon guided
their steps, but Hugh was still slightly spooked by the
extraordinary events at the monastery; he didn't bound
up the path with his usual enthusiasm. Aivlys also was
drained from the experience and stumbled and needed
to stop to rest frequently. Here and there they found dis-
carded Firozian implements, no weapons but shields,
clothing, empty water containers, all cast aside to
lighten the load of the climbers.

"Too bad," Hugh observed. "They'll need these later
on."

"There's only two more battles to be fought. We'll
lose the first but win the second," Aivlys announced.

Hugh stared at her in surprise. "What makes you say
that?" he asked.

"What?"

"What you just said."

"What did I just say?"

"That there'd be two battles, and we'd lose the first
and win the . . . hey, what's with you?"

"I miss my father," Aivlys said, which wasn't an answer to Hugh's question but was all he was able to get
out of her. *Strange girl,* Hugh thought. *She lives in two
worlds, and I'm privy to only one.*

"Did you see Beroth come through with the Firozian
army?" Hugh asked her.

"No, did you?"

"No. I wasn't looking for him, but I suddenly realized I would have seen him if he came this way."

"Maybe you missed him. He's changed, you know."

"No, I would have seen him, funny girl." Hugh was relieved that Aivlys was recovered enough to joke about what had happened to Beroth, the giant turned dwarf. They continued to climb and rest alternately for several more hours, and it was near dawn before they came to the high plateau where the Firozian army had made its encampment. General Sticer had chosen the spot well, Hugh observed. The relatively level meadow was rimmed by mountains and was accessible from below only by a single trail that threaded its way through an easily defended crevice. The Vargans would be hard put to gain entry to this natural fortress, which had the additional favorable quality of a plentiful stream of water running through it. The most difficult task now facing the Firozians was supplies. An army of several hundred needs huge quantities of food on a daily basis, and even the abundant wildlife of the mountain park would soon be depleted by the demands of the soldiers. As the sun rose over a nearby peak, Hugh and Aivlys walked warily through the camp of sleeping men. They were challenged twice by vigilant sentries, but battle, followed by the long flight and climb, had tired out the Firozians, most of whom were still asleep. Here and there an early riser was seen making tea in a blackened pot over an open fire.

At General Sticer's tent they expected to wait for him to rise, but found him already awake and in the process of having his whiskers trimmed by an attendant. The general greeted them warmly and thanked them profusely for their aid in the retreat.

"Boisset, you've covered yourself in glory twice over, first by sinking that Vargan vessel in the harbor and then with your outstanding delaying tactics."

"I had a lot of help, sir. Aivlys here was responsible

for sending the entire Vargan army into a panic. They fled down the hill and I doubt that they've completely regrouped yet."

"Hmmph!" the general grunted. "I'm not surprised. You've proven yourself as well, Miss Platho, though in our Firozian tradition women do not get involved in battlefield action, I'd have to say we'd make an exception for you."

"Thank you, General."

From the general they learned what happened in the city, and the fate of Beroth, who had volunteered to lead the fleeing Gnomonese into the hills. Perhaps it was because he felt more comfortable with people his own size. He had certainly distinguished himself in the battle before the city fell. Reports of his exploits were already legendary among the Firozian troops, who were in awe of his ability to wield his (now) oversized sword as though he were still the man of robust proportions they remembered. Some reported having seen the undersized warrior fighting and defeating four and five Vargans at a time, using his small stature and enormous strength to his advantage by coming up under their defenses with a peculiar lunging upward thrust he had developed on the spur of the moment. At the end of the battle, rather than retreat with the rest of the army, he had chosen to make himself available to the Gnomonese people, who were grateful for the guardianship he offered. From this encounter Aivlys learned that her father had worked with Basco Fournier, Henri Blouchette, and the other Gnomonese leaders to formulate a plan for the evacuation of the city, and that everyone was headed for the defensible position at the Impasse, where a few Firozian and Gnomonese troops still held the high ground. Their situation was desperate, but as Hugh had predicted, the Vargans were more interested at that point in quelling the revolt by the main Firozian army than in seizing fleeing civilians. Like the Firozians, however, they would soon face the problem of maintaining a refugee population at high altitude without adequate sources of food. Their sheep and goats and fowl would fall prey to the looting Vargans, along with their granaries, their larders, their wells, their fields of vegetables, and their orchards, everything that made possible the comfortable existence they had enjoyed until the coming of the enemy.

"They'd steal the fish from the ocean, too, if they could get at them easily," one of General Sticer's aides grumbled as they talked about the situation over a meager breakfast of tea and hard biscuits.

"They don't need to, since they've driven us from the water we can only fish the streams and lakes. That'll provide some sustenance, but not enough to feed two armies."

"We'll raid our own villages, though it'll be dangerous work," one of the Firozians suggested.

"That might work the first time, but not a second," said Hugh. The meeting broke up without a resolution to the difficult problem. Hugh and Aivlys were issued a pair of army tents for lodging. Aivlys was still wearing the same rough farm clothes she'd had on since she left Zentina Wraight's house. Was it only yesterday? She requested and received an oversized pair of breeches and a shirt from one of the general's aides so that she could at least wash her only other outfit. "Come, Aivlys, let's take a walk through the meadow," Hugh suggested. The sun had risen and the splendor of the mountains was all around them. Smoke was now rising from a hundred campfires lit by the men of the Firozian army (mingled with a few clusters of Gnomonese soldiers who had ended up in the Firozian camp during the chaotic retreat). Aivlys recognized a few townsmen among the Gnomonese and stopped to say hello. As one of the members of the Guild she enjoyed a certain status. Several of the men came up to her to inquire what she thought would happen next, but she had no answer for them except to encourage them to keep their spirits up. She and Hugh left the encampment behind and wandered out into the farther reaches of the meadow, whose golden grasses glowed in the early-morning light. A stream meandered its way through the meadow carrying runoff from the still snowcapped higher peaks. It was several degrees cooler up here than along the coast. The air was crisp and clean smelling, now scented with the fragrance of the burning pine boughs and cedar chips of the campfires. Kestrels and crows soared in the air above the meadow on the lookout for squirrels and mice. Yellow spanglias, blue and white mountain lilies, and red penstemon added bright splashes of color to the predominant green-and-gold scene. The man-made fury and terror of the previous day seemed far removed from them, yet Aivlys knew that in a matter of days or even hours this peaceful vale could become the site of another bloody encounter.

"Hugh, when are men going to stop killing each other?" she asked plaintively.

"When generosity replaces greed as our fundamental nature," Hugh answered. "When we learn that we are not merely animals but creatures of grace."

"And when will that happen?"

"You should know better than me, old soul, since you can see into the past and future."

"I can't see that far," Aivlys said dejectedly.

"Look over there." Hugh pointed to a small herd of deer bounding among the smaller trees at the edge of the forest. "Those beauties had better hurry or they'll be this evening's dinner for the Firozian army."

Aivlys was about to say "They wouldn't!" when she realized that of course they would, there was no alternative, unless she could come up with one. As a farm girl, she wasn't that squeamish about killing animals for

food, but the sight of these wild creatures running free
made her sad to think that they'd end up as soldiers'
fare. She determined to give the matter some thought
and see if she couldn't help supply the camp with food.
But one couldn't conjure food out of thin air, could
one?

"Come along, Aivlys, let's climb," Hugh called to
her.

"Wasn't last night enough climbing for you? My legs
are sore. When are we going to sleep?" she wondered
aloud.

"That wasn't for pleasure, though. Now we can take
our time, hike leisurely, at least for the morning. If we
get up just a little higher we'll have a great view. Then
we'll come back down for a nap."

"All right." Actually Aivlys felt pretty good, consid-
ering all she'd been through in the last twenty-four
hours—the mad dash on the *Salazar*, the battle at the
monastery and her magical intervention, the long
night's journey. Like Hugh, she was maturing as the
war progressed. Her rapid education under the tutelage
of Zentina Wraight had changed her, but the experience
of battle had altered her more quickly and profoundly.
She recalled with amusement how nervous and surprised she had been when Basco Fournier first attacked
her with a sword. Since then she had been through numerous attacks by cannon and sword, she had abandoned a ship moments before it exploded, she had
witnessed the ferocious bloodiness of battle, and seen
men die. Only reluctantly would she let her guard down
now. She wanted to make Hugh happy, though, and saw
that he had some reason for wanting to get away from
the masses of men huddled in their tents on the field
below. She allowed him to guide her up into the scrub
pines that grew in the clefts of the higher rocks. The
encampment of the Firozians was peculiarly sedate
looking from this height, as if the men were on an out-

ing, not weary refugees from war's horror. Hugh kept climbing after Aivlys would have stopped, until he finally gave up and let his feet dangle over the edge of a dizzying drop. Aivlys sat a few feet away in a more secure perch. *Always the bravado,* she thought with a smile.

"I was hoping to see the ocean," he admitted, "but I guess you'd have to scale that peak there to catch a glimpse of it."

"Please don't."

"I won't. Look how peaceful things are in the meadow."

"But how long will they stay that way?"

"Not long, I fear."

"You and I, we have to live every day as if it were our last. Do you think everyone lives that way?"

"Not at all. Many people think they've all Eternity to squander, then one day they wake up and they're old, and they haven't done anything. Aivlys, I've grown quite fond of you," Hugh started to say, but then he lost his courage and mumbled something about the loveliness of the meadow.

"Yes," Aivlys answered, knowing without his having said it what he wanted to say. She smiled at him. He withdrew his legs from the overhang and sat down beside her with their backs to a cool rock, and kissed her, fumblingly, as young lovers are wont to do. Like two birds they fell asleep together on the high perch.

12

IN A MATTER OF TWO DAYS FIROZIAN archers downed all the teal, mallards, and geese that flew overhead, while other soldiers snared the quail and doves that inhabited the low brush at the meadow's edge. The delicate, skittish deer had fled to inaccessible higher crags and thus avoided the fate of the birds. Squirrels and rabbits, the largest remaining animals in the surrounding forest, were soon hunted out of existence. The stream in the meadow was quickly depleted of fish, turtles, and even the small crayfish that lived under the overhanging banks. Nature, which seemed so bountiful in the fields of Gnomon, here was rapidly stripped bare by the demands of the army. After a day and a half the soldiers were anxious and restless. Hunger is a powerful stimulant to action, but for now they were bottled up in this beautiful but desolate highland. Fights broke out over the petty theft of stale biscuits and rotting scraps of meat. The complaining groan of empty bellies was almost audible. A general lethargy set in as the troops' energy was sapped by lack of sustenance. The situation was deteriorating from serious to calamitous; if something wasn't done soon, the army would be forced to make desperate and dangerous raids or surrender. General Sticer came to Aivlys as she lay in her tent in a lassitude born of fatigue and hunger. After receiving permission to enter he stood awkwardly at the tent opening, his head scraping on the low canvas roof. It was apparent that he was unused to requesting help, especially from a woman. It was a mark of the perilous circumstance of the army that he was there at all.

"May I importune of you, young lady?"

"What is it, General?"

"Er, I was wondering, that is . . ." The general was unable to articulate his request. After an uncomfortable moment he tried again. "It has been said that you possess . . . that you are endowed with . . . certain powers—"

"That I'm a witch."

"Yes." The general looked relieved that Aivlys had said it, not he.

"Well, it's true."

"But can you help us."

"I've been thinking on it. I can't make something from nothing, but I do have one idea. It involves a risk."

"The risk of doing nothing is greater," the general said gravely. "Our pickets have seen the Vargans probing our outer defenses. They haven't figured out a way to attack us yet, but they will. With our troops in their weakened condition it wouldn't be much of a battle, but if we can find some way to feed them my men will fight like the true warriors they are."

"Of course they will, General. All right, I'm going to try my idea, but you'll have to tell your troops, all but the sentinels, to remain inside their tents for the next hour."

"It shall be done." With a nod and a stiff, formal bow, the general withdrew from the tent opening to issue his commands. Minutes later Aivlys heard the bugle blow and listened to the scurrying of feet as the soldiers of Firoze and Gnomon obeyed the order to remove themselves to within their canvas quarters. When all was quiet, she ventured outside to find the camp empty of visible inhabitants. Even Hugh had apparently withdrawn inside his tent. All was ready—anticipation hung in the air like an electric charge. What would the witch do? Aivlys wandered into the middle of the meadow, as far as she could get from the camp. Conscious of the unseen but attentive presence of hundreds of men, she raised her hands dramatically and began to dance as she had in the monastery the night she had summoned the ghostly monks of MainSpring. She added a quavering song to her steps, then began to run wildly through the meadow as if possessed. All this was for show, however, and to impress the eyes that she was sure were peeping at her performance through tent flaps and holes in the canvas. All that was really required for the spell was a few words quietly repeated:

> Come rain, come spout
> Draw it up and suck it out,
> Ocean's bounty fall from heaven
> Fields' grain, that we may leaven
> Give us sustenance divine
> In the spell of Harvest Time.

The sky darkened rapidly, unnaturally so. The wind came up, whistling through the lower canyons. A few wicked drops of rain splattered the canvas tents with splotches. Then, from afar, a black whirling funnel-shaped cloud rose, spinning violently and lurching crazily from side to side. It was huge, malevolent looking, a storm that would shred the tents of the soldiers like leaves if it touched down in the meadow. It rose higher in the sky than the surrounding mountains; then, as if wrenching itself apart, it spun out a line of rain clouds that covered the meadow and began to open up in a downpour, but mixed with the rain were creatures from the sea: many kinds of fish, lobster, shrimp, crabs, eels, mollusks, a cornucopia from the ocean. The grass of the meadow was littered with flopping marine life, enough to fill many bushel baskets. A second twister followed, this one dumping loads of swirling oat hay and wheat stalks, their heads of seed still attached. The Firozian soldiers, unable to restrain themselves, rushed from their tents with any containers they could muster to collect the sudden treasure. They avoided Aivlys, who remained standing in the center of the meadow while they dashed madly about in pursuit of the scattered grain and seafood.

That evening the camp was pungent with the smell of dried, smoked, and freshly grilled fish and baking bread. A feast was prepared in Aivlys's honor, though she was still the object of much fear and speculation among the troops. In some ways this distancing was healthy, since she was the only woman among several hundred warriors. Aivlys had enhanced her performance of the spell for that very reason. At the feast, however, she dressed in a simple black robe she had fashioned from materials General Sticer had provided her with, and she wandered from group to group with Hugh at her side, to let the soldiers express their appreciation. There was enough dried fish and piled-up grain to supply the entire army for several weeks. Pickets posted on a skirmishing line down the mountain from the meadow reported no sign of the Vargan army. It was a night to relax, to try to forget for the moment that they were refugees, that their families were under oppression in Firoze or in hiding in Gnomon. The Firozians sang their folk songs and the Gnomonese answered with their own melodies. Some of the grain had been brewed into fresh beer at General Sticer's command—he knew what his troops needed. As the beer supplies diminished the singing became louder and more off key. Firozians and Gnomonese sang together, each trying to learn the others' tunes and words. General Sticer responded to repeated imprecations from his officers by dancing a gimpy jig for which he was famous, to the roaring drunken approval of his men.

The general planned to send some of the men over the mountains to fight in Firoze itself. These were the most coveted positions; there was considerable competition among the officers and men to be appointed to them, even though the Vargans held the country in a tight grip and assignment there was an almost certain death sentence. Aivlys was proud to observe that several Gnomonese volunteered to accompany the small invading force into Firoze. Hugh wanted to go along *(Of course,* she thought, *he always wants to be where there is the most danger and excitement),* but General Sticer asked him to remain in camp.

"This is where we'll make our stand," the general pronounced as they sat with a group of inebriated but respectful foot soldiers around one of the many fires in camp that night. "This is where the Vargans will attack, eventually. We control the high ground. Thanks to young Miss Platho," he said, with a gentlemanly nod in her direction, "we're well supplied. If we're going to defeat the Vargans, it'll be here." Aivlys said nothing, but in her heart she knew differently. Still, she felt it was not her place to contradict the general, especially in front of his troops. Hugh remembered her prediction, made as they climbed up from the monastery the night of the great retreat, that there remained two battles to be fought, and that they would lose the first but win the second. To change the subject, he turned to Aivlys.

"What is this place called?"

"To our people it's known as Hawk's Heart Meadow," Aivlys said somewhat curtly. This name pleased the bold Firozians, who grunted and clapped their approval that the soon-to-be killing ground was graced with such a striking description.

"I sense that you know something more about this place," Hugh prodded her. Aivlys looked at him in surprise.

"Well, yes."

"What is it?"

"This spot has been the site of one previous battle," she said hesitantly, as if she didn't really want to talk about it, but Hugh missed her cue and pressed on.

"Oh? When?"

"Many years ago, before the formation of Gnomon and Firoze as we know them now, when the monks who lived in the monastery below were attacked by outsiders whose name has been lost to history."

"The monks left their fortress to fight here? Why?" Hugh wanted to know. The fire flared up suddenly, as if someone had thrown powder on it. The faces around the campfire were suddenly illumined for a brief instant, then returned to darkness, but in that moment of light Aivlys saw the Firozian soldiers draw back, in fear that she, the witch, was going to perform some more magic. She smiled to herself, a mixture of amusement and chagrin.

"It was winter. There were no supplies. Both armies were starving and freezing. The monks hoped that by abandoning the monastery to their attackers they would be left alone. But the invaders pursued them up here." Aivlys stopped, hoping that no one would ask the obvious question, but Hugh did just that.

"What happened? Who won?"

"It was a general slaughter. The monks succeeded in decimating the invaders' forces, but in the process almost all of them were killed. They never reestablished the monastery, and soon afterward the people who are the ancestors of both the Gnomonese and Firozians came to the island and met no resistance. So you see, history is in danger of repeating itself."

"No!" said General Sticer, who realized the ominous suggestion in Aivlys's tale of the historic encounter. "There are many differences. First of all, we are not a single isolated monastery but the peoples of two strong nations who have occupied this island for many hundreds of years. We are now the rightful owners of Firoze and Gnomon, or at least its lawful caretakers, for who can truly own the earth? If the Vargans had even come to us and said, 'Our land is poor, our water dwindling, can we share your bounty with you?' we might have said yes, come here and live, we'll make room for you somehow, but instead they came pillaging and shooting their modern cannon, for which we swordsmen and archers have no reply except to disparage their cowardly ways."

"Archers!" Hugh exclaimed, taken by some sudden thought, but then he fell silent again.

"You haven't seen them, my friend, because we consider that form of weaponry also to be less than manly, useful only for hunting, but if the time requires we could send out such a hail of feathered fury that it would seem the air was too thick with them to breathe."

"And do your bows know their owners as well as their swords do?" Aivlys asked. Endimin had told her of the special bonding between swordsman and blade in the Firozian weapons shop.

"Indeed. We have a saying in our country: 'An arrow once released can only be recalled once.'"

"Ah. I would have said it can never be recalled."

"Exactly. Therein is our little magic."

Aivlys was intensely curious but sensed that now was not the time to ask about it. The revels continued. Now that their tongues were loosened and their spirits raised by the application of spirits, the Firozian soldiers lost their timidity around Aivlys and vied with each other to be close to her. Men who hadn't seen their wives and sweethearts for weeks now were thankful merely to look upon the female form from a distance, worshipful and respectful. Aivlys for her part knew her unique station in the camp, and was careful not to display affection for Hugh in the presence of the other men. In this way she remained aloof but accessible, a symbol of all womanhood, a rallying point, a reason to keep fighting.

"Can ye fetch us some grape next time, sweetie?" a bewhiskered veteran called out to her. "I favor Feeruzian wine to the hops."

"Let's hope we'll all be back on our farms and in our homes before I have to perform such feats again," said Aivlys. Her answer moved the men to cheers and tears. They sang their favorite songs to her, offered her the choicest bits of flaked fish and the headiest brew, and went to bed dreaming of beautiful witches.

Later that evening, before they slipped into their respective tents, Hugh asked Aivlys if there was a mountain trail that ran on the Gnomonese side of the Impasse along the spine of the mountains.

"Yes," Aivlys answered. "But it's pretty rugged, and there's no telling what the earthquake and lava flow did elsewhere along the ridge."

"Do you think you could reach the place where your father and the other Gnomonese are camped, without descending into the occupied territory?"

"Maybe," Aivlys said doubtfully. Though she was eager to try, she knew that on these narrow, precipitous mountain paths, one dislodged boulder could create an impassable blockade.

"We need to link up with them somehow," Hugh continued. "The Vargans won't leave them there forever. It would be much better if we could bring them down into this protected meadow with us."

"I'd like that, of course, I'd love to be with my father. I'll go," Aivlys agreed, though somewhere in her sensitive psyche she had a feeling of foreboding about the endeavor.

"Could you leave in the morning?" Hugh asked, and suddenly Aivlys realized why he wanted her to leave: he sensed that the battle was upon them and wanted her out of the meadow before it became a slaughtering ground again, as she had told him it had been once in the past. She began to protest, but then remembered her desire to see her father, and reluctantly agreed to make the trip.

"I'll provide you with a couple of Firozians as bodyguards," Hugh offered, but Aivlys said she preferred to travel on her own. Hugh knew better by now than to try to dissuade his headstrong young love.

"Someday, when there's peace, it'll be very different between us," he said. Their lips brushed together in a light kiss, and they parted for their separate tents.

Aivlys left the next morning without waking Hugh. She took only a gourd full of water, a loaf of bread, and a couple of pieces of salted fish. The sun hadn't crested the mountain peaks yet, there was still a night chill in the air as she walked through the dew-wet grass to the edge of the meadow and found the trail head that led out of the valley. The path started as a gradual gentle ascent, but quickly turned into a series of deep switchbacks as it rose from the valley floor. At every turn Aivlys caught stunning views of the golden meadow, glistening as the first rays of the sun felt their way down the mountainside to touch the grass. She startled a pair of sleepy but watchful Firozian sentries guarding the upper pass in the unlikely event that anyone should try to enter from that side. (No army could advance over the ridge—the trail was far too narrow for the baggage and equipage of a full-sized fighting force.) Except for the few score tents set up in one corner of the open space, Hawk's Heart Meadow looked as it had for hundreds of years, a peaceful glen far removed from the turmoil at sea level. Yet there was a hint, an echo of violence that perhaps only a sensitive soul such as Aivlys could feel, but was it past or future horror that sent shivers through her, or was it only the brisk morning air? To amuse and distract herself, Aivlys began to observe the plants growing along the side of the trail, to see how many she could identify from her schooling with Zentina Wraight. Stifled bluebells with round heads and drooping leaves, those were good for the spell of Discontented Lovers. Spiky thistlefoot, that was useful for taming truculent sheep. Delicate curling bindlestaff—Zentina had made a delicious stew from the tender tips of that fern and by eating it Aivlys had improved her memory several times over. Yes, Zentina had endowed her with an encyclopaedia of knowledge, and the means to use it. The greenery soon gave way, however, to the exfoliated granite of the mountain peaks, where only a few shrubs and patches of green and orange lichen grew among the boulders and rock faces.

At times Aivlys was so high up on the ridge that she was almost on the edge of the Impasse itself, and if the trail had been able to scale the last few score feet she would have been able to look on either side into both countries, but it was called the Impasse for good reason—there was never a place where any but the most daring rope climber could have reached the top of its jagged, saw-toothed crest. The trail stayed firmly on the Gnomonese side of the Impasse. She encountered no one on her trip, except for one curious incident. Nearly halfway through the journey, she heard a clear baritone voice singing in the distance. The smooth tones of the unseen singer bounced off the nearby cliffs and echoed all around her, so that she couldn't identify the source of the deep, round voice.

"Hello!" she cried out, and at once the singing ceased. "Hello!" she tried again, and this time her call was answered by a sung reply:

> Beautiful traveler, why hast thou come
> Up to the mountains under the sun?
> Where dost thou goeth, maiden alone
> Here among lofty cathedrals of stone?

Aivlys didn't know how to respond to this unseen voice—certainly not in song, and perhaps not at all, for how was she to know if the vocalist was friend or foe, despite the sweetness of his words and tone?

"Show yourself," she called out, but the voice did not respond. Though as a farm girl Aivlys was accustomed to walking alone in the hills, she was made nervous by the idea of an unseen stranger observing her. She momentarily regretted turning down Hugh's offer of an escort of soldiers. As she proceeded along the trail she hummed to herself and turned around occasionally to see if anyone was following her, but she never caught sight of anyone. At midafternoon, well over halfway into the trip, she came to a rock slide that buried the trail. To cross it she would have to either descend several hundred feet and work her way across the hillside, or risk a perilous climb over the jumble of house-sized boulders that blocked her path.

As she debated her alternatives, the same distinctive, pleasant voice that had sung to her before addressed her from somewhere very close by: "There's an easy way through, if ye can only see it."

Aivlys jumped back and whirled around but saw no
one.

"Who are you? Where are you?" she demanded in a
tense voice.

"Din't yer godmother tell ye about us?" the hidden
speaker replied teasingly.

"Godmother? I have no godmother."

"Ah, how quickly they forget."

"You mean, Zentina? Oh," said Aivlys, suddenly remembering the snatch of lore that Zentina Wraight had
mentioned to her, about these hermetic mountain people. And Zentina had told her by what means they lured
unwitting guests into their secluded world, but Aivlys
couldn't quite remember how they did it now. She
searched her memory frantically, all the while talking
calmly.

"Uh, come on out, I'm harmless," said Aivlys.

"You perhaps, but there's terrible goings on down
below. You'd do better to stay up here with us," the invisible voice replied.

"I can't. I'm on my way to see my father. Do come
out," Aivlys begged.

"All right, but no tricks now."

"And none from you, either," Aivlys said smartly.
This brought a chuckle from the impish character, who
materialized in front of Aivlys almost out of thin air.
He was small, much smaller than Aivlys had made
Beroth, and he had a puckish face with sharply angled
eyebrows, a pinched nose, and sandy hair. He was
wearing odd leggings and a fringed jacket and felt cap
with a feather in it and heavy leather boots, and he had
a foot-long clay stem pipe clamped between his teeth.

"Ringus Swop's the name. What's yourn?"

"Aivlys Platho." Aivlys extended her hand but the
elfish Swop seemed reluctant to grasp it.

Instead he hopped back a step and said: "Roll up

your sleeve. I have to see if there's any weapons tucked up there."

"I'm unarmed," said Aivlys.

"Then ye're an exception among your peers, my lass, for they're a bloody lot. Explosions day and night we hear, resounding off these old mountain walls. Have ye done gone crazy down there and killed each other completely?"

"We've been invaded," Aivlys explained. "Tell me how I get over this rock pile, will you?"

"Ringus Swop will keep his word, in time, in time. First let's find out if you're a true Gnomonese girl. Let me see a little dance."

"What, here?"

"And why not? Where's a better place to twirl your feet than the mountains, where the air is light and the light is airy? I'll sing ye a tune to cavort by. . . ."

When he said that Aivlys suddenly remembered how the mountain people kept their guests, but she didn't let on. Instead she decided to use some magic of her own.

"I'll dance if you'll sing these rocks away, that are blocking the path to my father," Aivlys promised.

Ringus raised his eyebrows—they made a V on his forehead. "Ye're a clever girlie, aren't ye?" he said at last. "All right, then, first you dance, then I'll sing."

"No, no, you first," Aivlys countered.

"Together, then," Ringus proposed.

Only the two crafty combatants knew of the struggle that was being waged, right there on the narrow trail above Gnomon. Ringus Swop, a seemingly harmless doll-like creature, was trying to capture Aivlys for his very own, and Aivlys was doing her utmost to avoid the trap that would snare her into the world of the Gnomonese mountain folk, where she would be lost forever in the misty veiled recesses of their high hidden world. They circled each other like swordsmen, but there were no weapons on display and both were smiling, though Aivlys's grin was forced. She felt her feet twitching, as if she wanted to cut a caper, and she tried to make them leaden and lifeless, while at the same time she tried to make Ringus sing the song that would move rocks.

"Ye had a good teacher," Ringus grunted after some time had passed and the two of them remained in a standoff. "She taught you well. But really, ye must come and pay us a courtesy call, at least."

"I can't, Mr. Swop. I'm on a mission to save my father and the other Gnomonese."

"Save them? So that they can join in the general massacre later, I suppose?"

"I told you, we didn't start this war. We were attacked. You should be helping us fight these foreigners," Aivlys said crossly, getting rather exasperated.

"Us, become soldiers? Not a chance, m'dear. We avoid bloodshed by avoiding all lowlanders, friend or foe, unless perchance they happen by, as ye did; then we treat them as honored guests. Won't you at least stop in for a cup of tea?"

"I'm touched, honestly," Aivlys answered, trying to be polite, "but I really must be on my way." The magic tug-of-war continued for a few more minutes. Ringus was a devious elf, but he was no match for the youth, strength, and precociousness of Aivlys. Finally he gave up.

"Very well then, you little witch, you win. It's too bad, ye would have made a nice addition to my collection." He made a pouty face, stuck out his tongue, then began to sing in that sonorous baritone:

> Rock wall, take a fall
> Down the dipsy hillside
> Spill your boulders, one and all
> That little miss may pass us by.

A rumbling noise began somewhere under the landslide. Soon the rocks began to pop and crack, as if they were being heated, and they started to roll away off the path and down, creating another thunderous slide into the next valley below. Aivlys waited until she thought it was safe, then dashed across the rubble-strewn trail. When she turned back, Ringus Swop was gone.

13

"ABOUT THESE ARCHERS . . . ," HUGH began, speaking to Commander Rutger, an aide and confidante of General Sticer's. Hugh had seen the man carrying a finely varnished wooden bow into the woods one morning, and had observed him returning with several fat partridge later in the day.

"Yes?"

"Could you demonstrate?"

"What?"

"The special properties of the arrows the General mentioned."

"Ah." Commander Rutger scowled at Hugh, loath to carry out the order his general had issued him, that if the navigator asked, but only if he asked, Rutger was to initiate him into the secrets of Firozian archery. Rutger was a swarthy man with black flashing eyes and little patience. He was especially muscular in the chest and upper arms, qualities that made him a great archer. Two men of ordinary strength would not be able to string his tightly sprung bow. "Very well, then, come with me." He turned his back on Hugh and marched toward the far end of the meadow where Aivlys had vanished into the forest a little earlier.

"Where are we going?" Hugh asked as he hurried behind the commander.

"Hunting!" came the curt reply.

Hugh followed after as fast as his gangly legs would carry him, but the commander was in no mood to make concessions, even to this brazen outsider who had been so instrumental in the few successes the Firozians had thus far achieved against the Vargans. This secret was a direct transmission from his family line, and he resented having to share it with a non-Firozian. Still, the navigator had proved himself several times a worthy ally. Begrudgingly he slowed up and allowed Hugh to catch up with him. They came to a smaller upper meadow, a narrow remove with sloping walls that was a perfect spot to flush birds into a controlled shooting pattern.

"I took quail here yesterday. There should be others," Rutger said in a low voice. "Now sit quietly, and watch."

Hugh was amused by the solemnity of his companion, but he obeyed. Minutes passed. Rutger remained impassively staring at a corner of the meadow where several bushes clumped together into a dense thicket. His arrows remained in their quiver, slung loosely behind his right shoulder. The bow, a marvel of tension, he held at the ready in his left hand. He whistled loudly. The birds lifted, and in a movement faster than a flash Rutger reached behind him, plucked a feather from the quiver, put notch to string, drew, and fired! His first arrow struck the lead bird of the covey, and a second whistled after and caught the next bird rising up. Then an odd thing happened, magic! The birds began beating their wings backward, though they were already dead, each pierced through the heart. The arrows' feathers bristled and ruffled in the reverse breeze, and flew back toward Rutger, dragging their targets along with them. One of the birds dropped off a few feet before it reached the two men, the arrow clattering harmlessly to the ground. The other tumbled into Rutger's outstretched arm, the bird still warm, blood trickling from the fatal shot. He extracted the arrow from its mark and handed it to the amazed Hugh, who examined but could see nothing that should have made the thin projectile reverse its course.

"You've just witnessed the Firozian Fetching Arrow at work," Rutger said with a touch of smugness, pleased at having dazzled the navigator.

"How does it—I mean why . . . ?"

"Like our swords, these arrows are bonded to us when formed. A good archer is at one with his bow, and at one with his shafts. The darts that I send out will come back only once. The second time I loose them they will stay where they fall, or where they strike. But the first time, they seek me out to retrieve for me the fruits of my shooting, or so that I might send a second volley if at first I failed."

"That's better than training a bird dog. Now, it brought back a little game bird. Would a human also come flying back to you if you'd hit him?"

"Or his heart, ripped from his chest, if that's where the barb struck," said Rutger with a pleased smile as he plucked speckled brown feathers from the lifeless quail.

Hugh pondered this gory image for a while before asking another question:

"And if I were to use your bow?"

"You are not connected to the arrows. Your flights would be ordinary archery, without the magic."

"I see. And has this magic ever been used in battle?"

"You heard the general. Archery is not for mass combat, its effects are too deadly, and it's unmanly to fight from such a distance."

"The Vargans seemed to have no such compunctions."

"The Vargans are cowards."

"Or realists, perhaps. When you have such power, it must be hard to resist using it." Hugh toyed with the arrow in his hand. "May I try a shot?"

Rutger shrugged and handed Hugh his bow. The navigator found that he could pull the string back only far enough to bring the arrowhead within a few inches of the leading edge of the bow; Rutger had been able to cock the bow fully until the pointed barb met the wood at the handle. Since there was no game in sight, Hugh aimed at a nearby tree, and succeeded in embedding the missile a few inches into the pulpy wood.

"I'm not the bowman you are, Commander," Hugh acknowledged as he handed the Firozian back his weapon, "but I must know, how many men in the Firozian army are magically gifted like you?"

"Of the men here in the meadow, at least a hundred. Many more are bonded to their swords, which are the true pride and glory of the Firoze people. Archery is merely a hobby, a boy's plaything."

But it may prove decisive in the coming strife, Hugh thought, not wishing to share his idea with the commander who held his own talents in such low esteem. Still, who else was there to test his theory against? "I have an idea that might help us defeat the Vargans, but it involves using these magic arrows. Will your troops use them if ordered?"

"A Firozian always obeys orders," Commander Rutger sniffed.

"Fine," said Hugh. He saw no need to apprise his hostile companion of the gambit he planned for the archers of Firoze. Without another word to each other the two fighters wheeled and headed back down toward the main meadow, leaving the smaller golden field to the birds and small animals who crept back into the idyllic silent grassy space by ones and twos to catch the last rays of the weak afternoon sun.

Aivlys had little time to savor her victory over Ringus Swop in their curious contest of wills. That strange struggle, which seemed to have lasted only a few minutes, actually consumed most of the afternoon. Shadows were lengthening down the canyon walls as Aivlys picked her way across the final twists and turns in the trail. The territory had become more and more familiar to her as she traveled north, because this part of the mountain range was closer to her home. Once or twice she hopped up on a promontory to see if she could catch a glimpse of the fields of her childhood, but a layer of clouds had drifted in from the sea and obscured the lower reaches, while the mountains were still lit by the rosy fading light at the end of the day. As she looked out over Gnomon, it seemed as if the sea itself had surged inland as a gray-white wave breaking over the Gnomon coast and smothering everything in its path. It was breathtaking to stand above the cloud level and see this vast white level layer rising slowly toward her, but Aivlys knew that she would be in trouble if she didn't reach the Gnomon camp before darkness or clouds made travel along the narrow trail exceedingly dangerous. She hurried on, unsure of how much farther she had to travel; as she rounded the last of a taxing stretch of switchbacks onto a straight stretch of trail a commanding voice from somewhere in front of her stopped her, and an enveloping mist had overtaken her.

"Halt! Who goes there?"

"Aivlys Platho of Gnomon," she answered in a clear, fearless way.

"Come forward!" It was a Firozian guard, one of the small party of soldiers who had accompanied the fleeing Gnomonese with Beroth.

"What are you doing out there?" he demanded of her. "You know that all civilians are supposed to stay within the confines of the camp."

"I'm not from the camp. I'm a messenger from the army in Hawk's Heart Meadow."

"And I'm the king of Firoze," the guard scoffed.

"No you're not. General Sticer is the military leader of your country, and I left his tent this morning." The guard, astounded by Aivlys's courage and intimidated by her personal knowledge of the general, lowered his sword and let her pass by. A second sentry accosted her a few yards farther up the trail, but she was spared a second round of interrogation when the man turned out to be Henri Blouchette.

"Aivlys! Bless my heart! How did you get here? Your father will be overjoyed!"

"I walked the Ridge Trail from the place where the Firozian army is camped."

"Come in, come in, I'll have someone take my place so I can lead you to your father."

"Don't bother, Henri, I'll find him. How are things here?"

"Very poorly, Aivlys." Henri Blouchette scratched at his beard. "We've little food and nothing to do. The Vargans harass us from the Firozian side of the Impasse but they haven't tried a full-scale attack yet. Your father and Beroth, an unlikely alliance if I ever saw one, have held things together so far, but we can't live up here forever. As soon as the first snows come, this place'll be uninhabitable."

"Things can't go on this way," Aivlys agreed. "I'll find my father. You stick to your post." The portly (but somewhat slimmer, Aivlys noted) Blouchette saluted her and resumed his vigil. Aivlys wandered into the camp. Unlike the neatly ordered tented field in Hawk's Heart Meadow, this makeshift village was a ragged collection of lean-tos and improvised shelters set up in no particular order, wherever the pitching ground allowed. Women and children lay listlessly within, their faces pinched by hunger. A few recognized Aivlys and waved weakly, but a languid torpor gripped them—none came out to embrace her. Across this desperate scene she saw her father, in discussion with a Firozian solder she didn't recognize, and called out to him. He lifted his head, and she saw that the intervening days had aged him, or perhaps that process had already begun during the strife down below and she hadn't noticed. As he came toward her, his shoulders were slumped with despair and his face was drawn with care, but his eyes were bright with pleasure at the sight of his only child. Aivlys greeted him with a hug but then asked the question that had been on her mind as soon as she saw conditions in the camp.

"Father, why is everyone hungry?"

"There's no food, daughter."

"Haven't you practiced the spell of the Rain of Fish and Grain? That's what I did for the army."

"I tried, Aivlys, but the waterspouts wouldn't reach this high. All we did was create an abundance for the Vargans who are living in our homes, and feeding themselves from the bounty of our farms."

"Ah, what a shame. Perhaps I can do something—"

"Now, now, child. Come, you must rest, you look very tired."

"But the need is so great, Father," Aivlys protested, though all of a sudden she did feel weak and exhausted from her long walk and her spirit contest with Ringus Swop.

"Oh, we'll make do for another few hours. Come to my tent. It's not much more than a sheet thrown over two lines, but it does keep the wind out."

"All right." Aivlys let herself be led to Endimin's humble quarters, and almost as soon as she lay down she fell into a deep sleep and did not wake until sunrise of the next day. Endimin was nowhere to be found when she rose, so she busied herself thinking of another spell that might provide some food for the Gnomonese people, but try as she might she couldn't come up with one. At last it occurred to her what she must do. She bounded out of the tent and was met by Beroth! An awkward moment ensued; neither party knew quite how to start a conversation, but while they stared at each other Aivlys realized that an enormous change had come over Beroth, even more striking than his short-ened stature. His visage, formerly that of a tough, hard-ened warrior, had softened and mellowed. He was almost saintly looking. Aivlys wondered what great event had altered him, and couldn't keep herself from remarking on his changed appearance.

"Yes, it's true, I've become more like a Gnomonese," Beroth answered with some embarrassment.

"How did this happen?"

"Well, first you shrunk me, and then—" Beroth was about to respond when a woman from Gnomon (whom Aivlys knew to be the widow of a man lost at sea some years ago) came running up to Beroth and grabbed him by the hand.

"Come, Beroth, the women need your help, they're raising a tent pole for a laundry room."

Beroth shrugged, gave Aivlys a deferential smile, and allowed himself to be led off. Aivlys watched after them in astonishment. *I've heard it said that love con-quers all,* she told herself, *but I never would have be-lieved it if I hadn't seen it.* It was difficult for her to reconcile the meek character she had just met with the brute who had (directly or indirectly) caused her broth-er's death. She was still shaking her head in wonder-ment when Endimin returned from some errand.

"Ah, I see you've encountered the man in love," he said quietly.

"Yes."

"You did him a big favor when you cut him down to size."

"He didn't think so at the time. Funny how things have worked out. But, Father, I have a plan. I'm going!"

"Not before breakfast."

"But is there anything?"

"Oh, we're not completely starving, yet. Come, I've made you some porridge."

"All right," Aivlys agreed, "then I'm off. I know where we can get some food, right up here in the mountains." After breakfast, and without explaining her idea to Endimin, who knew better than to question his remarkable daughter's intuition, Aivlys set out on the path back toward Hawk's Heart Meadow. She had traveled only a little ways before she heard the same strains that had serenaded her yesterday:

> Beautiful traveler, why hast thou come
> Up to the mountains under the sun?
> Where dost thou goeth, maiden—

"Oh, it's you." The singer, Ringus Swop, suddenly broke into ordinary talk, and rather peeved, ill-humored speech at that. "What do you want? Go away."

"I won't. The Gnomonese people are starving. You must help them."

"I, help them? Darling girl, I've made a lifetime of avoiding the lowlanders. They're nothing but trouble to me. Why should I suddenly come to their aid?"

"Because they're your kinfolk."

"Distant relations," Ringus answered in a cranky tone.

"Because if you don't, then I'll make you sing until

you're hoarse and can't sing anymore, and then I'll tell everyone exactly where you live."

"Ye wouldn't."

"Oh, I certainly would. Now show yourself again or I'll start spelling—"

"All right, all right, no need to threaten." Ringus Swop appeared again, as suddenly as the last time, still bedecked in his quaint mountain finery. "Now what's all this? Why don't they go back to their lowly homes?"

"Believe me, Mr. Swop, there's nothing we'd like to do more, and as soon as we rid ourselves of these invaders we'll leave you alone, but until then, you must help me feed the refugees, they've nothing to eat."

"Ye think I have food enough to feed hundreds?"

"The legends say you have secret fields of plenty," said Aivlys.

"Ye're not a girl to be denied, are ye?"

"When it comes to helping my people, no."

"And I thought loyalty was a trait the lowlanders had forgotten, in their greed and avarice. Well, let's see what we can do. Are ye prepared to visit the land o' th' mountain folk?"

"Temporarily."

Ringus Swop smiled a sly smile and winked her a wink. "Temporarily, o'course, miss. Once you've had the better of Ringus Swop, he won't try ye again. Come along." With that, Ringus disappeared, leaving Aivlys no clue as to how to follow him, but soon thereafter she heard him humming a little way up and off the trail, so she began to scramble across country in pursuit of the rapidly receding echo.

"Wait for me!" she cried out, but she knew that Ringus Swop would not make it easy for her. She chased him up the slopes as fast as she dared, clinging to the loose rock and pressing herself flat against the steep incline, using all fours to keep herself from sliding back down onto the trail, or worse, into the canyon below the trail. After a few minutes of scrabbling ascent, she came to a spot where the talus from a rockfall had left a jumble of huge boulders, still well below the topmost ridge of the Impasse itself. As she began to climb over them she saw a strange light in the distance, glowing from the ground. She worked her way across the boulder field toward the source of the light, which she assumed to be the mouth of a cave. When she reached the opening she discovered that it was not a cave at all but a narrow steep-walled canyon covered by a canopy of sheets of translucent mica, where the weak rays of the sun were intensified by passing through the thin sheath. Inside, the air was much warmer, and moist. Most amazing of all, row upon row of fruits and vegetables grew in pots on tables lined up in the steamy den. Bulbous squashes and ripe gleaming red tomatoes, their skins nearly bursting with juice, vied for space with succulent-looking peaches and plums on miniature trees. It was all so incongruous, up here in the harsh, barren terrain of the upper mountains, that it quite took Aivlys's breath away.

"What magic—" she started to ask, but Ringus Swop appeared at her side to exclaim, "No magic at all, merely good indoor gardening techniques."

"The Gnomonese at sea level could use this idea—"

"You lowlanders don't need it, ye have rich crop land and sunshine for most of the year. It's up here that we've had to be creative."

"It's wonderful," Aivlys said, speaking her admiration plainly.

"Ach, and ye haven't seen the grains from which we make our breads and our ales, ah, that's our finest product, it is."

"Where are the others, the rest of the mountain folk?" Aivlys asked, looking over the deserted greenery of the unlikely farm.

"Ach, do ye want to tussle with each and every one o' them?" said Ringus Swop. "They won't come out. They're a shy lot."

Aivlys realized that she was unlikely to see any of the other little people who inhabited and tended the secret gardens of the mountains, though she would dearly have liked to have met them. "But how am I going to carry enough to supply the village?" she wondered aloud.

"We'll place it on pallets and leave it on the trail, but ye must caution the others to wait until we give the signal before coming to fetch it."

"I will. Now show me around. I'm a farm girl, you know, and I'm fascinated by your growing techniques."

Later that day Aivlys led a group of Gnomonese men back to the spot on the trail where she'd met Ringus Swop. Sure enough, stacked there was a load of the finest-looking vegetables and fruits one could ever imagine. That evening, just as when Aivlys had provided the army with fishes and grains, a feast was prepared and Aivlys treated as a heroine. The women of the camp set to work preserving the abundant supplies that weren't cooked and eaten immediately. Bellies were full and hearts content for the first time in many days. That night Aivlys sat at a campfire with her father and a few of the other members of the Watchmakers' Guild, roasting potatoes over the open fire.

The next morning Aivlys and Endimin left camp, father and daughter on a leisurely stroll through the high country, a walk that would have been pleasant if the situation weren't so desperate.

"The aid of the mountain folk is wonderful, and that you secured it is ingenious," said Endimin, "but it buys us only a few weeks' time. The Vargans can strangle us slowly up here. How are we going to rid ourselves of them?"

"We have to make ourselves so distasteful, and the

effort to subdue us so painful, that they give up and go away," Aivlys answered.

"Do you think that's possible?" Endimin wondered.

"Yes, but we lack leadership. Aside from the few members of the Guild, the Gnomonese people aren't very good at it. There aren't enough of us. Hugh has been a good addition, and of course the Firozians can take control when necessary, but if the Vargans find out how few of us there are and go after us, I'm afraid all resistance will crumble."

"Should we attack?" Endimin asked, and it might seem strange that father was asking daughter for advice, but the elder Platho had come to realize his daughter's superior powers; she was extraordinary even among the Gnomonese race of magic-makers.

"That would be Hugh's impulse," said Aivlys, "but I don't see how we can. In direct conflict they've defeated us at every turn. It's only by the protracted method of harassment and delay that we've scored any successes."

"And that requires time, which we don't have."

"Imagine that," Aivlys said wryly, "Gnomonese without time. It's almost sacrilegious."

"I'm glad to see you haven't lost your sense of humor through all this," said Endimin.

"Oh, Father," she said, and they hugged, tenderly, both thinking of that first day when Endimin brought Runny's broken body back from these same mountains.

After a while Endimin composed himself and continued the conversation. "We need to find out what they're up to down there."

"Yes, I've been thinking the same thing. I'm going to visit the city, and maybe the old farm."

"But how? They capture and kill any Gnomonese they find, even old women and children, I've heard."

"I'm going to disguise myself."

"As what, a Vargan?" Endimin asked, dubious that

this feat was possible even given Aivlys's considerable powers of enchantment.

"No, as something they would never harm." Instead of returning to camp with her father, Aivlys climbed higher into the mountains, until she was among the tallest peaks, where the wind was chill and there were patches of snow that never melted, tucked in crevices among the scrubby pines that clung to the bare rock. There she found a flat rock overlooking the landscape of Gnomon, and sat down cross-legged to summon a visitor by unheard plaintive calls. She waited a long time, until the cold crept into her bones, but still she sat unmoving, until the shadow of huge wings passed across her and she held her hand up to block the dim sun and saw a frigate bird looping around to brush his wings against her face.

"Sister, may I fly with you?" she asked in a language without words. The gorgeous bird, whose wingspan was longer than Aivlys was tall, dipped her wings in assent, but Aivlys did not climb on the back of the creature in flight. Her soul rose invisibly from her body and joined with that of the aerial gymnast who swooped and turned. Then Aivlys was looking down on her own inert body and feeling the pleasant sensation of feathers at the ends of her fingers, and for a moment she was giddy with the dipping, diving, soaring freedom of flight, but soon she controlled her dizziness and let the gliding sensation take over, and together the bird and the spirit of Aivlys plunged down toward Gnomon, while her body, stiff and insensate, protected by a spell, remained motionless on the rock ledge.

When the big bird appeared in the skies over Gnomon, a careless Vargan soldier notched an arrow in his bow to shoot it down, for sport. As he was about to let fly with his thoughtless shot, a Vargan sailor stopped him.

"Don't kill that one, it's a frigate bird. Good luck for seamen."

"Ah, you don't believe those old superstitions, do you," the soldier scoffed.

"I do, and you'd better, too, if you want to see your wife and children again. It's a long passage back to Vargas, remember that."

"All right, old salt, for you I'll let this one go, but if I see a fat partridge—"

"Hunt all the birds you want, just don't kill that one," the sailor repeated. The frigate flew on, unaware of how narrowly it (and Aivlys) had missed becoming the target of a fatal arrow. It circled and finally came to roost on the crumbling ruins of the old Clocktower, which had been destroyed during the shelling before the invasion. From her perch on the shattered structure Aivlys could see all of Gnomon. Her eyes were sharper than she had ever experienced in her human body. She could see far out over the ocean, and back up toward the mountains, and everywhere within the town she could pick out details that would have escaped her human eyes. What she saw troubled her greatly. The Vargans were clearly making preparations to colonize the entire island. They had occupied all the farms and homes that hadn't been blown apart or burned. A cleanup was under way already; work teams of soldiers were busy clearing rubble and charred timbers from the streets of Gnomon. There were indications that the Vargans planned to rebuild the Clocktower. Scaffolding had been erected around the last freestanding wall where Aivlys the frigate bird now clung. The pier was crowded with ships, as the Vargans had moved the flagship *Regina* and part of their fleet into the harbor, no longer fearing retaliation from the scattered Gnomonese and Firozian forces. All that was left was for them to remove the remaining inhabitants and the island would be theirs. Aivlys spread her wings and prepared to launch herself from the precarious ledge where she stood (on thin legs whose toes were horny claws) but just then her piercing vision caught sight of a curious movement near the water. She gripped the edge of her perch more tightly and turned her far-reaching eyes toward the spot. A child was dancing frantically in the street—what would cause him to twist and jerk so? Then she realized, he was on fire! Nearly invisible flames and thin smoke rose from his twitching body. A group of Vargan soldiers and sailors were gathered around the frenetic youth, who was beating himself with his arms and rolling on the ground violently in an effort to put out the flames, which must be burning him horribly, yet none of the onlookers was attempting to help him. With two great wing beats Aivlys cast herself into flight and pulled back on her feathers to streamline her form and hasten her dive toward the boy. She swept down on the crowd, all the while croaking loudly, though she hardly recognized her own bird voice. With outstretched talons she plucked the boy from the earth and struggled skyward. The rushing wind put out the flames, but her talons dug into his smoldering clothing and broke the skin—it must be terribly painful! As fast as she could, Aivlys climbed in spiraling circles, catching the updrafts from the ocean breeze, and soon reached the mountain redoubt where she had left her body. As quickly as she could she reentered her human form and laid the bleeding body of the boy on the rock beside her.

"Thank you, my sister," she said to the frigate bird, who cawed her approval of Aivlys's daring rescue and flew off. Aivlys turned her attention to the boy. His burns were not as serious as Aivlys had feared—a heavy coat had protected him from worse injury.

"What's your name?"

"H-h-herve?"

"Herve? Herve Josthen? I know your mother,

Gislen." The Josthen family was one of the poorer ones in the city, but respectable. Christo Josthen worked as a porter in the sailors' lodgings.

"She's dead," the boy answered in a small voice. "They're both dead. I been living in the trash dump. 'Til they found me."

Aivlys wanted to hug the frightened, hurting little boy but his burns prevented her from the human contact they both longed for; she squeezed his left hand, which was unharmed.

"From now on," she told him, "you're my brother. My father Endimin and I will take care of you." The boy said nothing, but Aivlys felt a pressure from his hand in response. As soon as Herve had recovered sufficiently, Aivlys hoisted him onto her shoulders and started for camp. She walked as gingerly as she could, but there were places on the steep trail where she was forced to clamber over boulders or slide down gravelly slopes, and he moaned in pain when she jostled him too much. When she reached camp she was quickly surrounded by a crowd of anguished women who wanted to help her tend to the boy's wounds, but Aivlys brought him directly to Endimin's tent. She applied salves carefully to Herve's reddened skin, and held a bowl of warmed milk to his lips so he could drink. Endimin came in and knelt next to the youth. He stroked Herve's singed hair and passed his hand softly over the boy's forehead.

"He's a plucky little fellow," said Aivlys.

"Actually, he got plucked, the way I hear it," Endimin commented, looking at his daughter with pride.

"She was a bird," Herve said simply. "She picked me up."

"Yes."

"Why were those soldiers hurting you?" Aivlys asked.

"I heard 'em talkin'," Herve said. "They're gonna 'tack tomorrow."

"Are you sure?"

"'That's why they burned me when they caught me," Herve whispered. "They din't want me to tell nobody."

Endimin and Aivlys looked at each other. If the battle started tomorrow, there was no way either of them could be present to lend the aid of Gnomonese magic to their side. Hugh and the Firozians were on their own.

14

THE PENULTIMATE BATTLE IN THE WAR
for the island of Firoze-Gnomon began as a skirmish on the trail below
Hawk's Heart Meadow. Vargan advance troops probed the pickets General Sticer had posted. The Vargans
were looking for another way up the
slope to the meadow, but there was
none; if they wanted to encounter the
Firozian army they would have to
fight their way up the narrow pass
onto the level plain. Before attempting a frontal advance, the
Vargan command sent a messenger
forward to offer terms of surrender,
for the second time in the invasion.
General Sticer was in no mood to
consider giving up; he sent the envoy
back to Vargan lines without even
opening the envelope containing the
demand for submission. Privately,
however, he knew that his position

was hopeless. He was outnumbered, and there was no place for him to retreat, his troops were backed up against the impenetrable mountain wall. A single hiker like Aivlys was able to move across the Ridge Trail, but an army, with all its baggage and accoutrements, would never be able to escape by the higher path.

With General Sticer's permission, Hugh had assembled a company of Firozian archers at the front. Usually archers are positioned behind the lines, to launch their flights of arrows over the heads of the foot soldiers engaged at the battle line, but Hugh had a different idea, based on the special magic he had seen in Commander Rutger's demonstration. When the first wave of Vargan assault troops stormed up the trail, crowding and jostling each other double and triple abreast, Hugh's archers let loose a volley that was timed and aimed to follow the sinuous snaky path in a narrow range. The arrows whistled in and found their mark, then magically spun backward and returned to their senders, most of the shafts with their flint heads dripping blood. The Vargans had never seen arrows act in such a fashion, and were momentarily stunned, but their commanders, at their backs, pushed them forward over their fallen comrades, and the second hail of lethal missiles hardly deterred them from their forward surge. When the Vargans reached the steep wall at the base of the cliff protecting the meadow, they fanned out, produced hidden ropes with metal grappling hooks attached to them, and tossed the hooks upward until the barbs caught in crevices or dug into trees. Then the attackers started to scale the rock wall. By this means they widened the perimeter that the Firozians had to defend, and forced General Sticer to redeploy his troops along the cliff to keep from being outflanked. The Vargans were easy targets as they tried to haul themselves up the sheer face. Some were dashed back to earth when the Firozians loosened the hooks that had held the ropes in place.

Others were bombarded with rocks and logs until they
lost their grip and fell screaming to earth, but the diversion was enough to permit the main body of troops to
push up the trail and force an opening in the defensive
line. The Firozian troops gradually fell back as more
and more Vargans reached the meadow. Soon they were
pouring through the gap like a swarm of angry bees.
The Firozians regrouped in the center of the meadow
and formed a second line of defense using the contours
of the field as their perimeter.

Now the Firozian swords came into play. They had
been patiently waiting release from their scabbards,
hungrily smelling the blood drawn by the arrows, eager
to leap at the hated foe. Blind though they were, they
recognized foreign steel in the counterpart swords of
the Vargan adversaries, a threat to their own supremacy.
As soon as they were drawn, they struck out, lashing
and swiping, eager to slice, cut, maim, kill. The Vargan
troops had seen these strangely alive weapons before,
and feared them, rightfully so, but the odds were in
their favor and their officers pushed them forward relentlessly, so that even as those in front fell, the ones
behind them were forced to engage, often stepping and
even fighting on the fallen bodies of their comrades.
The thin mountain air was filled with the screams and
moans of the wounded and dying, while the forest
around fell silent as birds and animals fled or withdrew
into hiding. The stream that ran so peacefully through
the sward turned red and the mead grass was slick with
blood. Slowly the Vargans began an encircling action
that threatened to surround the Firozian army entirely.
Hugh, fighting at the very perimeter, saw what they
were up to and called out to Commander Rutger,
"They're trying to cut us off. Fall back! You know
where!" for Hugh didn't want to announce to the
Vargans that there was an upper trail out of the swale.
Hugh watched from the corner of one eye as Com-

mander Rutger communicated Hugh's message to General Sticer, and saw the general shake his head as if to say that the Firozians would not retreat a step further, but would make their stand here in the meadow.

Stumbling and falling and tripping over fallen bodies, his hair matted with sweat and foamy, frothy blood, Hugh fought his way across the front until he could shout to the general, "There's one way out. We must take it or we'll all perish!"

"Go, then. You've done enough. The Firozian army stays here," the general replied grimly. Hugh could see that there was no arguing with the man, he was beyond reason. Caught up in the death throes of his army and his country, General Sticer could see only one path for the Firozians, a fight to the death.

If only we had some magic as a diversion, Hugh thought, knowing well that Aivlys would not appear on this day to save them. He looked around him wildly, in futile desperation, then saw the apparition he had hoped for. An old woman was tottering toward him, oblivious to the carnage that raged around her. It was the spirit of Zentina Wraight.

"Help us!" Hugh pleaded.

"I cannot help you win, but I can save a few souls," she answered, her voice hollow. No one else in the battlefield seemed to see or hear her, and for a second Hugh thought he had gone mad from the insanity of the battle and was hallucinating, but Aivlys had shown him enough of Gnomonese magic that he believed what he saw.

"Please hurry!" he cried.

"Tell the men to lie down," she said.

"What? The Vargans'll slaughter us."

"Tell them to lie down, then get up and run for the mountains. And tell that general that if he doesn't obey, Firoze will fall."

"When should they get up?"

"They'll know." The old woman vanished before his eyes. Hugh rushed through the tumult to General Sticer's side, slashing left and right with his sword to clear a path through oncoming Vargans. He was almost exhausted when he reached the small clearing where the general's personal guard had ringed the leader of the Firozians for a hopeless last stand.

"General, help has arrived!" Hugh burst out.

The general looked around wildly with a frenzied expression of sudden hope, then turned to stare at Hugh.

"I see none!" he yelled.

"Trust me," said Hugh. "The Gnomonese are going to work some magic. Order your men to lie down."

"Are you out of your mind?"

"I thought I was, but I'm not. Do it! Now!"

In the midst of the fighting and turmoil, the general glared at Hugh. Then his face softened, and a strange look of bewilderment came over it. *Zentina Wraight must have shown herself to him,* Hugh thought, for in the next second the general was shouting the order to his men, "Get down, lie down!" As soon as they complied the astonished Vargans raised their swords to apply the final killing thrusts to their foes but then the air was suddenly filled with vapor, a thick, choking mist that settled in to all but the two feet above the ground where the men of Firoze lay. The Vargans were like ants trapped in honey—they couldn't move their limbs, while the Firozians scurried beneath the dense fog until they reached open air.

"Now, run!" the general shouted. Hugh and Commander Rutger led the men up the trail toward the Impasse. The effect lasted only a few minutes, but long enough for the remnants of the Firozian army to flee unseen out the upper end of the meadow and toward the safety of the mountains. When the fog lifted the Vargans looked around in amazement. The meadow was littered with casualties from both sides but the fighting was over, and their opponents had fled while the Vargans were under Zentina's spell of Mist Time. Hawk's Heart Meadow was in Vargan possession and the Firozian army was defeated and dispersed. The war for the island was essentially over, the decisive battle having been fought on a remote mountain field far from the cities and farms that were the prized possessions of the contest. Three hours after the end of the fighting a Vargan scout discovered the rear trail toward the ridge, but the Vargan commander disdained to chase the retreating foe.

"We've routed them. Let the weaklings starve or freeze to death up there."

Along the ridgeline, the decimated Firozian army limped and faltered its way toward the refugee camp. Aivlys's prediction of the outcome of the battle had come true. Would her second prophecy also be realized? As the first beaten and bedraggled soldiers dragged their feet into camp, she searched every face for Hugh, and found him helping a badly injured soldier lie down among the wounded. The two lovers embraced, a small light of hope amid the human misery around them.

"You were right, Aivlys. They defeated us easily. If it hadn't been for your friend, we would all be lying slain in the meadow."

"My friend?"

Hugh told Aivlys of the mysterious appearance of Zentina Wraight and the paralyzing fog that helped them flee. Aivlys said nothing but thanked the old woman silently from her heart. Somehow, though, she knew that the final conflict would be hers, and hers alone to win or lose. The disheartened Firozians were in no condition to mount another offensive; in fact they were resigned to subjugation and possibly exile. When all the wounded had been tended to and the troops fed from the bounty of Ringus Swop, the leaders of the

Firozian and Gnomonese people gathered in Endimin's shabby tent to discuss the possibility of surrender. General Sticer and Hugh had not yet divested themselves of their bloodstained battle clothes; they looked fearsome, like apparitional butchers from some horrible dream. Endimin and Aivlys were haggard from the rigors of living in the outdoors. The other Firozian commanders and Gnomonese citizens such as Henri Blouchette and Basco Fournier all displayed expressions of concern on their faces. General Sticer opened the meeting: "I never thought I'd say this, but I believe it's time to ask for mercy at the hands of the enemy."

"General, we should ask for peace but not resign ourselves yet to defeat," said Aivlys. Her remark puzzled the group, but most of those in attendance had learned to listen to the wisdom of this girl who was wise beyond her years.

"You have a plan?" Commander Rutger asked her bluntly.

"I have an intuition, a feeling, that everything will turn out well for us in the end."

"I wish I could say the same," General Sticer said wearily. "In all my years of military service I have never suffered a worse defeat than the one inflicted on my troops today. Nor have I ever run from a battleground. It was humiliating."

"To run away is better than to die, because it means you can fight again, when circumstances favor you," Hugh pointed out sagely. "If we had been overwhelmed, we would have had to surrender. By fleeing, we avoided complete defeat, and we still have a chance to win."

"In any case," Endimin broke in, "we've no choice but to ask the Vargans what their terms are going to be. We can offer to work for them, as servants if need be, if they'll let us stay on our beloved land, or we can submit to exile, the gods know where."

"It won't come to that, Father," Aivlys promised, and her conviction reassured the group as they dwelt silently and morbidly on Endimin's words. "Let's just approach them and see what happens." There was little dissent from the Gnomonese citizens, who were weary and sick of war. The Firozians resisted for a while, but they had no alternative plan to offer, no military tactic or strategy that would allow them to keep fighting without an organized army and having been driven far from their homes and cut off from their supplies. At the last General Sticer agreed to accompany a truce party down to the city of Gnomon to request terms from the Vargans. The Firozians insisted on wearing full battle dress, which was risky even though they would walk in under the white flag.

"If I must hand over my sword to Admiral Francisco, I'm going to do so with my uniform on."

"It'll balk at his hand, won't it, General?" Endimin asked.

"It'll do what I tell it to," General Sticer replied.

"In the morning, then," said Hugh, calling an end to the grim meeting. He was eager to spend a little time with Aivlys. After the men left the tent, she boiled water and made him strip down so that she could wash his clothes while he cleaned himself of others' blood. When he took off his shirt she saw that he had suffered two light sword cuts that left searing red streaks across his chest. She reached out to touch them with her healing ways, but he pulled back.

"No magic," he said. "I want these scars to remember this day by."

"That's silly," she said.

"To you, perhaps."

"Tomorrow we're going to save Firoze and Gnomon," Aivlys insisted, repeating her prediction.

"What makes you so sure?" asked Hugh.

"The ghost of Zentina Wraight told me," Aivlys
joked, even as she winced while trying to clean the
crusted blood from the sword scratches on Hugh's
chest. When he pulled away again, she scolded him:
"Don't worry, I won't heal you, I just want to make
sure there's no infection."

15

ADMIRAL FRANCISCO RETREATED BE-
lowdecks and locked himself in his
cabin. In one corner of the neat, com-
pact quarters stood a chest of dense,
dark woods, teak and mahogany, with
squat legs and iron filigree decorating
its front. Taking a key from a chain
that hung around his neck, Francisco
moved to open the chest. Before
doing so, however, he knelt before it
and uttered words of prayer, or were
they an enchantment? After bowing
deeply, Francisco inserted the key into
the ornate lock and turned it to the
right. The door opened with a clean
clicking sound. Within the chest was
a vase or urn of porcelain, deep black,
not shiny but dull, unreflective, as if it
were absorbing all the light around it.
The cover of the vase was secured by
an elaborate brass clasp that fit tightly
to the top lip of the vessel. A look of

deep respect crossed Francisco's face as he stared at the container. With extreme care he lifted it from its resting place and carried it to his writing desk, a tiny fold-down piece of planking hung from chains off the bulkhead. He seemed unwilling to let go of the jar because the ship was rocking slightly despite being at anchor. For several long minutes he sat in contemplation of the strange cask.

A knock on the door disturbed his reverie.

"Who is it?"

"Lhosa, sir."

"Enter."

Lieutenant Lhosa opened the door and stooped into the cramped room, then flattened his back against the wall in terror.

"Admiral, sir!"

"Yes, Lieutenant?"

"Is it safe, sir?"

"As long as the seal is not broken there is no danger, Lieutenant. Relax."

But the lieutenant did not relax, he remained with one hand on the door and his body rigid with fear. For the Vargans, too, had magic. Contained within the ceramic pot on Francisco's writing desk was the only spell known to the Vargans, a single malevolent force known as the Black Wind, which was (as it sounds) a fiercely destructive whirlwind they could summon to attack their enemies. Its effects lasted only a minute or two, but could be directed to a specific target. The Vargans tended to use it only in extreme need, for it was so violent and unpredictable that it sometimes turned against those who summoned it and decimated them instead of the enemy. This is what caused the lieutenant to flinch at the sight of the open chest. In an earlier campaign he had seen the Black Wind in action, on the lonely, disastrous field at Druhorst, when the vile storm wiped out an entire regiment of the opposition, but carried off half his men as well.

"We are going to use this against the islanders, sir?"

"If necessary. What do you think?"

"I'd rather fight them than unleash this horror," the lieutenant said plainly. Another leader might have been offended, but Admiral Francisco valued his lieutenant's frankness.

"I appreciate your concern, Lhosa. I too was at the battle of Druhorst when that catastrophe occurred. But we don't have time or the supplies to maintain a lengthy siege against these obstinate people. We need a decisive victory, and the Black 'Horror,' as you call it, can provide us with that advantage."

"Then you've made up your mind, Admiral?"

"I have. Now I seek only the proper opportunity for an action. What do you suggest?"

"Hmmm. I do have a suggestion. Don't use it on their army as a whole, it puts us in too close proximity. Lure their leaders out on some pretext, and destroy them with it. Without leadership their defense against our siege will collapse quickly."

"A good idea, Lhosa. Let me think on it. You are dismissed."

Lhosa left without bringing up the subject that had initially brought him to the Admiral's cabin. Outside, a summer storm was building, darkening the horizon with savage-looking clouds, but Lhosa hardly gave them a glance. However, he ordered the mainsails furled and the outer hatchways secured, almost absentmindedly. His thoughts were on that other, mystical whirlblast, whose fury he had witnessed once before. Such enchantments were against his religion, against the religion of all good Vargans. The queen had sent them off with great hopes, to be sure, and she expected them to make sacrifices, even give up their lives if necessary, for the greater well-being of the realm, but not at the expense of their souls. Surely not. At some point a man must decide for himself whether the glory of the empire was justification enough for his individual actions, and to Lhosa's mind, the use of the Black Wind was shameful—no, he would have no part in it. If Francisco wanted to take that decision upon himself and sully his own soul with it, so be it, but he, Lhosa, would not acquiesce. Let them hang him for treason, he would die easier knowing that he had not been the one to let loose that evil thing. He had made up his mind. If the opportunity arose, he would prevent his own admiral from committing that sin, by force if necessary.

Word of the Vargan victory at Hawk's Heart Meadow reached Admiral Francisco that very evening. The indigenous people of the island had been vanquished at last. Their military high command and some scattered troops had escaped by means of some devilishness, but they had made known their willingness to bargain for terms of surrender. Here was his chance to annihilate the leadership once and for all. With their rulers out of the way, the rest of the inhabitants could be led by the nose onto transport ships and dumped in some wasteland, he didn't care where, while this beautiful, bountiful, pleasant island would be his, for the glory of the empress and the empire, of course. He issued orders for the representatives of the conquered people to meet him at the knob of land they called by the unimaginative name of Headland Cove, but which he would, that day, rename in honor of the empress's consort, Prince Madrido. How fitting, that the destruction of the headmen of Firoze and Gnomon would take place where they had had the audacity, the rank gall, to set ablaze a ship of the realm. He would set the Black Wind on them, and wipe them off the face of the earth forever.

"Bring me my sword," he shouted to his cabin boy, "and tell Lhosa to prepare a landing party." With a curiously cruel delight he returned to the cabinet, where the blackest magic in the Vargan repertoire waited with all its fury contained within a single vessel of hardened clay.

The Firoze-Gnomon truce party waited on the bluff above Headland Cove. They had wandered out to the edge of the point, where they could look down one side into the peaceful bay of Headland Cove and down the other onto rocky wastes. On the Firozian side of Headland Cove the cliffs dropped straight into the water. A single sandbar that barely raised its scraggly head from the choppy water was the only feature that distinguished the rugged coastline. There wasn't much left to say; what they had seen in Gnomon had left them all pessimistic about the outcome of the talks between themselves and Admiral Francisco. The Vargans were settling in for a colonization of the Island, and their plans did not include allowing the Firozians and Gnomonese to coexist with them.

"I saw them eating the flesh of animals we wouldn't touch," said one of the Firozians, pausing to spit after he spoke.

"There's nothing wrong with differences in their habits," Endimin pointed out gently. "It's their intolerance, and their brutality, that make me think we'll be better off if we have to relocate to another land. They—"

Endimin stopped in midsentence. He was watching a strange low cloud, funnel-shaped, blacker than any rain cloud he had ever seen before, that had appeared far on out on the horizon but was moving toward them at frightening speed.

"What the devil?" said General Sticer, who had now seen the thing, too.

"The devil's work is right," Hugh said, panic evident in his excited voice. "That's the Black Wind!"

"What?"

"Vargan magic. The only one they possess, but it's wicked. They use it against their enemies only when they want to completely annihilate them."

"Why haven't they used it against us in battle?"

"It's unpredictable. It might have turned on their own troops, it's been known to happen. But now they have us out here alone, it's perfect."

Aivlys had been staring like the others at the black menace bearing down on them. She started toward the Firozian side of the bluff to get a better look at the incoming cloud, and wasn't watching her step when she wandered too close to the edge and lost her footing. Suddenly she was falling, tumbling through space, and the water was rushing up at her. Instinctively she threw out her arms and performed an awkward impromptu dive, luckily plunging into the deep water between the cliff's edge and the sandbar. When she surfaced, gasping for breath, she swam slowly to the sand and pulled herself onto it. Looking up, she saw the others peering down at her from a great height. Dizzy and out of breath, she lay down on the sand and closed her eyes.

Up above, Hugh was beside himself. "A rope! We need a rope—where can we get one?"

"The old bells at the monastery, MainSpring, they have ropes connected to them!" Endimin remembered.

"Come on, we've got to get her out of there before the Black Wind hits, or she'll die!"

Hugh led a charge up the hill toward MainSpring, the site of his brilliant delaying action (with the help of Aivlys and the ghost army of monks) against the Vargans. He reached the bell tower first and yanked at the ropes but despite their age the tightly wound hemp fibers were still intact and he succeeded only in set-

ting the bells to ringing wildly. Dashing madly up the
stairs to the belfry, he was again the first to reach the
turret where the bells hung. It was impossible to reach
the ropes without climbing out onto the bells themselves, so Hugh jumped across empty space and
landed on the largest brass fixture. Oblivious to the
threats to his own safety, he slid down the bell, which
fortunately for Hugh had been cast with handholds for
transport, until he could maneuver his way like an ac-
robat into the inside of the huge musical chime. He
had to hang upside down a hundred feet in the air, his
legs wrapped around the immense clapper, in order to
loosen the tight knot where the rope was affixed. It
fell to the ground like a severed serpent, coiling in a
pile where Firozian soldiers lifted it up and looked up
at Hugh questioningly.

"Yes, go, go, I'll catch up!" he shouted, and they
obediently ran off with the hefty rope looped over their
shoulders. Hugh swung to and fro to send the clapper
into a pendulumlike movement back toward the edge of
the casting. He leaped for life and caught hold of a handle by one hand, and there he dangled, unable to reach
the other handle or haul himself up. Commander
Rutger, who had followed Hugh up the bell tower, arrived at that moment and saw his predicament. Without
a moment's hesitation he too vaulted across nothingness
onto the bell. His landing caused it to swing dangerously and threatened to shake Hugh off his precarious
handhold and send him crashing to the floor below, but
somehow Hugh hung on. Rutger worked his way down
the side of the bell until he was able to offer his hand
to Hugh and pull him to safety. The two men clutched
each other for balance on the swaying bell, then one at
a time bounded back onto the platform surrounding the
bells.

"Thank you, Commander."

"For what?" the Firozian asked.

"For risking your life to save mine."

"We need you," Rutger answered simply, but there was the hint of a laugh in his voice.

"Come on, then, help me save my betrothed's," Hugh cried out, and ran past the Firozian to race down the stairs. The soldiers made slow progress under the surprising weight of the lengthy rope; Hugh caught up with them by the time they had reached the open space that led out onto Headland Bluff. Fetching the rope had taken only a few minutes, but by the time Hugh reached the bluff the Black Wind had swelled as it ascended until it blotted out the sun and hung over the earth like a huge, dark anvil about to drop on them. The wind was rising; the outer edges of the deadly cloud swirled in advance of its dense center. Hugh ran to the dropoff and took one look to see that Aivlys was still there, then helped the soldiers tie off the top end to a nearby rock. They pushed the bulky coil off the cliff, where it plummeted as Aivlys had and dangled into the water.

"Come on!" Hugh yelled. "Everyone down the rope. We'll be more protected there anyway than up here on the bluff."

One by one the group lowered themselves to the water. Hugh was first off the rope and rushed to Aivlys's side. She looked at him dreamily, as if she were still stunned from her fall. Her father also came to kneel beside her, but she assured them that she was fine, the water had broken her fall, she wasn't even bruised.

"You were flying again," Endimin managed to joke, though he was frantic with worry over their plight.

The rest of the rescuers splashed out onto the sandbar and collapsed in fatigue. Above them the sky had turned furious, and it seemed as if night had descended, yet it was still midafternoon. A frightening noise could be heard in the distance, as if the sky itself was about to be shattered.

"We may as well lie down and die. The situation is hopeless," one of the Firozians moaned.

At that point Endimin rose wearily to his feet and looked around him at the brave group huddled under the overarching cliffs of Headland Bluff on this stretch of inaccessible sand. His eyes fell on his daughter Aivlys, clutching the arm of Hugh Boisset.

"There is one possible solution, but it is fraught with danger," he said.

"What is that? Speak up, man, now is the time!" General Sticer responded.

"Or now is not the time."

"Don't play games, what do you mean?"

"I think now is the time for No Time."

"And what is that?"

"The most powerful spell in the repertoire of the Gnomon. No Time is when we take a slice of existence and make as if it never happened. The sublime second chance that all of us wish for at some time or another—of all the peoples in the world, we alone, the Gnomonese, can offer it—but at a price."

"What price?"

"The price of great danger, for if the spell fails, or if something goes wrong in the Second Pass—"

"Second Pass?" General Sticer had to shout because the approaching blackness was howling and the water turning frothy all around them.

". . . then there is no remedy possible—the people involved, everyone within the power of the spell will vanish, forever, as if they had never existed, and they and all their heirs throughout eternity will be voided, nulled out, removed from the ledger of the living."

"If we don't do something soon that will happen to us anyway—look there, the sky darkens, the Black Wind descends upon us!" Again the general raised his voice, he was nearly screaming in Endimin's ears, and no one else in the group could hear their conversation except Aivlys, who had come over to join them.

"Agreed. There is one more risk involved." Endimin paused, as if to gather himself, and Aivlys saw that he was trembling slightly. He too was shouting now, and they all had to fight to remain standing against the gathering gale. "The one who incants the enchantment may not be among those taken by the Pass."

"You mean—"

"Yes. If I do not go with you I may be left here to face the Black Wind myself."

"Then I will say the words, Father." Aivlys stepped forward, and before her father could refuse her, which he certainly would have done, she shut her eyes tightly and quickly uttered the words of the spell:

"Clock-ticking Time passes. Clock stopping, past Time, in No Time. Time and Time Again. One Moment, No Moment, the Eternal Moment. Now!!!"

There was a clap like distant thunder, and then a whooshing, swirling sound like a cyclone passing nearby, but softer, and without the effects of a ripping wind, and then silence. When Aivlys opened her eyes, her companions were gone. She was alone on the water-ringed beach, as she had been a few minutes ago, when she fell. The Black Wind, which just a few seconds before had been bearing down on them, was still a dot approaching in the distance.

But what do I do differently, that this dread hour does not repeat itself? Aivlys asked herself, for she knew that soon the band of rescuers would be arriving as they did before, to save her, and instead would be trapped with her again, unless she could change the course of events this time. She looked around her. This barren spit of sand offered little inspiration. There was no place to hide, and nothing useful to make into weapons or defenses. All she had gained was another chance—what she made of it was up to her, and her alone. Already the Black Wind was a dark blotch on the horizon, hurtling toward her like fate.

From above she heard a shout—it was Hugh Boisset, just as before, leading the effort to rescue her. The same rope was lowered down the cliff face. Aivlys could climb up the rope, but that would leave her and the others in the same predicament as before. Aivlys tugged at it to see if she could yank it down and thus prevent them from ending up trapped with her on the beach, but it was firmly in place. She tried to shout to them, but as before the rising wind drowned out her words, so it didn't make any difference that this time she was saying something quite different. It was happening all over again. Aivlys panicked and ran screaming up and down the enclosed beach. Then she looked back and saw her footprints in a looping pattern on the sand, and an idea came to her.

She carefully smoothed over the exposed surface and began to trace words in the sand: DON'T COME—FATHER—TIME. Would they get it? Would they understand? She was sure that Endimin would make the right decision, but could he stop Hugh, the headstrong navigator, from plunging ahead and bringing down the whole rescue party with him?

Up above on the cliff edge the rescue team was preparing for the descent. Endimin was already troubled, his Time sense twitching with a nagging awareness—hadn't he experienced this already? But it's all so subtle, this playing with Time. He couldn't be sure—how would he know? He wanted to tell his comrades "Stop! There's something wrong here!" but what could he say to make them believe him. He peered over the edge at his daughter, his only remaining relative and heir, trapped on a tiny sandbar and threatened by rising tides. Would they reach her in time? Ah, that word again! *But look,* he thought, *she's acting very strangely, running around on the beach like a crazy woman. Now what?*

She's gone insane, the danger has driven her mad—no, wait, she's dragging her feet deliberately ... making shapes ... she's—

"Wait! She's sending us a message!" Endimin yelled as Hugh Boisset began to let himself down over the cliff onto the rope ladder.

"We've got to hurry, man! The tide rises fast here—we've only got a few minutes."

"Wait, I tell you! What's that? 'Don't come'! She's telling us to stay up here."

"Do you want her to drown, then?" Hugh shouted, halfway off the edge and already swaying on the perilous rungs.

"She's warning us—"

"All right, you all stay. I'm going down to get her."

"Hugh!" Endimin cried, but it was too late, Hugh Boisset was already climbing down toward his beloved. When he was three-quarters of the way down, the ladder let loose from above and sent Hugh plummeting, but fortunately for him the tide had risen sharply enough that he landed in the water, narrowly missing having his skull broken open by nearby protruding rocks. Dazed and out of breath, he swam weakly to the sandspit where Aivlys helped him to flop onto his back and rest.

"I never fell so far before—knocked the wind out of me. Ooomphh!" he said, gasping between breaths.

"Why are you here? Didn't you read my letters on the sand?" said Aivlys, rather crossly.

"That's a fine thank-you for your would-be rescuer."

"Rescuer? Now you're merely trapped down here with me, and those above are short one fighter. I suppose it's better than the first time, though."

"The first time? What are you talking about?"

"Never mind," said Aivlys. "I'll explain it to you later, if we get out of this alive. What are we going to do?"

Hugh looked around. Like Aivlys, he saw only a bare sandbar with nothing to recommend itself. "We're going to swim for the cliffs," he decided.

"But there's no way we can scale them now; the ladder's gone. We can't climb that sheer wall without it."

"Well we can't stay here. I think I see an opening there, near the promontory. We'll make for that." Unconvinced but without a suitable alternative, Aivlys allowed herself to be pushed into the water.

Hugh had stumbled into a bit of luck. The crevice he had spotted would have been inaccessible at low tide when they first descended, but the rising tide had brought it within reach. First he pushed Aivlys up into the narrow gap, half drowning himself in the process as he hoisted her, then scrambled up after her. There was barely more than a tiny crack in the cliff wall, but it was big enough for the two lovers to squeeze through together. Astonishingly, the hole did not dead-end after a few feet but continued into the interior—it was the opening of a cave! They were actually inside the Headland Bluff. The passageway twisted and turned, narrowed and threatened to peter out altogether, but eventually opened up into a limestone cavern. Water dripping down from the cliff top for untold years had created this vast interior hole in the seemingly solid earth. As they ventured farther into this hidden landscape the light from the outside grew dimmer, until they were almost swallowed up by the blackness and were hesitant to take even a step for fear of falling into some unseen precipice. But they were not the first visitors to this underground wonder world. On the cavern floor they found strings stuck into bits of animal fat and fashioned into candles, and with the aid of Hugh Boisset's flint they managed to light a couple of these ancient tapers and dispel the darkness somewhat. What they saw astounded them: huge formations of water-carved rock in fantastic and weird shapes. In places the crystallizing sediment had formed into tiny pearllike excretions, thousands of them, littering the floor like spilled treasure. Elsewhere the rock walls glittered as if studded with diamonds. Other dripping deposits hung from the roof of the cave like icicles, and where they fell to the floor, upside-down icicles rose up to meet them like pairs of matching teeth. The air was heavy, musty, still, full of dampness and the odor of decay. In the flickering light of crude candles the high-walled cavern seemed like the abandoned palace of fairies or giants.

"What strangeness," Aivlys whispered. The hollow chamber echoed her words.

"We're lucky there's not bats," said Hugh. "The twisty entrance must keep them from using this as a nesting place."

"Who do you suppose left these stubs of wax here?" Aivlys wondered aloud.

"This is a perfect place for sea pirates to hide out. Maybe we'll find some of their booty," he said. Aivlys looked at him oddly. For all she knew, he might be a pirate himself. The Vargans certainly thought so, they'd had him locked up for trying to make off with one of their ships, though Hugh had sworn to her that he was only trying to escape captivity.

"All I want to do is to reach the surface and help my father and the others to defeat the Vargans. We're useless down here in this dungeon."

"We'll have to go deeper in, then. We know where the way out leads down here. We'll have to follow the path out the other side of the cavern, if there is one." They followed a dim trail of footprints, undisturbed for untold ages, across the grotto floor. Sure enough, on the other side of the shadowy lair there was another tunnel-like passageway leading out and up. It was slimy and slippery, but there were enough footholds for Hugh and Aivlys to scramble up, sometimes on hands and knees, sometimes clinging to the damp wall. Now there was no other light besides their fragile tallow sticks, which were difficult to hold as they clambered and scurried their way toward an uncertain destination. Hot wax dripped onto Aivlys's hand and made her drop hers momentarily, but Hugh, climbing behind her, caught it before it could slither away down the chimneylike hole. It was suffocatingly close, being in the middle of the earth, surrounded, encased by thousands and millions of tons of rock. Aivlys had to fight the urge to scream as the mute pressure of the stone pressed in on her. She must have been panting, or not breathing at all, because Hugh called up to her, "Breathe steadily," and made her relax with a few deep breaths before they continued their ascent.

If we ever get out of here, I'm never going in a cave again, Aivlys swore to herself. At one point the passageway narrowed until they had to contort their bodies to twist and slither through. Just above this spot a shelf of loose rock gave way beneath Hugh's feet. He grasped wildly for a fingerhold, then pulled himself up as several tons of stone cascaded down beneath him, sending up a plume of choking dust and piling up and collecting at the narrow spot—they were now sealed off from the caverns below.

"Only one way to go now," said Hugh, trying not to let on how worried he was that their escape route had been cut off. "Let's keep climbing."

Their precious candles had dwindled to stubs when, far in the distance above them, they glimpsed a faint glow. As they climbed, the light consolidated into a blue speck, and then grew to the size of a porthole—the sky, with stars in it!

"Have we been underground so long it's night?" Aivlys asked as she struggled with all her remaining strength toward the freedom that tiny opening represented.

"No, it's just a phenomenon. When you're so deep in the earth all the other light around is blotted out and the stars appear," Hugh reassured her.

The last few yards of the climb were treacherous. Fewer handholds offered themselves and the rock was smooth, perhaps from rain washing and wearing away at it. Just below the surface a curious antechamber just off to the side of the opening to the cave, perhaps man-made, allowed them to stand upright for the first time in a long while. From there they hoisted themselves up, one by one, and they were out!

They emerged through a sinkhole at the top of the cliff, where they flopped onto their backs and lay exhausted for several minutes. Looking around, they blinked in the sudden sunlight and breathed the fresh air. Then Hugh turned to his companion with a questioning look.

"What did you mean, down there on the beach, when you said 'the first time'?"

Aivlys explained how she'd cast the Gnomonese spell and how Hugh had almost ruined everything by repeating his mistake.

"Boy, that gives new meaning to the phrase 'If I had it to do all over again.' But now what?"

Almost at the same time they spotted the others from their party, a few hundred yards away, still perched near the cliff edge. Endimin must have convinced them to stay close, though this left them exposed to . . . Hugh and Aivlys turned almost as one and stared into the face of the approaching Black Wind. Aivlys wondered what they had gained by her use of the most difficult magic spell in the Gnomonese repertoire. Instead of facing death on the sandspit below they now were confronted with it on this barren bluff.

"Let's join them!" she shouted, raising her voice to be heard over the freshening breeze that represented the leading edge of the Black Wind.

"No!" Hugh yelled. "Signal them to come over here!"

Aivlys was perplexed by this suggestion. What difference did it make? But she waved her hands and caught her father's attention. He led the rescue party on a mad dash across the brush-covered heath to her side.

"Daughter, thank the gods you're all right!"

"Yes, but look, there's the Black Wind still bearing down on us."

"I've a thought," said Hugh.

"Have at it, lad. Give it your best effort," Endimin urged him.

"If we could lure the Black Wind into this cavern we could bottle it up and prevent it from spreading havoc on our land."

"That's brilliant, Boisset! Simply brilliant! We'll just set ourselves up for targets and let the Vargans blow us right into the center of the earth," said one of the Firozians.

"Exactly!" said Hugh. Someone had finally appreciated his ingenuity.

"There's no time," another among the Firozians protested. The Black Wind was only a few hundred yards offshore and would be upon them in a minute.

"There's always time," Endimin responded calmly. "How do you propose to do this, Hugh?"

"We'll just stand here until the last second, and let it find us, then duck down into the tunnel. The Black Wind'll follow us. There's a little side chamber just beneath the entrance. We'll hide there 'til it passes down into the depths of the cavern, then we'll jump back out and roll a boulder over the hole."

"And what if it finds us in the chamber?"

"It won't. Wind is like water, it seeks the path of least resistance. I'm sure it'll take the main route down into the cave."

"And if it doesn't ... if it finds us?"

"Then we'll die there instead of out here," Hugh said grimly.

"All right, then, let's give it a try. Everybody, help roll this big stone into place next to the entrance."

Everyone, even Aivlys, lent their backs to shoving the massive rock closer to the cave mouth. The wind was ripping up the low scrub brush and flinging it around like chaff, and the sky was growing steadily darker, but there was still enough time for them to position the boulder next to the sinkhole and duck down into the side cave before the full force of the life-seeking Black Wind struck. As they cowered in the declivity, the densely compacted wind hurtled by them, diving into the main shaft as Hugh had predicted. They could hear it raging deeper and deeper into the rock with frightening intensity.

"All right, everybody out!" Hugh shouted. They poured out of the hole and leaped to shove at the huge rock, which proved more difficult than they had imagined, to tip it in. They were stuck just a few inches from the lip of the depression when the receding roar of the Black Wind began to reach their ears again.

"It's coming back!" someone shouted. Frantically they strained at the rock, but it wouldn't budge until Endimin, at the extreme last moment, just before the Black Wind was about to explode out of the hole in full fury, uttered another spell—Time Flies: *"Time Flies light as a feather, Rise up all together!"*

Suddenly the rock, and everyone pushing against it, rose weightless in the air. Standing on firm earth, Endimin tipped them forward gently so that the rock hovered over the opening, then canceled the spell: *"Open your eyes, at the end of Time Flies."*

The boulder dropped into place, filling the hole perfectly, and the people leaning against it tumbled to the ground. A second later the Black Wind reached the surface. They could hear it beneath their feet, and the ground shook like an earthquake, but the stone did not budge. The Black Wind surged downward again, seeking an outlet for its rapacious force.

Hugh's trick seemed to have worked. There was a stillness in the air, a calm like none other Aivlys had ever experienced. Then the ground beneath their feet began to tremble again, as the trapped Black Wind struggled to free itself deep within the earth.

"We'd better get off this point," said Hugh, and the whole party dashed for firmer ground, inland from the shaky salient on which they stood. They had barely crossed the line where the protruding land jutted out from the coast when the hollow bluff gave way with a rumbling noise and slid into the sea. The waters around the heap of rubble grew muddy.

Everyone shouted and laughed, but the Black Wind was not finished. Out of the rubble of the bluff it rose again, re-forming and coalescing, even more violent and erratic than before, but instead of plunging inland it veered wildly and charged out to sea. Those vessels of the Vargan fleet that hadn't moved into the harbor, well over half the ships under Admiral Francisco's command, lay in the path of the chaotic cyclone. Hugh, Aivlys, and the others watched in horror as the black terror tore through the ships at anchor. Even at this great distance they could chart the wake of devastation as masts toppled, hulls collapsed, powder rooms exploded, and fires broke out. The Black Wind dissipated and dissolved as it passed through the fleet; by the time it reached open water it was only a thin line of storm squalls, but the damage had been done.

From far away came a sound like a sigh, or a soft

groan, but so indistinct in the distance that it could have been cheering, as at a sporting event.

"What's that?" Aivlys asked no one in particular, and no one answered her. The men averted their eyes and shifted on their feet, evasive and uneasy. "What's that?" she asked again. Hugh took her by an elbow and led her off to one side.

"You see," he began hesitantly, "sound travels far across water. What you're hearing are the cries of the Vargans, calling for help, but no one is going to come, they're drowning. Even if it's the enemy that's floundering out there, these Gnomonese seamen can't stand hearing the agonies of their fellow sailors."

"Can't we do anything?" Aivlys asked, but by now the sound had diminished. They gazed out to sea at the shattered ruins of the greater part of the Vargan fleet. The sudden turnaround in their fortunes left them with mixed emotions. It provided them with hope for defeating the Vargans, but at the cost of so many human lives.

One thing was certain—the Black Wind was vanquished. In its place the sky was filled with benign-looking slate gray clouds, stacked one on top of another until they reached the heights of the firmament. Here and there patches of blue peeked through from behind the incomplete cloud cover, and pure white, straight shafts of sunlight streamed through one of these openings. On the horizon a glorious rainbow arched its back and dipped both ends into the yet-roiling sea, creating a multicolored halo.

"You've done it, Boisset!" the men called out. "You've saved Firoze and Gnomon!"

"No, the Black Wind regenerates in its bottle. In a few hours they'll be able to use it again, though it's doubtful they would after today's debacle."

"It depends on how desperate they are," Endimin cautioned. "We've denied the Vargans one of their major weapons, but we still have to fight one more battle with them."

"I have a plan for that," Hugh Boisset said with a determined look on his face. "When the clock strikes three, our swords will come out."

16

ON THE DAY AFTER HUGH BOISSET HAD
tricked the Black Wind, the leaders of
Firoze and Gnomon approached the
flagship of the Vargan fleet with an
offer of tribute. It was a gesture of
surrender, an admission that despite
Hugh's valiant and clever effort, they
could never match the military might
or the savage ferocity of the Vargan
invasion. Trunks and boxes were piled
in the forepeak of a small Firozian
vessel and sailed out toward the flagship of the Vargan fleet, the *Regina*.
Admiral Francisco, in full battle regalia with all his combat medals crowding for space on the breast of his
uniform, stood at attention on the
forepeak of the *Regina* to greet them.
Once again a rope ladder was lowered
to the much smaller Gnomonese boat.
The visitors scrambled aboard; steve-
dores behind them hauled the treasure

in chests, cabinets, and cloth bags up the rocking walkway. On shore a crowd of Gnomonese had gathered to watch the ceremony. The rest of the Vargan fleet (what was left of it) had moved off to give the *Regina* clear maneuvering room for the triumphant promenade it would take down the channel once the papers of conquest were signed.

Endimin, Aivlys, Basco Fournier, and Henri Blouchette represented Gnomon. General Sticer, Beroth, Commander Rutger, and a few trusted aides made up the Firozian contingent. Never in recorded history had the Firozian or Gnomonese people submitted to rule by others. Some among the populace thought that their leaders were being hasty in acquiescing to the Vargan demands, but there were many others who had lost loved ones in the skirmishes and battles that had already been fought, who were willing to accept defeat if it meant peace.

The men from Firoze and Gnomon were dressed in their finest soldierly outfits also, with the striking visible difference that they carried no swords. This was one of the stipulations of the Vargans for agreeing to receive the contingent from the island on the invaders' ship. For Hugh Boisset this was a revisit to the site of his long imprisonment.

"I feel naked," General Sticer mumbled under his breath to Beroth, who accompanied him as an unofficial aide-de-camp. Beroth had redeemed himself in his commander's eyes with his heroic actions in the last battle.

"My sword is my better half," Beroth agreed. "I feel less than a man without it."

In return for the offer to surrender, the Vargans had made two concessions—they no longer demanded that the Gnomonese and Firozians be forced into exile—the conquerors had decided they could use the native people for chattel, and they had promised not to press for Boisset's return or for the seizure of the Celestial Compass, which a Gnomonese court had ruled to be the property of Hugh Boisset alone. The Vargans had agreed to abide by this decision, perhaps as a sop to the Gnomonese for their willingness to submit without further loss of life. In all other respects this ceremony would mark the complete annexation of the island for the queen of the Vargan people.

"It will go hard on our people to see another flag fly over the city," General Sticer sighed. "We have always been free."

"And shall remain so," Beroth muttered.

"What's that?" General Sticer asked, but Beroth turned away as if the subject were too painful for discussion.

The Vargans were making the most of this opportunity to humiliate and further oppress the conquered Firozians and Gnomonese. The visiting officers were seated well below their Vargan counterparts, in a row of small, uncomfortable stools, or made to stand, while the conquerers lounged on more comfortable deck chairs. Despite many setbacks, Admiral Francisco had forced a difficult enemy to capitulate. When he returned to Vargas, great glory would be his, as well as a goodly share of the plunder now stored away in the holds of his fleet. He was going to enjoy the ceremony of relinquishment of power by these intractable people. Soon they would feel his boot on those proud necks. There remained only the formality of the signing of the treaty of surrender. Admiral Francisco examined the so-called treasure that had been brought aboard. A bunch of useless trinkets, as far as he was concerned, except perhaps for one case full of Firozian swords, which had shown themselves to be fine weapons, though he still preferred his own Vargan blade. He picked up one of the gift swords, hefted it, tested its balance, then tossed it carelessly back into the box.

The ship's bells rang out, two, four, six. Six bells.

Three o'clock. From somewhere within one of the trunks a Gnomonese clock chimed in with three mellifluous strikes. A strange quiet came over the gathering, an empty, anticipatory silence like the absence of sound that precedes the oncoming of a driving rain. Hugh turned toward Aivlys and winked, and caught General Sticer's eye and, outrageously, winked at him also. Then he turned back to Admiral Francisco and, with insouciant panache, goaded him carelessly.

"So, you have won a costly victory over a tiny and ill-equipped enemy."

"I care nothing for the odds," Admiral Francisco answered. "My charter was to secure this island for my empress. I've done so."

"I suppose," Hugh said, his expression blithely untroubled. "Oh, I forgot to tell you one thing about these Firozian swords."

"What's that?" Francisco growled.

"They're asleep right now."

"Asleep? Swords don't sleep!"

"These do. Would you like me to wake them up?"

"I don't know what you're talking about." Francisco showed signs of impatience.

Hugh, as if to mollify him, said, "You're right, we really shouldn't give you sleeping swords, should we? It's not polite. *Swords! Wake up!*"

At his command the box of swords stirred, then each one leaped up and flew through the air into its owner's hands!

"Trickery! This is an outrage!" Francisco cried.

"No more than the obscene cruelty you have exhibited in your unprovoked attacks on our island!" Endimin shouted from Hugh's side. The two opposing sets of troops clashed swords on the pitching deck of the *Regina*. The Vargans, though greater in number, were caught off guard by the suddenness and ferocity of the surprise attack. Their greater numbers also

proved a hindrance, as they crowded their side of the
deck and prevented free swinging of their weapons.
Many of the soldiers were trapped belowdecks and unable to join the fray. Firozians quickly lashed shut the
hatches or jammed them with belaying pins.

The treasure trove of Gnomonese ingenuity also suddenly metamorphosed. Innocent-looking timepieces became explosives, blowing up in Vargan hands. Cleverly
spinning clock faces hypnotized their viewers into a
stupor. Delicately tinkling music boxes began to emit
distracting blares and sirens. Devices that were wafting
perfume suddenly discharged noxious smoke bombs.
Zentina Wraight's Scents of Time filled the air around
the Vargan soldiers' heads, making them dreamy and
disinterested in the here and now. The effect was dis-
orienting and alarming, as if the world had lost its bearings. Everything seemed out of kilter and on edge,
except to the Firozian soldiers, who had been warned of
the dazzling display and wore rags over their noses and
mouths to keep out the undesirable effects. Some of the
Vargans became convinced that the ship was sinking;
they threw themselves overboard and began to swim
away so as not to be caught in the vortex when the vessel turned bottom up and went under. Others slept
through the excitement, lured to drowsiness by enchanting music. All in all it was a disorganized, fragmented,
and dispirited Vargan contingent that faced the Firozian
assault. The Firozians had one goal in mind: to capture
Francisco and the urn containing the Black Wind. If
they could accomplish this they would be able to hold
hostage the rest of the fleet and prevent a counterattack.

Nor was Francisco ignorant that he was the object of
their attentions. Flanked by Lhosa and several other officers he put up a gallant defense, backing up and giving ground grudgingly. Swords rose like startled birds
flashing underwings in the sunlight, and fell as if
arrow-struck. Some of the blades were stained and drip-

ping with bright red blood, and the waters below were lightly dyed with the precious fluid of life. The rocking ship made for a dangerous, pitching, unsteady fighting platform. A mistimed thrust sent one of the Firozians tumbling over the rail into the sea with a scream, where he joined thrashing Vargans in a death struggle.

Francisco knew that if he could retreat to his cabin for just long enough to conjure up the Black Wind again, he could send it whirling among his enemies, though at these close quarters he would lose some of his own men as well. Lhosa too was contemplating the probable result of the admiral's actions, and remembering his vow not to let this fiendish flaw fall upon his own men. As they backed toward the hatchway that would lead to the admiral's cabin, Lieutenant Lhosa foundered in the throes of his dilemma, all the while battling the Firozians who pressed their advantage relentlessly. What should he do? The Firozians surged forward, hacking at him with their superior battle swords. Lhosa found himself behind Admiral Francisco, backing down the passageway toward the room where the cursed urn lay under lock and key.

"Open the door, then hold them off, Lieutenant," Francisco ordered him between breaths, slipping his lieutenant the key to his cabin.

"Yes, sir." Lieutenant Lhosa turned to place the key in the lock, leaving himself momentarily unprotected. A Firozian swordsman saw his opportunity, jumped forward, and ran his sword through Lhosa's body with such force that the point protruded out his back and impaled itself into the paneled wood of the door. Admiral Francisco responded by beheading the now unarmed assailant with a single sword swipe, but it was too late for Lhosa, who bled at the mouth and began to slump down, blocking the doorway.

"Out of my way, dammit!" Francisco shouted, but Lhosa, as the life drained out of him, fell heavily against the door and bent the key in the lock, jamming the door shut. Francisco's last hope for defeating the Firozians was lost. He fought on for another minute, then called out, "Desist! I'll give the order for surrender!" and raised his sword in a gesture of resignation. Three soldiers led him quickly at sword point back to the quarterdeck, where Endimin and Hugh were already mopping up the last of the Vargan resistance.

"Put up your swords," Admiral Francisco ordered his men, who were all too willing to comply. The Firozian-Gnomonese surprise was a complete success. Within minutes the roles of the conquerors and conquered had been reversed. The Vargans were shoved and shunted into a despondent crowd at the stern of the ship.

With their commander a captive and the Black Wind in the possession of the enemy, the rest of the Vargan fleet could do nothing, though they still held an overwhelming edge in men and matériel. A general retreat from Firoze and Gnomon was ordered. Admiral Francisco would be held until the Vargan fleet and all the invaders were well offshore, then escorted out to sea in a small boat. A promise not to reinvade was extracted from him with little difficulty. Within hours a stream of Vargans passed through the port cities of Gnomon and Firoze. The people of Firoze watched in hostile silence as the invaders boarded their landing craft and returned to their ships. The islanders' long ordeal was over.

While the battle was taking place, General Sticer had been safely shielded by Firozian soldiers, who refused to let him take part in the fighting, even though he had drawn his sword and waved it at them furiously. When the hand-to-hand combat was over, and he and the others in the boarding party had been ferried ashore and stood again on solid ground watching the first of the retreating Vargans leave, he shoved his way past his own guard to confront Beroth.

"Why didn't you tell me of your plans?" General Sticer asked, though he found it hard to be too severe with the victorious soldiers.

"We wanted you to play your part to the hilt, sir, that of penitent and defeated enemy. We knew that if you got wind of the uprising you'd have wanted to lead it yourself, sir," Beroth answered to spare Endimin the embarrassment.

"Well, perhaps you were right. I would never have countenanced such a devious maneuver. Fortunately it was suggested and conducted by a non-Firozian, an out-islander, who cannot bring too much dishonor to us. Nonetheless, it goes against all military codes of honor, not to mention strategy and tactics."

"On the contrary, General," Hugh interposed, "there is a famous legend about just such an episode. To gain entry to a besieged city, soldiers hid in a—"

"Not in our culture, Boisset," the general interrupted him. "Be thankful you were successful. To attempt such artifice and fail, that would be true humiliation."

"But we did not fail."

General Sticer looked past Hugh Boisset toward the ocean, where the Vargan fleet would soon recede toward the horizon and fade into a bitter memory. This young hero had risked everything for a people who didn't know him. The general searched for understanding in his heart. The old ways were changing. He himself was on friendly terms with several Gnomonese, whom he had formerly scorned. Who was to say that in the future he, General Sticer, might also need to adopt other military tactics and strategies, ones he now abjured? *You are never too old to change, there is always time to learn, if you are receptive,* the general thought.

"And what of you, young adventurer? Does this mean you'll be off to new lands, using your Celestial Compass to chart new waters?"

"Not right away, General. There's plenty for me to

experience right here in Firoze-Gnomon. The adventure of marriage, for instance." Hugh winked at Aivlys, who blushed but kept her composure. She and Hugh had made a pact—she would not keep him from roaming, as long as she could accompany him. There would be time for settling down, later.

General Sticer gave Aivlys a good looking over. Halfway through the battle he had seen the girl, one hand wielding a sword and the other behind her back, fending off two Vargans with astonishingly quick steps, spinning out of the way of their whirling blades so quickly that he thought he was hallucinating in the heat of the moment. "Ah, marriage. Yes, there's a terrifying sea to sail. That's why I make port as infrequently as possible. Give me a rolling deck awash in white foam before you make me stand and fight in those dark and deep waters."

"Oh, some comely lass may catch you yet, General," Endimin chided him in a friendly way.

"Well, after all I've seen, I won't say never. Now, if you'll excuse me, I'm going to make preparations for my return to Firoze. It's been a long time since I set foot on my native soil."

"This, too, is your native soil," Endimin pointed out, and the general agreed quickly.

"Yes, you're absolutely right, thank you for correcting me. We must never again view ourselves as separate nations. We're one island, one people. What I meant to say is that I haven't been home in a while."

"Have a good trip, General. Come back soon."

"Come back for the wedding," Hugh invited him.

"It would be my honor," said the general gravely, then he saluted Hugh and Aivlys and wheeled about in military fashion to take his leave.

Into the night and through the next morning the Vargans returned from the farms they had appropriated and the fields they had seized. They wore the stunned look of soldiers in defeat, though they had not lost a single battle on the island. The villagers who had been in hiding or in the camp in the mountains returned to Gnomon to reclaim their houses and barns, their shops and stores. Spontaneous dancing broke out in the streets.

The wedding of Hugh Boisset and Aivlys Platho was a grand affair, an opportunity for the community to celebrate not only a marriage but also the return to its peaceful ways. A special delegation of Firozian soldiers held their drawn swords aloft to form a canopy under which the bridal couple entered the ceremonial ring, where all marriages in Gnomon took place. All the bells and chimes of all the clocks in Gnomon rang in a chaotic symphony of joy. Hugh and Aivlys, bedecked in colorful costumes, were married before the entire population of Gnomon, with many visiting Firozians also in attendance. Herve Josthen was the ring bearer, and of course Endimin Platho gave his daughter away.

Later, at the reception, a lavish outdoor banquet held in the grassy yard in front of the Platho farm, Endimin spoke again with General Sticer, who looked relaxed and distinguished in his full-dress uniform, amply decorated with ribbons and medals across his chest.

"Perhaps we would even have liked the Vargans," Endimin suggested, "if we had the chance to get to know them. They approached us in their worst role, as invaders and conquerors. If we met them over some fine Firozian brew and a Gnomon lamb feast, like we are enjoying today, might we not have found them amiable companions?"

"Your heart is too generous, Endimin," the Firozian general chided him.

"My heart was heavy, but it's lighter now," Endimin replied; he stroked the hair of Herve Josthen, who stood beside him. The boy had quickly won his way into Endimin's favor, and though he would never erase the memory of Endimin's own son Runward, Herve had many of Runny's charms, including a fierce sense of loyalty. He was almost always seen now either holding Aivlys's hand or in the company of his adoptive father Endimin.

It would take many weeks and months to repair the damage done to the streets and buildings of the cities, and the wounds and losses suffered by the people would take even longer to heal, but a spirit of cooperation now existed between the two formerly separate worlds of Firoze and Gnomon. A new flag flew over the united island. Blazoned on a field of green was a clock face decorated with the distinctive hourglass shape: ∞. The hour and minute hands of the clock were gleaming swords, sweeping cuts through Time.